THE SERPENT'S CIRCLE

' "I've got a lot of faith in you, Tom," The boy's cheeks turned red again, for different reasons. "And that's why I'm going to entrust you with the secret. Are you willing to hear it? To share the burden of knowledge? Make no mistake, Tom, knowledge can be a thing of terror, to be taken up like a sword. There's no going back."

Unthinkingly Tom grasped the left arm of the crucifix, as if to brace himself for a blow.
    "Yes. I'm ready."

Joachim spoke gravely and with great deliberation. "First you must swear not to tell a living soul what I am about to tell you, which is a secret passed down through the centuries from the time of Christ."
    Tom was pale but resolute. The words came out in little more than a whisper.
    "I swear." '

'Fascinating . . . speeds towards a genuinely exciting climax'
                                    Books and Bookmen

About the Author

Patrick Harpur was educated at Cranleigh and at St Catharine's College, Cambridge. He has worked as a dish-washer, fisherman, journalist and postcard-seller in Africa; and in England as a teacher, in market research, and as an editor for a book-packaging company. He is currently at work on his second novel and lives in Wiltshire.

THE SERPENT'S CIRCLE

Patrick Harpur

CORONET BOOKS

Hodder and Stoughton

Copyright © 1985 by Patrick Harpur

First published in Great Britain in 1985
by Macmillan London Limited

Coronet edition 1986

British Library C.I.P.

Harpur, Patrick
   The serpent's circle
   I. Title
   823'.914[F]   PR6058.A6876

   ISBN 0–340–39706–3

Printed and bound in Great Britain for
Hodder and Stoughton Paperbacks, a
division of Hodder and Stoughton Ltd.,
Mill Road, Dunton Green, Sevenoaks,
Kent (Editorial Office: 47 Bedford
Square, London, WC1B 3DP) by
Cox and Wyman Ltd.,
Cardiff Road, Reading.

For Nique,
as promised.

PART I

The Burial Mound

1

The dry wood burst into flames, crackling and spitting and throwing up huge sparks into the night air. The steep banks of the Ring became clearly visible. The giant yews which stood like sentries around the parapet bent closer over the clearing. A thousand shadows darted in and out of their branches. The Firelighter withdrew and surveyed his handiwork. He was curiously shapeless, obscured in a long, dark-blue robe. A deep hood concealed his face.

He bent down and abruptly picked a burning brand from the fire. Holding it aloft, he turned towards the centre of the Ring where the mound was, humped like a dinosaur against the cold. The wind rushed through the trees, setting their branches clashing. But within the shelter of the glowing crater, everything was as quiet as the eye of a storm. The only sounds were the hissing of the fire and the rustle of dead leaves as the Firelighter moved unhurriedly towards the entrance of the primordial mound.

Two ranks of figures stood in front of the opening, four on either side. Each figure was identically dressed in a long robe; each was equally faceless. All of them were turned towards the fire, watching, as in the Old Days, when at dead of winter men kindled miraculous flames to foster the rebirth of the sun. Without a word, the Firelighter took up his position at the head of the two rows. The row nearest the fire turned inwards to face its opposite number. The Firelighter lowered his head and walked towards the black space which marked the doorway of the mound. As he passed through the human passage, each figure touched him once on the shoulder. He stepped through the entrance, and almost immediately the light from his fiery torch disappeared, as if snuffed out by the sheer mass of blackness.

The robed figures silently dispersed and reassembled in pairs at each approximate corner of the oblong mound. Their heads were tilted upwards. They seemed to be watching the smooth, bluish-grey column of stone which stood on, or thrust itself through, the roof of the mound. At first only the muted roar of the fire could be heard, and the distant conspiracy of wind. But, gradually, a low sound seemed to emanate from the dark motionless men. A resonant hum rippled across the clearing and washed against the waiting trees. In sudden alarm, a night bird beat off through the branches.

Imperceptibly, the humming grew louder, swelled and burst into a chant. No words could be discerned. The chant seemed older than words; it seemed as old as fire. As if in response to the sound, the ancient stone began to glow.

He had not visited the remote copse – it was strictly out of bounds – for a whole year. It had been warmer then, and darker, and George had been with him. Lodged in the cleft of his tree, his eyes fixed on the patch of ground thirty feet away, Tom Reardon remembered his friend's excitement at the emergence of the pure white, almost mythical beast. It had been like a sign, an augur of good fortune. But now nothing stirred except the wind that whispered in a hollow way around the copse, like a genie trapped in a huge glass jar. A big moon dipped through scudding clouds. Tom shivered and, more out of habit than anything else, began to pray.

Our Father who art in heaven . . .

It was the only prayer he really trusted since it came directly from the Lord. He had set himself the task of repeating it as a preparation for his first vows, which could not take place until his seventeenth birthday, still three months away. He had told no one about it (apart from Joachim, of course) because he knew how pious enthusiasm was held in suspicion. Religious fervour flared up in the most unlikely boys at school – and died down just as quickly. His had to last a lifetime. Joachim had made no comment on his resolution, but his sad marvellous eyes had lit up for a moment with approval and, possibly, a hint of pride.

Thy will be done, on Earth . . .

A gust of bitter wind excited the trees, making them sway woodenly and clash their branches together. Tom was afraid that the rare white creature would not come after all. Perhaps, sensing the onslaught of winter, it had already begun to hibernate; maybe its sensitive nose had got wind of him despite the precaution of climbing the tree. It was more of a blow than Tom liked to admit; if the albino badger didn't come, it would be like a blessing withheld.

He shifted his gaze to the hilltop where the Abbey buildings were dimly silhouetted like a concentration of the night sky. He fancied he could see the flicker of candlelight from inside the chapel where George was keeping his solitary night-long vigil. After the harsh Year of Abstinence, this was the last hurdle of his initiation into the Order – the actual ceremony must have finished an hour ago or more. While Tom's own private vigil, poised above the badger's sett, was essentially a token of sympathy and support for George, it also contained an element of envy. It was intolerable to have to wait so long before he too was tested and found fit.

And deliver us from evil . . .

Tom realised that he had not been concentrating on the prayer. He would have to start again from the beginning. It was his rule to make it a kind of meditation, so that each burning word was given absolute attention until it sank into the bottom of his soul and cauterised a tiny part of its

5

corruption. Sometimes it took twenty minutes to say a single Our Father.

Tom suddenly stiffened. Above the metallic whisper of the dying leaves, another sound was echoing the wind, the unmistakable sound of voices. Yet there was something inhuman about them, something excruciating. All thought of prayer or badgers was instantly banished from his mind. He swung his legs out of the tree and, dropping lightly to the ground, stood absolutely still with his head on one side, listening. His stocky body naturally adopted a kind of wrestler's position, with his short muscular legs planted firmly apart and his broad shoulders hunched slightly forward. The moonlight sharply defined the strong bones of his face, out of which clear green eyes scanned the darkness like a cat's. Over the treetops the weird voices drifted in the wind.

He moved silently to the edge of the copse. Across a frosted expanse of field, gleaming like steel in the bluish light, lay Bloxbury Ring. Tom caught his breath: he had never seen it at night before. By day the ancient earthwork was just an obsolete landmark; but at night it came into its own. The massive rampart, fortified by its black phalanx of yews, was lit from within by a faint glow that quickened and faded in concert with the wind. The voices were clearer now, chanting in unison, compelling him towards them. But the Ring was forbidden ground and he was frightened by what he might find there. He hesitated, wishing George were with him now. The voices shifted into a higher more insistent pitch.

Tom slipped out of the shadow of the trees and loped stealthily across the open field, his footsteps leaving dark scars on the light powdering of frost.

The four altar candles cast a wavering circle of light over the small cross. The rest of the chapel was dark and empty except for the tall thin boy, dressed in cassock and white surplice, who was kneeling in front of the altar. George's black eyes, wide and unblinking, shone in the candlelight. They were unfocused and seemed to be directed upwards, at the large crucifix half hidden in shadow that hung outside the frail net of light.

After a while he shut his eyes tightly for a moment and began to tear at his bottom lip with his teeth. It was cold in the chapel, but not cold enough to explain the violence of his sudden bout of shivering. Abruptly he stood up and, without genuflecting, turned his back on the cross and walked quickly along the central aisle to the doors. He eased one of them open and paused, peering to left and right through the crack. Outside, the vaulted colonnade hummed softly in the wind. He slipped silently between the columns, through the deserted cloisters and into the warmer building where the silence was heavy with the breathing of sleeping boys. One of them cried out from the depths of some nightmare, causing the boy to press himself into the shadow of a doorway.

Alone in his room he switched on his bedside light and gazed at the photograph next to it. His Italian mother smiled out at him from among the orange trees which grew around their farm in Tuscany. Underneath she had written 'To darling Giorgio'. His English father called him George. He turned away from the photograph and flinched as though someone had aimed a blow at him: waiting for him at the end of his bed was a dark-blue robe. George glanced around wildly to see if anything else had been touched. Then, quickly pulling out the bottom drawer of his desk, he laid it on the floor, reached into the empty space and took out an old leather-bound volume. The Book.

With a sigh of relief, he was about to replace it when he paused and opened it. The words NOT TO BE REMOVED were printed in red on the inside cover. Hurriedly he turned over to the frontispiece which was a complicated geometrical pattern, annotated in Latin. The core of the design was seven concentric circles. Thoughtfully he traced the outer circle with his finger and then turned to the beginning of the text. *Primum Circulum: Caveat aspirans*, it began – 'First Circle: Let the Aspiring One beware!' He began to translate:

> Here begins the first Dark Night of the Flesh. Tortuous as the Serpent is the Way out of the *Tumulus*, grave are its dangers. But through its narrow portals straight the Soul like a phoenix from the ashes of the Body can rise . . .

George gnawed at his lip. No need now to puzzle over the word *tumulus*; it meant a barrow or burial ground. Yesterday the Book had been little more than a quaint work of fiction. Now it was plain that the rites it contained, far from being imaginary, were real and had to be endured. George brushed away the beads of sweat which had formed on his top lip. He remembered bitterly how he had assumed that the initiation would be a matter of course. How could he have guessed what an abyss lay between him and the dark-blue robe? He had foolishly believed himself prepared; but what could possibly have prepared him for the power he had witnessed and the knowledge he had to accept?

He went to his cupboard and pulled out a light travelling bag. He could not accept it; he had to get out, get away. He placed his mother's photograph face down in the bottom of the bag.

A barbed wire fence stood between him and the Ring. Conscious of being dreadfully exposed, Tom took a chance. He grasped one of the wooden posts and vaulted over the fence. The thump he made on landing sounded frighteningly loud. With hardly a pause he ran on, down into the wide ditch which surrounded the Ring like a moat and up to the foot of the steep embankment. He crouched on his haunches, panting for breath. A grey cloud washed over the moon, smudging it like a watercolour.

8

The chant was building to a climax. He tried to identify the language, but it was certainly not English nor the Latin so familiar to him from the Mass. The stream of incantation was not even smooth and solemn; it was harsh and primitive-sounding, and the voices – unlike anything he had ever heard – were strangely nasal, controlled yet ecstatic. They affected him physically so that he was surprised to find himself shaking and, for a second, unable to move.

He began to inch his way up the face of the bank. Towards the top he had to negotiate the huge exposed roots of the yews which creaked like old hinges in the wind. Light flickered dimly through the branches overhead. At last he reached the edge and, bracing his left foot against a root, peered over.

Unprepared for the blaze of light in the clearing below, Tom could see nothing at first except the smooth moss-covered mound in the centre. He recognised it as a long barrow, a burial mound built on the far horizon of history by Stone Age men. On top of the mound, a single massive finger of stone accused the sky.

He searched the clearing for the source of the weird sound. Two figures stood at the nearest corner of the mound; they were shrouded in full-length robes of deep blue. Tom drew in a sharp breath. The robes belonged to the Little Brothers of the Apostles, the Order of monks who ran the school. Four more – no, six more – stood in pairs at the other corners of the mound. They were perfectly still but their chanting was growing higher and wilder, producing impossible discords which seemed to bypass the ear altogether and directly pierce the solar plexus. Tom felt the breath knocked out of him, heard it hissing between his teeth. The incantation climbed to a single unbearable note – and then died away sharply to a thin blade of sound.

Each monk stretched out an arm towards his neighbour until their fingertips touched. Their bodies strained upwards, almost on tiptoe. Slowly they extended their

9

free arms in front of them, palms upwards in greeting or supplication. Then they fell silent. Tom felt oppressed as if the air around him had become heavy, charged with an invisible force. His eyes followed the direction of the outstretched arms. They were pointing to the column of stone which seemed to glow for a moment – or was it catching the light from the dying fire? Tom could not be sure. But he was quite sure that someone was standing in front of the stone; someone in a long robe which rippled and stirred as if with a life of its own. The cowl was thrown back to reveal the face.

At first Tom was at a loss to recognise it. From the defiant tilt of the chin to the incandescence of the face, the man who stood so gloriously before the stone barely resembled the monk who only yesterday had taught him boring geography. But there could be no doubt: it was Brother Paul. The young schoolmaster had been uncannily transformed into a different being.

'Oh,' Tom whispered. 'Oh God.' His foot slipped from its supporting root and he slithered several feet down the bank. For some reason, the spectacle in the clearing had unleashed a deep uneasiness, as inarticulate as a groan. Breathing in short gasps, he threw his head back and stared across the light years. In the space between two winks of a star, the terrifying thought flashed through his mind that God had withdrawn Himself infinitely and for ever. Hurriedly he pulled himself back to the brink of the Ring: with a jolt of surprise he saw that Brother Paul had vanished.

The fire had burnt right down but the moon was throwing its light full on to the entrance of the burial mound. Silently the monks formed themselves into two rows in front of it. Out of the mound came a man. He passed between the rows and, pausing, turned to look up at the enigmatic stone, now bathed in deep shadow. It was Brother Paul. His face was still bright with joy, perhaps, or triumph.

Tom was troubled. What was the point of it all? Paul's

behaviour was especially puzzling: he must have scrambled down the mound like lightning, gone inside, waited for the other monks to form up, and then come out again. Why on earth would he do that? The monks were moving in procession around the long barrow and heading for the narrow gap in the Ring, directly opposite to where Tom was hidden. They were absorbed like shadows by the encompassing darkness, leaving the Ring empty and silent. The last sparks from the fire whirled into the air on a blast of wind. Tom realised that he was numb with cold.

2

The Abbey bell began to toll the villagers into early Mass. Brother Ambrose closed his study door against the clamour of several boys who were waiting in the cloisters before their breakfast. He was a short man, powerfully built, with a swarthy, almost Mediterranean complexion and close-cropped hair that was already turning iron grey. He crossed the bleak airy room and stood at the bay window. It was a small indulgence of his to watch the faithful obey the summons of the bell. They were already emerging out of the dawn mist which lay like white smoke in the dark valley, and were straggling up the long graceful curve of the drive.

The view from the Abbott's eyrie embraced the whole of Bloxbury. Across the valley, he could see the length of the high ridge, crowned with woodland and, lower down, patched with fields. They were still full of placid cows, like painted toys, soon to be brought in for the winter. Smoke rose from the chimneys of the farmhouses – a few of them Protestant – which were dotted over the hillside.

To the west, the village was fringed by the river which looped behind the Abbey, while far away to the east, beyond the labyrinth of narrow lanes, he could just discern the grey ribbon of motorway. Cars beetling along it, flashing pink now in the first light, were oblivious of the pocket of houses and farms hemmed in by hills. If any tourist, lured by the promise of an Abbey, did stray off the main road, he was disappointed – the name was only a token. The original Abbey had burnt down long ago and been replaced by an unremarkable collection of buildings which housed an international school for Roman Catholic boys.

The Abbot's eye fell on the village, an almost absurdly picturesque cluster of cottages at the foot of the hill. Someone as small as an insect was leaving the larger, detached cottage at the far end of the main street, and was heading towards the gates of the Abbey. Ambrose narrowed his eyes; even at that distance he knew who it was.

There was a knock at the door. He made no sign that he had heard it; he was busy watching the insect as it disappeared behind the high walls of the Abbey. A monk entered the room. At first glance, he was unexceptional: a mild, modest-looking man with fair hair. He crossed over to the desk and stood in front of it. Although only of middling height, he was several inches taller than the Abbot. His habit was worn and grubby, the sleeves rolled up as if he had been interrupted in some manual task. His hands, clasped in front of him, were rough and looked too large in proportion to his wrists; a dark band or ring was just visible on the third finger of his left hand. Without turning round, the Abbot spoke in a musing tone of voice:

'So far, all the political angels of death have passed harmlessly over our heads, thanks to people like these.' He pointed out of the window at the approaching villagers. 'It wouldn't do to forget that.' The monk made no reply; nor did Ambrose seem to expect one.

'Did you know,' he went on, 'that during the Reformation the Little Brothers were hidden in the village? The King's self-appointed agents, full of Protestant righteousness, did their best to root us out – there were the usual tortures – but not one of us was betrayed. More than a century later, Cromwell's Puritans also caused considerable unpleasantness. They didn't succeed either.' He turned to face the monk. 'But can our believers be trusted *now*, when we need it most? You know, of course, that I'm going to make the announcement at Mass.'

'I'm sure they'll take your words to heart, Brother Ambrose.' The formal statement was delivered with the trace of an accent. There was a slight stress on the word 'your'. Ambrose looked sharply at the monk, who raised his eyes. They were unusually luminous and, in spite of their obvious humour, they carried an indelible impression of melancholy. It would have been difficult to guess his age: his features and movements were youthful, and yet there was some quality in his face or bearing which made him seem older by far than the Abbot's fifty-odd years.

'We must make sure of it,' said Ambrose decisively. 'Incidentally, I'm meeting the most prominent among them in private, after Mass. I've decided to grant their request for the old crucifix – I see no reason to refuse since your work will shortly make it redundant.'

'May I ask what they want it for?'

'Have you forgotten the annual Remembrance, Joachim?'

'No, Brother Ambrose, I hadn't forgotten.' The monk's voice held a disapproving edge. 'But it's a barbaric custom. It encourages the worst kind of sensationalism.' Ambrose clicked his tongue.

'You're right, of course. But you haven't considered how vital it is – especially now – to cultivate the proper spirit of reverence. Besides, there's something touching about their devotion to the martyrs . . .' He smiled. 'However, we have more important things to discuss. Tomorrow the boys will be leaving and our preparations can begin in earnest. A simple announcement is inadequate – I must be certain of the believers' obedience. You and I will visit every one of them – '

'Forgive me, Brother Ambrose,' Joachim interrupted. 'Can't one of the other Brothers go with you? I'd planned to spend as much time as possible in prayer and fasting. They are absolutely essential if – ' Ambrose cut him off.

14

'They are superfluous if the villagers can't be relied on. I need you because you inspire affection and trust in their plodding souls, God help you. I'm well aware that I inspire . . . rather different emotions. It's an elegant arrangement: between us we will close their mouths and enlist their eyes and ears.'

'Surely that won't be necessary. They're good people.'

'Good?' echoed the Abbot. 'What has that got to do with it? They are weak and thoughtless – that's enough.'

'We are all sinners,' the monk remarked without emphasis.

'Quite. But the believers are not my only concern. We must consider the outsiders, too. Take that Dutch woman up at the hotel . . . you've heard about her? She wants to examine Bloxbury Ring for some book she's writing. Can you imagine! How many other tourists must we deal with? Every movement in and out of this area must be closely monitored – not least because I've promised our Visitor total security. He must have faith in our arrangements. Fortunately, I have a small strategy that will make the task a good deal easier . . . It'll require some of the old skills, but it's high time I rehearsed them.' He laughed briefly. 'However much our poor flock lacks spiritual insight, there are still advantages to living amongst farms. We begin tomorrow, Joachim. That's all for now.'

The monk remained motionless in front of the desk, ignoring his Abbot's dismissal.

'It's not quite all, Brother Ambrose,' he said. 'I came to ask you about last night.'

Tom paused by the Abbey gates to catch his breath. Ahead of him, vague figures were strung out along the tree-lined drive, moving through the thinning mist as in a dream. He preferred to celebrate Mass with the villagers because he felt a closer affinity with them than with his fellow pupils – nearly all boarders – who

15

dispersed at the end of each term to places as far apart as France, America or the Philippines.

When he first joined the school, he had felt otherwise. The prospect of friendship after a lonely childhood filled him with an almost unbearable excitement. He didn't know that day-boys belonged to a lower caste, nor that the additional stigma of a scholarship would make him virtually an untouchable. He soon learnt from the élite, fee-paying boarders that clever little bastards were passed over when teams were picked, and had to cope with their homework alone.

Thanks to George things had improved. At the start, they were merely thrust into each other's company by the force of their common calling. It marked them out as an embarrassment and, like informers, best avoided. But luckily, companionship had deepened to a friendship which had even survived the older boy's arduous year as a novice. Whether it would survive last night's initiation remained to be seen. For the moment George had become an unknown quantity, lost to that other world of long robes, ceremony and silence. Would he make the meeting they had arranged for that morning? It was suddenly urgent that he should, for who else but George could be trusted to explain the disturbing events at the Ring?

'Last night?' Ambrose was not listening; he was looking out of the window once more and seemed preoccupied with the latecomer who had stopped briefly at the gates and was now hurrying up the hill. 'Oh, last night was satisfactory. Brother Paul safely attained the third circle. Promising, don't you think?'

'I meant before that,' said the monk patiently. 'At Woodward's initiation.'

'Ah yes. Woodward. I was a little disappointed with Woodward,' Ambrose remarked vaguely. He continued to follow the boy's progress towards the Abbey. 'I'm more interested in your pupil, Joachim. How is young Reardon coming along?'

'We haven't settled down seriously to doctrine yet,' he replied cautiously.

'There's time enough for that. You above all know that the doctrine can't alter or confer the essential qualities. What of those?'

'Well, from what I've seen of Tom he could be exceptional . . .' In his enthusiasm, Joachim lost his caution. 'He's still unaware of his own strength and independence, I think – they will make obedience harder for him than most. But once his will has been directed, he could go a long way . . . even as far as the sixth circle. It'll depend on how well he uses the knowledge to increase the power of his faith.'

Ambrose nodded thoughtfully and with obvious satisfaction.

'Good, Joachim. Now that your coming has ended the days of the Twelve, we shall need a good many dedicated Brothers. Tom Reardon will be an invaluable asset. But I want you to see less of him for the time being. You have too many other responsibilities and I don't want him to form any attachments which will hamper his first vows. You needn't worry about his future instruction – I shall personally attend to it during his Year of Abstinence.'

'If you think it's for the best, Brother Ambrose . . .' The monk did not seem certain.

'I do, Joachim.'

'What about Woodward?'

As the Abbot turned his back to the window his large head was framed in a nimbus of pale light.

'He's no concern of yours. Woodward is not the first to be a little upset by a revelation of the Order's power and purpose. That's what the initiation is for, after all. We'll take care of him.'

'Perhaps if I were to talk to him – '

'No! You're forgetting yourself, Joachim. How long have you been here? Three, four years? It's nothing. Your unique position here does not mean that you can interfere with the laws of the Order – or question my decisions. Is that clear?'

The monk stared at the floor. 'Of course, Brother Ambrose. I beg your pardon.'

'We'll say no more about it. Mass is about to begin. I must go and bear the glad tidings to my flock . . . You're not joining us, I take it. Perhaps you find the Mass too . . . sensational?' He smiled ironically and marched out of the room.

3

The service had already begun. Tom hurried along the colonnade, remembering to hitch up the trousers of his baggy second-hand suit and to smooth down his unruly hair. Its striking auburn colour was inherited from his mother and, as always, it refused to be neatened. He slipped through the double doors and took a seat at the back of the chapel which, unusually, was filled to capacity.

The interior was being refurbished: there was scaffolding around the doors, and the walls were shrouded in long dustsheets which billowed slowly outwards in an occasional draught. The high stained-glass windows failed to trap the early light; since no candles had been lit, the faces of the worshipping villagers loomed pale in the surrounding gloom. There was an expectant look about them as they exchanged glances or, more often, stared keenly at the low semicircular platform where the altar stood.

Affected by this curious air of unrest, Tom caught the eye of his neighbour, Miss Carroway, who ran the village post office. The elderly spinster shot him a sharp look and lifted a wizened hand to adjust her hat. She had never been seen without the hat which, with its wide brim and wild feathers, was one of Bloxbury's more outstanding features. Tom craned around the burly farmer in front of him to see who was officiating. It was Brother Anselm, the oldest of the monks and George's special tutor.

Tom realised immediately why the congregation was so restless. The Little Brothers of the Apostles were present in force, sitting in a row behind the altar with the Abbot in the centre. Dressed in identical habits, their faces lean and hard from long years of self-denial, they resembled some dire and unyielding tribunal. Behind and above them, a wooden, dispirited Christ sagged on his Cross. As far as Tom could remember, the last time all twelve monks had attended a villagers' Mass – or a School Mass for that matter – was on the providential day three and a half years ago when, out of the blue, Brother Joachim had arrived.

Until that moment Tom had never quite understood what his peculiar gift (or aberration) was *for*. How could he have guessed that it would be the means of an extraordinary illumination? For he had not only *seen* the newcomer with the shattering clarity which characterised the gift; he had also seen himself. He had looked into his own heart and clearly read there his vocation. Of course, he couldn't recall a time when God hadn't been, apart from his mother, the real Presence in his life; but this was the moment when all his vague intimations had congealed, like the sudden thickening of whipped cream.

He had applied to join the Order as soon as possible. To his surprise, the Abbot had raised no objection; indeed he seemed almost to expect it, even though Tom had not previously revealed any predilection towards the monastic life. Naturally, Brother Joachim was to be his special tutor until his novice's vow in the New Year; then, following twelve hard months of doctrine and self-discipline, he would be admitted (barring acts of God) into the Order.

Tom ran his eye eagerly along the row of monks, hoping to spot his mentor, the thirteenth Apostle. Joachim was not there. Brother Paul was assisting Brother Anselm; his thoughts instantly flew to last night's events at Bloxbury Ring. He was sure Joachim could provide a

20

simple explanation, but it would mean admitting to a wilful breach of the rules. Joachim was very particular about obeying rules. He would have to rely on George. But why hadn't George taken his place in chapel along with the other monks? Had the rigours of his initiation left him too exhausted? Tom settled down to the prayers. It was an indifferent monk who couldn't even concentrate on the Mass.

George rested his forehead against the window, enjoying the coolness of the glass. His head was throbbing as if it were connected to the lorry's engine. From his seat in the high cab he could see over the hedges to where the shadowy fields steamed in anticipation of the sun. The horizon ahead was flushed with a delicate rose colour.

'You want a smoke, pal?' The cheerful driver was holding out a packet of cigarettes.

'No. Thanks.' He knew it was a hitchhiker's duty to chat to the driver, but his throat was so swollen and sore that it hurt to talk. He smiled instead, grateful for the heat of the cab, grateful above all for having been picked up on a deserted road in the early hours.

It still seemed nothing short of miraculous. When, after his escape from the school, his flight through the woods, his arrival at the wall and freedom – when, after all that, the five dark shapes had materialised around him, he had been close to screaming point. It would have been more bearable if the monks had grabbed him, shouted, cursed – anything rather than the frightful icy silence in which they brought him before the Abbot.

Of course he had lied, desperately, knowing all the time that it was useless to lie to Ambrose who (all the boys were certain) could see through walls. 'A visit to my parents,' he had said, pleading homesickness; 'A short rest,' pleading illness and overwork. Ambrose said nothing, only listened with half-closed eyes. Then, after an eternity, he suddenly agreed. He even offered a parting blessing. George's legs nearly went from under

21

him with relief as he received the Abbot's touch. But the worst moment was his dismissal, the way they all casually turned their backs on him; it was like ceasing to exist.

'My boss'd kill me if he knew.'

'What?' George was startled.

'Against company policy to pick people up.'

'Oh. I see.'

'I mean. You could be anybody.'

'Yes. I'm sorry.'

'No bother, pal. I have to pass the airport anyway. Going far?'

'To Tuscany . . . Italy.'

'Beautiful, pal,' the driver said vaguely as he wrenched the huge lorry into a lower gear. 'Bleeding lovely.'

'Yes.' George winced at the grinding of gears. Every sound registered harshly in his head. His whole body was burning, but without warmth. The heat seemed to spread downwards from a point on top of his head. He fancied for a moment that it was the spot where Ambrose had laid his hand in blessing. He smiled at his own foolishness; it was a simple chill, picked up on the long walk through freezing lanes to the London road. It was a small price to pay for escape from –

The image of Ambrose rose up in front of his eyes; not the image of the stern headmaster, or the revered Abbot, but the other, Unmentionable One who had presided over the initiation. He thrust the picture away – that madness was past. He could look at it again one day, perhaps, from the safety of another country. He found himself grinning stupidly at the driver. His head was singing.

'I'm going home. To see my mum and dad,' he remarked with an effort. The driver nodded slowly.

'Good for you, pal. Good for you.'

The climax of the Mass was imminent. There was no special warning: the Little Brothers liked the ceremony to be as austere as possible, in keeping with their traditional simplicity. There were no elaborate accoutrements or clothes, no swinging censers, no chanting. The Host was not a pitiful wafer but a loaf of real unleavened bread which Paul placed on a salver while Anselm knelt before the unpretentious pewter cross. Tom carefully observed the young monk as he poured the wine into the chalice. There was nothing in his face to link him with the radiant figure who had stood on top of the burial mound. If anything, he looked rather bored.

Tom forgot Brother Paul and became wholly absorbed in his hands as they prepared the Sacraments. He marvelled at how easy it was to make ready for the presence of God; yet somehow it was the very home-liness, like laying a table, which made it so awesome.

Anselm rose and with a single graceful movement lifted the salver high into the air. Tom suffered a fleeting sensation of vertigo, and experienced again the flash of panic and doubt which had tempted him at the Ring. Again he heard the inhuman voices opening a crack in creation, through which he glimpsed the abyss of the divine Absence.

Now, Brother Anselm was murmuring the words which infallibly summoned the Saviour to transform the ordinary bread and wine into His Body and His Blood. What if for once it didn't work? Tom was shaken by terror at the image of a world so abandoned – so *banal* – that bread could never be anything else but bread.

The farmer in front coughed and idly flicked through his prayer book; Miss Carroway moved her hat; far away a door banged, followed by the distant clatter of feet; Tom prayed.

There was a rustle in the universe. He sensed it rushing nearer at an inconceivable speed. With a sound-less roaring of wind, God, on huge invisible wings, traversed the infinite thickness of space and time to alight on the bread and wine.

No one seemed to notice; the crack was sealed up. Tom breathed freely again and moved out into the aisle with the other villagers to receive the Eucharist. He had seen the vast extent of the Power which could, he knew, burn up the world with a single kiss. Instead – and this was the mystery – It chose to put Itself meekly at the disposal of men, a sacrifice to be eaten up – or spat out.

He stood at the edge of the low platform, ready to receive the Body and Blood. The monks remained in their chairs. Brother Ambrose sat motionless and upright, his eyes moving under their half-dropped lids. As he knelt down, Tom noticed that the eyes had come to rest on him.

Brother Anselm pronounced the final blessing. There was a brief silence and then the coughing and shuffling began as the congregation got ready to go home. The Little Brothers were expected to file quietly out of the chapel before anyone else could leave, but only the Abbot stood up. The shuffling stopped. He marched to the edge of the dais and positioned himself at the head of the three steps which went down to the aisle. His head looked too large for his short body; a vein bulged on the side of his forehead. From the back of the chapel his eyes, deep in their sockets, could not be seen at all, except for an occasional glitter.

There was no preamble. The Abbot's command was such that he took the undivided attention of the villagers for granted. He was a Napoleon, addressing his troops.

'You will have noticed that this chapel is being extensively refitted. Such alterations are not accidental. They are, you might say, part of a small celebration. This year marks the seven hundredth anniversary of the founding of this Order.' The audience seemed inclined to applaud, but it was forestalled by Ambrose who swept on:

'We thought it fitting, therefore, that there should be a special blessing of the chapel, a re-consecration to inaugurate a new era in which the Order will, we pray, endure for another seven centuries. At least.' There was a general murmur of approval. The Abbot strolled along the edge of the dais, more Shakespearean actor now than military leader.

'There is one further circumstance which will make this ceremony of blessing a little out of the ordinary.' Behind him, one or two of the monks stirred in their chairs; the congregation picked up the movement and magnified it. 'I have been in two minds as to whether or not I should tell you. Any kind of extreme reaction would be anathema to the Order. However, my Brothers assure me that we can trust to your good sense – and your discretion.' Ambrose shot a sidelong glance at the monks and smiled thinly. A powerful current of expectation swept through the rapt audience. For a second they were left in mid-air, then the Abbot swung towards them like a searchlight. His eyes glittered.

'The blessing will be performed by Pope John the Twenty-Fifth during his imminent trip to this country.'

The villagers sat stunned. There was a collective exhalation and then a low hubbub broke out across the chapel. The Abbot silenced them with a single raised hand.

'I must emphasise that, in negotiating with the Vatican, I secured the Holy Father's gracious consent to come here on one condition . . .' His dense body radiated authority. '. . . that his visit will be strictly pastoral. He will not be on public view; he wishes only to join the Order in a private Mass during which he will bless our chapel.' The statement was issued like a challenge. The men looked down at their feet; Miss Carroway adjusted her hat, as if for protection. 'Nevertheless, in token of the close relationship between the Order and the lay community over the years, we have persuaded him to bless a representative of the congregation as a symbol of friendship and renewal. Afterwards, His Holiness has agreed to preside over a Service of Thanksgiving to which some of you will be invited. When we have decided which of you will attend, you will be notified; the Order's selection will, of course, be final. At the same time, *all* of you are responsible for

the success of the Pope's short stay. Is that understood?'
It was more a command than a question. There was a great
deal of eager nodding.

'There will be no publicity, no inappropriate excitement. Anyone who draws unwanted attention to the
event will not be welcome at the Abbey. Neither at the
Thanksgiving ceremony nor' – he dropped his voice – 'at
any time. That is all.' He marched out of the chapel at the
head of his Brothers. The villagers followed more slowly,
chattering excitedly to each other.

Tom stayed in his seat. He wanted a few moments on
his own to absorb the news. The Pope's visit was, he
supposed, a pretty thrilling event. He had even experienced it as such under the contagious influence of the
congregation. But now, alone in the draughty chapel, he
was infected by a chilly indifference.

He had once cut out a photo of him (the old Pope, of
course) from a magazine, and, for a fortnight after, the
kindly peasant face and snowy hair had become mixed
up in his prayers with God the Father. But that was long
ago. The Head of the Church – even the Church itself –
had not really cropped up since the days when he had
struggled to learn his Catechism. As far as he was concerned, the Abbey was synonymous with the Church;
and Ambrose, not the Pope, was head of the Abbey. He
resolved to set about stretching his imagination as far as
Rome – after all, on reflection, Pope John the Twenty-
Fifth was St Peter's successor; he, not Ambrose, was
Vicar of Christ.

The long dustsheets billowed mournfully on the walls.
He realised he had loitered longer than he intended. He
did not want to keep George waiting in this weather.

4

As Tom pushed quickly through the scrubby bushes and brambles which carpeted the slope, the wind gusted around him, making his open jacket flap wildly. Shreds of grey cloud passed intermittently across the pale wintry sun and he felt the dampness of impending rain on his face.

Beyond the stream he could see the deeper green of water meadows, paving the way to the river that marked the boundary of the Abbey's lands to the north. Away to his right the yews of Bloxbury Ring moved their branches ponderously up and down.

The tops of the willows came into view, marking the sheltered bend in the stream, at the base of the cliff between the two gentler slopes, which he and George had come to think of as their private meeting-place. Sure enough, George was waiting for him, dressed in a uniform dark blue.

At the next step Tom saw his mistake. The monk's habit, and his own expectation, had fooled him. The figure below bore no resemblance to George. It was Brother Ambrose. Instinctively he crouched behind a bush and peered through its leaves. Eight villagers, their backs towards him, were gathered in a respectful semicircle around the Abbot. At that distance only two of them were identifiable – one, John Hooper, by his height; the other, Miss Carroway, by her hat.

The odd little conference was drawing to an end. Ambrose strolled along the row of men and, as he passed, each of them executed a strange movement with their heads. When it came to Miss Carroway's turn, there was no doubt. Her unruly plumage bobbed and quivered in sympathy as she bowed – one, twice, three times – to the Abbot.

The group dispersed, Ambrose striding off up the far slope with the men following more slowly in a bunch. The old postmistress was left alone to look for a more gentle ascent. She walked unsteadily into the buffeting wind and began to follow the stream around the base of the slope.

Tom no longer expected to see any sign of George, especially in view of the initiation and vigil. He wondered if his friend would feel as indignant as he did at finding their place usurped by Ambrose and a handful of villagers. What did they mean by bowing to him?

As he turned towards the Abbey, he caught sight of a small drama being enacted by the stream. The wind had seized Miss Carroway's hat beneath its wide brim and blown it backwards into the water. The old lady, intent on intercepting it, was hurrying towards the stepping stones. If she had not been so obviously agitated, she would have looked comical. As the hat swirled serenely towards her on the torrent, she tottered out on to the third stone, leant over and snatched it up. The movement unbalanced her. Swaying on the wet surface, she hopped back to the second stone, failed to recover, hopped again – and slipped.

She keeled over sideways, her hat still clamped to her bosom, and landed with her body on the bank and her legs covered by foaming water. Tom could see her waving feebly at the other villagers but the last of them had already disappeared over the hill. Without a second thought he leapt down the slope like a goat and raced along the bank of the stream.

He jumped straight into the icy stream and prised apart the two stones trapping the old lady's leg. The water

28

gushed up to his knees and seeped through his shoes, making his toes go numb. He clambered back on to the bank and hauled her bodily after him. She lay on her side, quite still and clutching her hat so hard that her knuckles were white. Her round black eyes, bright with pain, regarded him with the darting glances of a wounded starling. He bent down to lift her but she held out the hat like a shield.

'Don't touch me, Thomas!' Her usual clipped tones quavered beneath her bravado. 'It's my leg. I think it's broken.'

He looked at her legs, amazed that such brittle-looking sticks could ever have supported her. There was something slightly sickening about the angle at which the left leg rested gingerly on the ground. The thick stocking had a long tear in it and Tom could see angry mauve marks where the skinny ankle and shin had been wrenched between the stones.

'You can't stay here,' he said firmly. 'I've got to move you into the shelter of that tree.' He pointed to the nearest willow. 'Then I'll get help.'

Miss Carroway closed her eyes and muttered irritably, but she did not refuse. She did not so much tremble with cold, as flutter from head to toe. He half-carried her to the tree and leant her back gently against the trunk. The drooping branches, stripped of their leaves, closed them in like bars. He took off his jacket and laid it over her, feeling the bite of the wind through his thin shirt. Her lips were tinged with blue and her long sodden skirts clung heavily around her thighs. He had heard about old people taking falls and he felt the first stirrings of panic.

'Don't . . . don't move, Miss Carroway,' he advised unnecessarily. 'I'll fetch Doctor Kelly right away.'

'Kelly!' The old woman snorted derisively. 'He's no good to me. Bring Brother Joachim – *Joachim*, d'you hear? And Thomas . . . be quick about it.' Her voice died away into a whisper.

Tom was shocked by her deteriorating condition. He only hesitated for a second. Then he began to run towards the far slope and Joachim's workshop.

At first the world was as it always was. The hill was steeper than he had reckoned and his legs ached intolerably but, head down, arms going like pistons, he forced himself on. Only when he was convinced his tortured lungs would burst did he stop to take a breath. It was then that it happened.

The grass was electrified by the kind of intense greenness that presages a thunderstorm. Above, the smooth brow of the hill melted into the air to form an unbroken sweep of more subtle colours, from green through clear blue and soft grey to the brilliant white of the huge clouds, piled against the sky and edged with gold. He had not known what beauty was until that moment. Yet the scene was flat, two-dimensional, like a picture. Everything seemed suspended. Even the smoke from Joachim's workshop hung like a painted ribbon above the shining roof. The wind was a faraway whisper.

Tom's heart beat slowly and heavily like a great bronze bell, swinging painfully upwards, hanging still for a second, and then gathering momentum to swing down with a long boom. The air was forced from his lungs in a sudden gasp. A bright gleam flashed briefly at the crest of the hill. He waited.

Against the natural background of grass and cloud and sky, a luminous body appeared, an exotic cocoon woven out of pure silver light. As it moved steadily towards him, the flat landscape outside it darkened and then lightened as it passed. Tom knew what it was. His legs trembled – not with fear, but with sudden exhaustion. He sank to his knees and, with closed eyes, found himself once more panting for breath. He heard the swish of grass and felt a faint vibration in the earth. He opened his eyes. In front of him were a pair of black boots, a scruffy dark-blue robe and, finally, the smiling quizzical face of Brother Joachim.

'Help . . . Carroway . . . river . . . bust leg,' he blurted out between breaths. Joachim grasped the situation instantly.

'Right. Show me.'

Tom clambered to his feet and, with the monk's help, retraced his steps. The lonely figure of the postmistress came into view below.

'Are you all right?' Joachim asked. Tom nodded. 'Good. Take your time. I'm going on ahead.' He strode off down the hill towards the stream.

By the time Tom arrived back at the weeping willow, Miss Carroway was in a bad way. The sun had been completely obscured by a bank of grey rainclouds and it was noticeably colder. The tree's encircling branches offered her little protection from the sharpness of the wind. She was shivering convulsively in her wet clothes, and her face had taken on a grim waxen quality. Joachim had persuaded her to take off her shoe and the effort had left her rigid with pain. Only her head shook feebly from side to side while little groaning noises escaped between her clenched teeth.

'Let's have a look at it,' Joachim was saying gently. He reached out a hand. She shrank from his touch and shook her head more emphatically.

'I won't hurt you. I promise.'

'No. Please. If I don't move it . . . if I can just leave it alone.'

'You can't lie there for ever, Miss Carroway,' Tom broke in. 'Let Brother Joachim have a look. He says he won't hurt you.' The monk raised his hand to silence him.

'Go and wait over there, Tom.' He pointed to a nearby tree.

Tom did as he was told. Leaning his back against the

31

tree, he shivered once at the touch of the smooth cold bark. He could see the monk and the injured woman through the cage of branches. Joachim crouched next to her and began to talk, but too quietly for Tom to catch the words. Gradually Miss Carroway ceased to shake so violently. She nodded her head in answer to a question and stared intently into the monk's face. She nodded again and smiled. Tom could just hear the comfortable sound of Joachim's low laugh. It was reassuring. He began to relax.

A faint lustre outlined the monk's head and shoulders. Tom could not tell whether it was an optical effect – an after-image accentuated by the growing gloom – or a trace of Joachim's brilliant light. The word was not adequate to describe the rich glowing colours which people radiated; but it was the word he had first used, and somehow it had stuck. Idly he remembered that first time. He must have been very young. His great-aunt Louise was staying with them. She had terrified him by walking into the room one day and apparently taking off her head; he did not know what a wig was, let alone that she frequently wore one. The shock had caused her light to come on. Her physical body was replaced by a body of coloured light, rounded into a kind of egg shape. It comprised most of the colours of the spectrum, but there was a predominance of pale blue tinged with orange. He thought of these as her colours. The effect surprised and pleased him more than anything.

But then he had noticed something truly frightening, far worse than the removal of her head. A brown, sticky, malevolent creature with too many legs was hooked on to her side, causing an ugly breach in the pretty light. Even as he looked, it had moved, crawling an inch further in. After that, he had cried and cried but no one could discover why. He was too young to explain, or even to know, that he had caught a glimpse of evil. Years later he learnt that Great-Aunt Louise had undergone, soon after, a painful and lingering death from cancer of the liver. Ever since, he had secretly suspected that the disease was as much spiritual as physical.

Tom drew in a sharp breath. He had noticed that the monk's hand was resting on Miss Carroway's injured leg. His stomach muscles tensed involuntarily as he waited for the poor old girl's scream. But there was no sound, not even a whimper. There was only Joachim's low voice. Her eyelids began to drop; she was quite still. Joachim's fingers began to probe the leg with the delicate skill of a surgeon. The old woman seemed to have fallen asleep. The monk was silent now, gazing at the leg. He moved his head closer, scanning the injury intently. Then with a sudden rapid movement, he brought his other hand across and gave the leg a tap. Two taps. He brushed the air around the leg with short economical motions of his palms, as if he were dusting a surface one or two inches above the skin. Finally, he took hold of the foot and casually straightened the leg. He stood up and beckoned Tom.

'Give me a hand, will you?' he said briskly. 'Put her shoe on for a start.' Tom looked nervously at the leg. Beneath the tear in her stocking there was no trace of the earlier swelling. It appeared perfectly normal.

'But . . . but is she all right?' he asked incredulously.

'Seems to be.'

Tom was astounded. He fitted the small shrunken foot into its shoe, hesitantly at first and then more firmly. Miss Carroway remained oblivious. Tom glanced nervously at her face to see if she were still alive. It had assumed its normal colour and she was breathing deeply and easily. He hardly dared to ask the question. Finally he did.

'But what did you do?'

The monk ignored him, issuing a sharp command instead: 'Help me get her up. No, go the other side. That's it.'

Once on her feet, Miss Carroway opened her eyes. They had a bewildered look. She stared stupidly down at her leg and then up at Joachim.

'All right now?' he asked. 'You haven't forgotten how to walk, I hope!'

She took a few tentative steps forward and the colour rose up into her face as though for a moment she had shed thirty years. Her bright bird-like eyes were shining. Impulsively she clasped the monk's hand and bent over it. Joachim quickly withdrew it and, picking up her abandoned hat, solemnly gave it to her.

The action restored her to her old self. She settled the hat on her head and brusquely tested the leg once more.

'Well,' she said. 'That seems more satisfactory.'

'You'd better get home before you catch your death. I'll come with you, of course,' Joachim offered gallantly.

'Thank you, Brother Joachim, but I won't hear of it. I'm perfectly all right,' she said briskly. She nodded at Tom. 'Thank you, Thomas. I shan't be needing your jacket any longer.' She handed it over and set off on her original course along the bank of the stream.

Tom was blazing with curiosity. As soon as the old woman had disappeared from sight, the words burst out of him:

'Miss Carroway said her leg was broken . . . !'

Joachim sighed. 'Oh, Miss Carroway exaggerates. Come back to the workshop, Tom. We'll dry your shoes and socks. Your mother is not going to be pleased.'

'Do you mean her leg *wasn't* broken?'

The monk looked at him sternly. 'Perhaps it was broken, perhaps it wasn't. What does it matter? It is not broken now.' His face relaxed into a smile.

'Listen, Tom. You think you have seen something, well, marvellous? You haven't. I have a knack for these things, these little tricks. That's all. I will explain it to you one day, but not now. So leave it alone, all right?'

Tom nodded reluctantly.

Joachim grasped his arm briefly. 'And Tom, I must ask you not to speak of . . . of what happened here. People don't understand. Promise?'

The thought of sharing a secret with Brother Joachim mitigated his frustration at being denied an answer.

'I promise,' he said.

The monk patted him on the shoulder.

5

'. . . I am still of the opinion that His Holiness might be better advised to travel by helicopter or, at the very least, by train on the third phase, especially as the roads in that part of England are, I am told, somewhat uncertain. Quite apart from which . . .'

Cardinal Carlo Benetti was not listening to the droning voice of Father Giulio. He had no need to. The chaplain was quibbling over details of the Pope's itinerary for the third – no, the fourth – time. He meant well, but he did not know that the Cardinal had already mapped out every part of the journey in his head. Too tactful to spoil the eager self-importance of the younger man, the Cardinal lit a fresh cigarette from the one he was smoking and gazed out of the window. There was a small brown bird on the flat roof outside. He was strangely moved by the creature, so tiny against the looming dome of St Peter's – so brave to have flown this far, through a country fraught with snares and guns. What kind of people are we, wondered the Cardinal, to have killed all the birds?

Father Giulio had finally stopped speaking. Suavely, the Cardinal intervened before any of the other four chaplains could prolong the meeting further: 'We are all grateful, I think, to Father Giulio for suggestions which will prove invaluable in the event that we have to adopt a contingency plan at any stage . . .' The chaplains made noises of agreement. Two of them were not altogether sure what they were doing on this committee, responsible

36

for organising the Pope's tour of the United Kingdom. Cardinal Benetti appeared to have it all worked out on his own.

'And now,' said the Cardinal, a concluding note in his voice, 'if there is no further business . . . ?' He looked round the comfortable room, indistinguishable from any modern boardroom, except perhaps for the crucifix on the wall. Outside the window, the brown bird had found something to eat and was pecking at it vigorously. Father Giulio coughed.

'Yes?' Cardinal Benetti asked politely, concealing his irritation.

'I have one question concerning Day Two. As we all know, His Holiness will arrive in London on the Friday evening, but his tour proper will not begin until the Monday, when he goes to Liverpool.' The Cardinal could hardly believe that he was going to begin all over again. 'On the Sunday he is travelling to the West Country to bless the Order' – he looked briefly at his papers – 'the Order of the Little Brothers of the Apostles – '

'Yes, yes,' the Cardinal interrupted. 'It is a pastoral visit – recognition of devoted service by the Order, and so on. We are not publicising it. It shall be officially designated as a day of rest.' He added wryly, 'As Sunday should be.'

'Quite, Eminence. But – ' the chaplain raised a portentous finger – 'His Holiness has asked me personally to ensure that he is fully briefed on this Order before he arrives. He is to make a short speech, you will recall. Nothing formal . . . a simple consecration.' The Cardinal thought quickly; Father Giulio had a point.

'Does anyone know any details of the Order?' he asked. There was a general shaking of heads. 'In that case,' he declared, 'we need Father Vittorio. He knows all the Church's nooks and crannies. I'm sure he will quickly supply us with the relevant data – I will see to it personally. Now, any other business?' There was not. The Cardinal eased his tall lean frame out of his chair. 'Until next week then, for the final briefing.'

The door closed behind the last chaplain. Carlo Benetti strolled over to the window. The bird was still there on the Vatican roof. Far below, the traffic of Rome hummed and blared. An exhausted party of tourists, stunned by the marble splendour of St Peter's, stumbled out into the vibrant Mediterranean light. They chatted among themselves, satisfied at having seen the living proof that the Rock on which Christ had built his church would endure for ever.

The Cardinal felt a headache coming on. He stubbed out his cigarette nervily. The small brown bird grasped the last morsel of food and flew off.

The workshop had once been a large stable and some of the beams in the low ceiling, one or two stalls and the big half-door still remained. A wide window had been knocked into the wall overlooking the fertile flood plain. A light spatter of rain tapped on the glass.

Tom was sipping hot tea in front of the blazing log fire which cast a friendly glow into the shadowy room. His wet shoes and socks steamed on the fender. The smell of damp leather and wool mingled pleasantly with the sharp clean scent of new wood. A pile of planks was stacked against the wall, in the corner where the wooden staircase wound up to Joachim's sleeping quarters. It was a peaceful place.

There was an eternal quality too. A craftsman from medieval Flanders, for instance, or even first-century Galilee, would have felt at home there. The monk himself would have been a familiar sight in his timeless robe, quietly sculpting his new crucifix for the chapel out of seasoned timber. Days, hours, minutes – the waterdrips of history – wore down the outside world; inside the workshop the brief pause between two ticks of a clock had been infinitely stretched into stillness. Only the powerful electric lamp, pulled down low over the workbench, was evidence of the twentieth century. It illuminated Joachim's head and shoulders when he bent forward over the wood he was carving. His large hands moved in and out of the pool of light, exchanging tools or brushing away shavings. Tom was reminded of some study in light and dark by an old Dutch master.

The questions which nagged at the back of his mind were gradually dispelled by the tranquillity and warmth. Even the Ring ceremony paled into insignificance. He had probably exaggerated its importance; he could always ask George tomorrow. Meanwhile, as he watched the monk's hands moving over the wood, he was reminded of a duty which pressed almost physically upon him: to confess about seeing the lights. If Joachim could mend a broken leg as easily as he joined two pieces of wood, he would surely understand the peculiar gift – or whatever – which might not be quite, well, *orthodox*. Before he had elected to join the Order, Tom had simply taken it for granted, like a talent for tennis or a knack for learning languages. But recently it had come to weigh heavily on him. What if seeing the lights were a sin? It would be a relief to tell Joachim, who could be counted on not to laugh or dismiss the gift. But he wouldn't confess it right now; it would be a pity to break the mood of calm intimacy.

A log flared momentarily and then cracked, throwing a glowing splinter on to the square of carpet in front of the fire. Tom jerked his chair and bent down to remove it. At the same moment he remembered that neither he nor Joachim had mentioned the pressing news of the day.

'Brother Joachim! Aren't you excited about the Pope's visit?' He watched the monk's face as it bent closer over the crucifix to examine a small knot in the wood. The features were sharply etched by shadows around the eyes and nose, making him appear fleetingly as a bird of prey. There were no signs of excitement, but he was quite unprepared for the stiffness of Joachim's impersonal reply.

'Naturally it is a great honour for the Order.'

At the root of Tom's question there lay a desire to

clarify his own confused reaction to the unique event, but Joachim was unwilling, it seemed, to help him.

'So you feel honoured?' he asked, with a hint of sarcasm on the last word. Joachim's words jarred the air between them.

'Why do you ask? His Holiness Pope John the Twenty-Fifth, Vicar of Christ and successor to St Peter himself, is stepping down from his throne and visiting us. Here. In the middle of nowhere. How can I not feel honoured?' Although the monk's annoyance was mild, Tom was shocked. He regretted his impertinence.

'I'm sorry. I just thought – ' He was cut off.

'Can you see no contradiction? You will learn what it is to be a monk. Sworn to poverty and humility. Forbidden every passion except one – the terrible unquenchable passion to be united with God.' The monk's voice grew low and bitter. 'You will learn how little *we* have to do with jet aircraft and limousines, with all the crowds and cavalcades, with pious retinues and finery for every occasion – ' He stopped short. The wind blew a flurry of rain against the window pane. 'Forgive me, Tom,' he said soberly. 'You see now how weakness lies in wait for us?'

Tom was bewildered. 'You mean you *envy* all . . . all that?'

'Envy?' The monk gave a hollow laugh. 'My sin is worse than that.' He looked sadly at his half-finished crucifix. 'It's pride, Tom, spiritual pride – the worst sin of all.' He smiled apologetically. 'You'll do well to remember this moment when you come to take your vows.'

Tom knew that he would remember it, but not in the way that Joachim meant. He was profoundly stirred by the monk's contrition over such a comparatively small outburst. He was appalled that such a man as this should ask his forgiveness. *His* forgiveness. Yet, at the same time, he was thrilled at Joachim's admission of fallibility. It had so often seemed to him that the man he admired so much was scarcely human. Yet it in no way diminished Brother Joachim – on the contrary, faced with his simple dignity and humility, Tom wanted more than ever to be as he was. He wondered vaguely if all sons must, at some time or other, feel this way about their fathers. He had never known his own father. Tom wanted to say at least some of this to Joachim, but the words would not come. He got up, poured himself some more tea from the pot on the hearth, and strolled across to the workbench.

'I think I'll start on His face tomorrow,' Joachim remarked, tenderly running his hand over the uncarved mass of wood at the head of the crucifix. Tom nodded. He was looking at the ring which Joachim wore on the third finger of his left hand. He had not taken special notice of it before. At a distance, it looked like a single dark band.

'May I see your ring, Brother Joachim?'

The monk hesitated fractionally and then held out his hand under the light. The ring was not made of any metal, but had been carved out of some dark, glossy stone. It felt hard to the touch, like jade, but much more brittle. Tom turned his hand over. The ring was carved in the likeness of a snake. On the inside of the finger the snake's tail was jammed neatly into its mouth to form the complete circle. The pattern on its body was minutely and delicately picked out, scale by scale.

'Will you take it off? So I can have a closer look?'

Joachim's reply was unexpected. 'I can't take it off.'

Tom laughed. 'Can't – or won't?' He looked up at Joachim's face and saw that it was serious.

The monk immediately broke into his delightful laugh. 'Both!' he said.

'Where on earth did it come from?'

'Ah-ha. Where it originally came from, nobody knows. It's old, though. Very old. And valuable. I got it,' he added, 'from my teacher.'

'Your what?' Tom found it impossible to imagine Joachim being taught. His face must have indicated as much, for the monk laughed again. It's a very long story, Tom – and a boring one.'

'Let me decide that. Please.'

The monk hesitated. Tom sensed that he wished in some way to atone for his earlier, harsher words.

'Well, Tom. All right. I'll tell you a small part of it at least.' He took up his chisel and began to make some fine adjustments to Christ's left arm.

'I was not much older than you when I left home – '

'Where was that?'

'It doesn't matter. Strictly speaking, a monk has no business recalling his former life, but I'll tell you a bit about it because you may learn something and because you asked. So, no more questions. Do you understand?'

Tom nodded.

Brother Joachim continued, 'The only important thing is that one day I began my search for, well, something. I didn't yet call it God.' He looked sideways at Tom. 'I was a Romantic in those days,' he smiled. 'I thought all searches began with travel.'

6

Father Vittorio di Rivera finished the sentence he was writing with a flourish, took off his spectacles and pushed back his chair. He yawned and absently scratched his paunchy stomach. It was on days like these, drafting a particularly delicate encyclical on the abuse of the Pill in Uruguay, that he felt ready to curse human ingenuity at devising means of contraception. He was ready for dinner. It would do no harm to have it early for once. He thought lovingly of spaghetti carbonara, *fruits de mer* with fresh broccoli, an aromatic zabaglione, a little blue cheese to finish. Tasty and satisfying, but not elaborate or heavy.

He read through the paragraph he had just finished and yawned again. To be fair, if it wasn't the Pill, it would be something else – hadn't they found evidence of intra-uterine devices amongst the ancient Egyptians? He would have to look it up. And when he considered the methods they used on Fernando Po . . . He shuddered at the memory of his mission to the pestilential little island, tucked into the huge steaming armpit of West Africa.

The plump little priest put his spectacles on again, rose awkwardly from his chair and crossed his study. He stopped in front of a cabinet set in the midst of a wall of books. They were written in a wide variety of languages and he had read most of them. He had a knack for languages. He spoke six fluently and read as many more, including the so-called dead ones – Latin, Greek, Hebrew. It had been difficult actually to like his hard Jesuit schoolmasters but they had certainly crammed the

Classics into him. It was the accounts of their missionary work, too, which had fired his youthful zeal and impelled him to follow in their footsteps.

He opened the cabinet and extracted a glass and a bottle of red wine. He had opened it an hour ago to let it breathe. He poured a glassful and sniffed appreciatively at the bouquet. A little young, perhaps, but by no means too fruity; it was most acceptable. On Fernando Po he had struggled bravely with discomfort – the unremitting sticky heat, the drenching rain, the vicious insects, the disease, the mud, the overpowering wall of jungle, and yet more heat in which the slightest movement drained the body of fluid and energy. A good bottle of wine, a lasagne and a fresh salad would have helped. A man could only do so much on charred maize, boiled plantain and the odd chicken that had died of old age.

On Sundays after evening Mass he had done his best to provide a meal for his flock. They were drawn exclusively from the poor plantation workers whose Spanish bosses paid them a pittance. Many of them were refugees from Nigeria – tribesmen who had fled from a regime determined to exterminate them. But when Church funds ran out, so did his flock. They dwindled to a handful, and, finally, on one terrible Sunday, no one at all came to the church. He had sat there alone at the back, listening to the rain crashing on the corrugated iron roof. When it stopped, he had walked miserably up to the plantations in the dark. He soon found his parishioners. They were drunk and dancing by the light of a fire. He could still see their glazed eyes, their black faces glistening with sweat. There were awful sounds of drums and tinny music blaring from an old record-player; bursts of stamping and clapping; the cries of fornicators in nearby shanties.

He had almost wept tears of joy when the Vatican wrote to suggest that his talents might be better employed at home. Even now, sadder and wiser as he was, he despised himself for his failure. He had lost something more precious than his self-esteem in that savage place; he had lost his faith. He knew deep down that if he had not been recalled he would have been forced to leave the Church. He had tried to make himself useful since then and, indeed, had gained a certain reputation for shrewdness and sagacity, but this did little to allay the withering emptiness he felt inside. He prayed every day that his faith might be returned to him. There was no contradiction. He did not doubt the existence of God; it was his own relation to God that he doubted, his vocation. It was as if he were praying for his lost youth.

Vittorio frowned and took another sip of wine. It remained satisfactory, but he thought he could detect a slightly bitter aftertaste. He was still frowning when there came a knock at the door.

'Enter,' he said wearily.

The door was flung open. The tall, energetic figure of Cardinal Benetti strode into the room.

'Good afternoon, Father. No, don't get up. What's this? *French* wine? Our own not good enough for you?' He clicked his tongue in mock disapproval.

The little priest had scarcely stammered a greeting in return before the Cardinal had waved it aside and rushed on. 'Look here, Father. A small request. The Little Brothers of the Apostles – heard of them? No? Well, the Holy Father is calling on them. In England, that is. A short speech is required. Find out what you can – history, notable members of the Order, the usual things. Can you let me know tomorrow? Good. *Ciao*.' He spun on his heel and swept out again before Vittorio could even nod.

The priest groaned inwardly. This would mean a late night. Thrusting all thought of an early dinner from his mind, he took a fat book from its shelf, opened it at the back and ran a podgy finger down the index, muttering under his breath, 'Apostles, Little Brothers of . . .' The wretched people had to be in there somewhere.

'. . . and it was in India that you met your teacher?' Tom had forgotten that he was not supposed to ask questions.

'No,' said Brother Joachim, 'that came later. In India I travelled high up into the foothills of the Himalayas. I've always had an affinity with mountains. I felt drawn to them; and, besides, I had heard of the strange men who lived up there. I thought that if I could find them, I might find some peace of mind at last. It's an old story, of course. Thousands have tried to do the same thing. On the law of averages alone some of them must have found what they were looking for – but we'd never hear about it if they had, would we?'

'You didn't find anyone, then?'

'Oh yes. I was very determined. And lucky. After four days, my guides would go no further. They said that only evil spirits lived on "the roof of the world". So I went on way up above the treeline, until I stumbled across some caves. Five men were standing in front of them as though I were expected. They might have been Tibetan, I'm not sure. They were small, dark, very silent. They looked hard at me – it was spooky, I can tell you! – and then they turned away. They didn't look at me again for six months. I moved into a cave of my own and waited. You can see that patience was something I learned early on.

'Then one day I became ill. Although it was nearly summer, it was still terribly cold and difficult to find enough wood to make a decent fire. After four days I was barely conscious – too weak to eat and with a fever which seemed to be burning up my body like dry wood. I just lay there in a heap of clothes and blankets, thinking how sad it was that I should die in a muddle, without knowing anything.' The monk paused and crossed over to where Tom was sitting by the fire. He poured himself three inches of black tea and sat down opposite the boy on a hard, straight-backed chair.

'They saved me, of course. The first thing I remember was that I gradually began to feel warm. From the outside, that is – the fever inside burned but brought no warmth. I opened my eyes to look for the fire. All I saw was one of the dark men sitting in meditation nearby. An incredible heat was pouring out of his body; I could feel it on my face. I remember laughing and laughing. I must have been delirious. The next thing I remember was a face bending very close to mine. It had eyes like a cat, narrow with tiny flecks of gold in them. I felt happy looking into those golden eyes.

'Some time later I was lifted up and all my clothes were taken off. I was being rubbed down with some sort of oil. The fever was being drawn out of me, brushed off me like cobwebs. I was given hot tea to drink. There was a lump of rancid butter floating in it. I soon recovered.'

'And you stayed? You found what you were looking for?'

'I stayed for a while. I thought these men were wonderful. They taught me – oh, I don't know how much. But there was something desperate about them too – for ever starving themselves, meditating for days at a time, standing all night up to their necks in freezing water, climbing the rocks until their bare feet were cut to the bone . . . They taught me a lot about gaining mastery over the body and how deep its secret energy runs. But I learnt as well that the body cannot be crushed. Its energies and passions cannot be uprooted without doing some essential violence to the whole person. There was something a bit frightening about those men – an animal look in their eyes, their matted hair . . .'

It had grown quite dark outside and the fire was low. The monk's face was hidden in shadow.

'One evening I told them that I was leaving. I could not explain why – explain that they were too . . . fierce or too unthinking. Anyway they didn't ask. The next morning my friend with the gold eyes took me on a long trek, even higher up into the mountains. He didn't say why, but I trusted him. At last we stopped. He pointed to a remote peak, covered in snow, the highest mountain for miles around. Right at the top I could just make out a dark patch. It looked like a dwelling of some sort with a black dot moving in front of it. My friend told me that up there lived the Puppet Master and that I should go and see him. I asked what he meant by "Puppet Master". He made strange movements with his hands. Apparently the man – or whoever – living on that mountain held the strings which were attached to all of us. We were acting out our lives according to the way he moved his fingers. In the mornings he lifted his arm and the sun came up; in the evening he lowered it and the sun sank. Standing in that remote, rarefied spot I found it easy to believe – but it was too late. I knew that my path lay elsewhere. I had decided to leave, and I did leave.'

Joachim leant forward and tossed another log on to the fire. It smoked for a few seconds and then burst into flame. The monk stared at it thoughtfully.

'So you went home,' prompted Tom.

The monk looked over at him. Twin flames burned in the depths of his eyes. He sat back and the miniature fires were extinguished.

'That was my intention. But I had not taken into account God's will. He led my steps to a small hamlet in Bulgaria, of all places. It lay on the lower slopes of the Balkan mountains overlooking a beautiful valley. Above the village there was a monastery. It was deserted. Communists don't like any competition, as you know. The monks had grown old and died and none came to replace them. In fact, there was only one left and he had gone to work in the hamlet as a carpenter.'

A light of understanding broke over Tom's face.

'He was your teacher! He taught you how to carve . . .'

Joachim nodded. 'Yes. And he taught me a good deal more. I can't begin to tell you. He even taught me English – I thought it was to do with the books we studied together. He had an astonishing collection. I was a poor pupil, I'm afraid. Unworthy of his attention. But he had no one else – luckily for me.'

'But you teach theology and all that pretty well,' said Tom ingenuously.

Joachim laughed. 'If I do, it's thanks to him. He never let me forget that theology is important, but that it's only partly to do with books. It's more the intellectual expression of a man's life. And in the end, it's all just a tiny footnote to the life of one person – Jesus Christ.'

'Why did you ever leave him?' asked Tom.

'I didn't really. He left me. He died.'

'Oh. How did he die?'

'If you mean "why did he die", that's easy. Old age. How he died is another matter. It was remarkable.'

'In what way?'

'One day we were both leaving the cottage of a peasant who was very sick. He was unlikely to last the night. My teacher could do nothing more for him although he was, shall we say, exceptional at performing cures' – Joachim noticed a question forming on Tom's lips and raised his hand to silence it – 'We won't go into that. Anyway, he turned to me and said nonchalantly: "This time tomorrow I'll be joining that poor fellow." I didn't understand him, of course. But it was true. The following evening we ate our supper as usual. Then he spoke to me for the last time, lay down on his bed and died. It was a remarkable death because it was so simple and so utterly unassuming. For a whole week the room was filled with the scent of lilies.'

Tom absorbed the story in silence. At length, he asked, 'But what about the ring?'

'Ah yes. The ring. It was my teacher's legacy. He always wore it. Just before he died, he told me that it could only be removed on his death. He told me that I should do so, put it on and . . . go to England.'

'What?'

'The Order he had spent his life in,' Joachim explained patiently, 'was called the Little Brothers of the Apostles.'

Tom looked at him blankly.

He smiled. 'You see, Tom, his Order was a sort of "brother" Order to this one. When he was gone, it would disappear. So he made me promise to take myself and the

49

ring to England, and ask to join this Order. Which, as you see, I did.' He chuckled at Tom's bemused expression.

'But why were there *two* in the first place?'

'That's easy. You must remember that the Order is extremely old. Way back in the Middle Ages the Church was not exactly holy most of the time. Priests and monks were corrupt and greedy, and so on. So, some French monks decided to return to the ideals of the early Church, to make a new start, as it were. Two of them founded the Order in the Balkans and two of them ended up here, in Bloxbury. They wanted to keep far away from the hypocrisy and showiness of the existing structures of the Church in France, Italy, Spain, and so on. That's why we keep everything so uncomplicated to this day. No inessentials in our services. There's even a tradition of worshipping out-of-doors without any church at all between us and God.'

Tom thought instantly of the ceremony at Bloxbury Ring. He only just remembered in time not to mention it. But he was a little reassured to learn that it might, for all its anomalies, be a quite usual event in the private worship of the Little Brothers.

Joachim interrupted his train of thought. 'Well, Tom. I have to go or I'll be late for Vespers. I don't have to remind you that eveything I say between these four walls must remain strictly between us?'

'Of course, Brother Joachim.' He was fully aware of the honour of being admitted into the monk's confidence. 'But there's just one more question . . . Can you really not take the ring off?'

'Well, I suppose I could. Really.' His eyes were dark, yet strangely luminous. 'But it would be more than my life's worth.'

Tom laughed – that was no answer. The monk's expression did not change. He looked grave. The boy's laughter died away.

As he walked unsteadily down the long bare tunnel, George had the distinct feeling that he was being swallowed up. The walls were a pale red, glowing with light from an unseen source. They seemed to pulsate at regular intervals like the working of a gullet. It was unnaturally stuffy and becoming more airless by the second. He began to feel dizzy. His legs could hardly carry him forward, while the small bag he was carrying was as heavy as a millstone; his shirt was sour with sweat.

Again the terrible voice, high-pitched and nasal, seared the air around him. He could not tell where it was coming from. It was disembodied, echoing and twanging between the stark walls of the endless tunnel.

'. . . Alitalia flight number 136, leaving for Florence, Trieste and Athens, is now boarding at gate number three . . .'

Florence! That was it! He clung to the word like an amulet to ward off evil spirits. 'Florence . . . *Firenze* . . . home.' He pictured his parents' farmhouse, buried in the warm vineyards of Tuscany. He would soon be there, if only he could hang on. His lips moved, soundlessly repeating the magic word, 'Florence, Florence . . .'

Suddenly there was someone at his elbow. A man. With a moustache. George veered away from him, stumbling slightly as he did so. The blood pounded in his head.

'Is anything the matter?' said the man with the moustache. 'Are you sick?'

'No . . . nothing's the matter. Who are you?' George heard an unfamiliar voice say. He recognised it as his own, and let out a forced, unnatural laugh. It hurt his swollen throat. Speech was becoming more and more difficult.

'Tell me,' said the man kindly. 'Tell me what the matter is.'

'I've sworn not to speak!' The words came out in a hoarse stage whisper. George found himself praying that the nightmare would end soon. Then he remembered the previous night and knew that he was awake. He saw

51

again the awful shape in front of the Stone, saw it gliding slickly down the mound to stand in the firelight; he saw the flash of the knife and heard the voice utter the unspeakable things.

'Pray for the Holy Father!' he whispered. The man's moustache twitched doubtfully; his eyes seemed very large and mournful. George felt hot tears of self-pity welling up in his own eyes. He hastily pulled himself together. 'I'm fine,' he said as normally as possible. 'Thank you.' The man still looked dubious but he nodded and walked on all the same.

'I know,' George confided to himself, 'I *know* that my Redeemer lives.' The half-remembered quotation gave him strength. He straightened up and walked with a lighter step towards the waiting aircraft. He even managed to return the smile of the air hostess standing in the doorway.

7

'Are you sure it wasn't some kind of hallucination?' asked Elizabeth Reardon, putting a plate of scrambled eggs in front of her son. She was thirty-seven and would have looked younger if her pretty oval face, framed by sensational red hair, had not been aged by its habitual expression of anxiety. 'It could have been all that running, you know. Too much oxygen to the brain . . .' Her smile was always slightly hesitant, revealing the tiny wistful lines around her eyes.

'No, I'm quite sure.' Tom was firm. 'As soon as I saw the brightness and the silver colour, I knew it was Brother Joachim. It was just like before, when I first saw it. You know, when he first arrived at the Abbey.'

'You never told me you saw it then.' Elizabeth was surprised.

'Well, I did.' Tom paused to take an enormous mouthful of egg. 'Actually, that was the first – '

'Finish your mouthful,' said Elizabeth absently. She was vexed that Tom had started up again with this business of seeing what he called 'lights'. She did not doubt him – at least, not since she had discovered the book called *The Human Aura*; but she found his gift unnerving.

' – the first time I saw a light by myself. Intentionally, I mean.'

Elizabeth was intrigued in spite of her misgivings. 'What do you mean exactly, Tommy?'

'It's hard to explain. It happened when Ambrose – '

his mother frowned – 'Sorry . . . *Brother* Ambrose was presenting Brother Joachim to the school at the beginning of his first term. He looked interesting and I wondered what he was like. I studied him carefully and then it came to me that I might sort of . . . *see* more if I stopped studying him. So I just pointed my eyes at him and used the inside of my head. Not my brain or anything – I wasn't thinking; I was concentrating my attention on him. It felt funny. I can't explain, but it was like retreating into my body to a quieter place. I could still hear everything that was going on, but far away . . . and there it was. A brilliant silver light all round him. I mean, I could still see the outline of his body, but it was faint. The light was the thing. Everybody around him looked very dull in comparison . . . unreal. It's the strangest light I've ever seen.' He took another mouthful of egg and toast and began to chew thoughtfully. 'It wasn't like the others in another way. His light *meant* something – as if it were just for me . . . as though I could see myself lit by it. That's when I knew I just *had* to join the Order.'

'So you don't actually see them with your eyes?' his mother asked.

Tom considered. It was the strength of them which mattered, and the colour. Most people's lights were not all that bright and, if the colour was pleasant, it was frequently tainted with a streak or an edge of some less pleasant hue.

'Well, the eyes obviously come into it. But it's behind the eyes that sees lights. I can't explain.' He put down his knife and fork and shrugged in the way that he had learnt from George. 'I mean, when I was young – ' his mother smiled. He gave her a withering look. 'When I was young and I saw old religious paintings of saints and people with haloes, I assumed that all painters could see lights, just like me. But since it's only saints who seem to have them I think maybe that some lights are so strong that everyone can see them – I don't know why they only paint them around the head. It makes me suspicious.

Maybe they can't see them. Anyway, it's true that lights are brightest around the head. And the stomach.'

'The solar plexus?' Elizabeth asked, remembering the diagram in *The Human Aura*.

'Probably,' said Tom, without really listening. He was thinking of the haloed saints. They might support his secret theory – that, although the lights were closely linked to the body, their ultimate source lay elsewhere. Deeper. Maybe in the immortal soul itself.

Elizabeth sat down at the round table and sighed. The previous day's rain had cleared and the morning was streaming sunlight through the low, wide windows of the kitchen – part of the cottage's extension which her inheritance (as well as providing a small income) had made possible. Apart from building on, she had not tampered with the original rooms. Her home was essentially the same one she had been born in. She poured out two cups of coffee.

'I had no idea you'd been seeing your "lights" all this time,' she said, pursing her lips. 'I thought you'd grown out of it – *hoped* you'd grown out of it. Do you remember when you were a child and you used only to see them when you were frightened or over-excited? It puzzled me for ages.'

'I still do. In fact, Mum, that's obviously what happened yesterday when I was running up the hill and saw Brother Joachim's light. I was in a terrible state over Miss Carroway – '

'What about her?' Elizabeth interrupted. 'You never told me if she was all right after that mad rush to get help.'

'Oh. Yes. She was . . . her leg was fine. After all.' Tom looked down quickly into his cup of coffee. It was almost the truth. His mother noticed nothing.

There was a silence, companionable but troubled as they both absorbed the implications of their conversation. They had never discussed the problem of the lights so explicitly before. Partly out of curiosity, partly

55

out of a desire to prepare the ground for her more serious request, Elizabeth asked, 'What colour is my aura . . . my "light"?'

'Oh, yours,' said Tom breezily. 'It's pretty good, Mum. Pale yellow mostly . . . clear . . . very nice – most of the time.' He smiled mischievously.

'What do you mean "most of the time"?' retorted Elizabeth.

'It gets a bit . . . sickly. When you're tired or when you have one of your migraines. And sometimes it grows reddish streaks when you're irritable.'

Elizabeth laughed. It sounded a little forced, betraying the anxiety which lay behind it. 'I'll have to watch my colours from now on, my lad. I can see that. I feel as though I were being spied on!'

Tom was idly making patterns in the sugar bowl with his teaspoon. He looked serious.

Elizabeth decided that it was the right time to lead in to her question: 'I hope you don't go round telling everyone about this . . . this gift of yours,' she said as lightly as she could. 'They could have you put away!'

'No. Only you know about it. I nearly told George, but he doesn't like that sort of thing. He'd think it was creepy. So I decided not to.'

He paused and then, unaware that he was forestalling his mother, he announced gravely, 'Mum, I'm going to confess the lights. Now that I've thought about them, it seems that they might be considered wrong . . . by the Little Brothers, I mean. I can't join the Order without mentioning that I can see lights. It might even be sinful, for all I know.'

Elizabeth Reardon thought quickly. This was a moment she had dreaded.

The blade of the knife – properly speaking, it was more of a dagger – was about eight inches long and tapered to a needle-sharp point. From time to time, the Abbot tested the sharpness absent-mindedly against the palm of his hand. There was a knock at the door. In response to Ambrose's curt exclamation, a monk glided into the room.

'There is someone to see you, Brother Ambrose,' said the monk apologetically, eyes lowered. 'A . . . Miss van Neef.'

The Abbot's impassive expression did not change. He merely opened a drawer in his desk, placed the dagger inside and shut it again.

'Let her come in.' The monk left the room, reappearing seconds later with a robust woman in a tweed jacket and skirt, thick stockings and heavy brown shoes. Her greying hair had been swept carelessly back into a bun so that several wisps had escaped, giving her an unexpectedly girlish look. Her broad face gave the impression of good humour and health; the red cheeks and hazel eyes were free of any make-up. She took longer strides than is usual for a woman of her weight and height, and her shoes clumped loudly on the floor.

'Good morning . . .' She paused momentarily, being uncertain how to address the Abbot. Her clear eyes flickered around the study, apparently without taking anything in. In reality, she had noted in a flash how the room served Ambrose's function as a headmaster – the usual large desk, the filing cabinet, the book-shelves, the telephone. She saw, too, that it had retained traces of the monk's cell. There were no carpets, for instance, only a threadbare rug; no drinks to welcome or appease parents; no school photographs on the walls. In short, it lacked the human touch.

Having failed to resolve the problem of Ambrose's title, she continued unruffled, 'My name is Hannah van Neef. You received my letter.'

It was a statement, not a question, delivered with calm assurance and, despite her Dutch accent, in flawless English.

Ambrose replied in kind: 'Good morning. You have not, perhaps, received my reply.'

He made no move, either to stand or to offer her a chair.

Hannah was not the least put out. 'But I have. And that is why I am here. I wish you to reconsider your decision to deny me access to Bloxbury Ring. I have reason to believe that it may prove of key importance in the research I am currently undertaking,' and she added diffidently, 'my book on the prehistoric sites of England, you understand.'

'I am familiar with your previous work on stone circles – the "sacred geometry" if I'm not mistaken? A thoroughly competent work . . .'

Hannah inclined her head in acknowledgement of what might have been a compliment. 'Thank you. You will appreciate, therefore, how pressing it is that I inspect your Ring as soon as possible. I am told that it is centred around a tumulus of sorts . . . ?'

'I seem to remember something of the kind,' Ambrose said vaguely. 'Of course, I am no expert . . . However, as I made clear in my letter, it is impossible for you to visit the Ring just now. We had to fence it off. Instances of vandalism, I'm afraid.'

Hannah flushed slightly at the idea that she could be implicated in such instances, and replied rather more hotly, 'But surely . . . in the case of respectable research . . . exceptions can be made? It seems reasonable – '

Brother Ambrose had raised his hand; the gesture was final. He spoke more earnestly: 'Miss van Neef. I must tell you honestly that if it were solely up to me, there could be no possible objection . . .' Hannah looked a little mollified. 'However, my hands are tied. I personally have no power to rescind this decision – all policy is decided collectively by the Order. Even monks have their committees, you know.' He drew back his lips into the semblance of a smile. 'But I will urge your case at our next meeting,' he added pleasantly, 'and I can confidently say that the Ring will be open to you shortly. A matter of a few weeks.'

'Weeks?' Hannah van Neef was taken aback.

'You must see that I cannot overrule the decision of the Brothers just like that! It would cause grave offence. Especially at a time when we are fully occupied with our own . . . internal affairs. But you may be sure that you will be able to examine our little mound to your heart's content. Eventually. I personally guarantee it. And now, will you forgive me? I have a great deal to do. I can contact you at the hotel? Good. I hope you are comfortable there . . .' and, all at once, Hannah was being ushered out while Brother Ambrose continued talking. '. . . I must say it is a rare thing to find someone taking such an enlightened interest in our national heritage . . . too little thought has been directed towards these ancient monuments. Goodbye . . . You will be hearing from me . . .' and the door closed behind her.

Hannah van Neef felt that, had she been a child, she would have stamped her foot.

It was Elizabeth Reardon's turn to look serious. The idea that Tom was about to confess his gift, his strange variation on the theme of second sight, made her request come out as an urgent demand.

'Tom,' she said softly. The unexpected intensity beneath the gentleness of her voice caused her son to look up, startled. 'You *mustn't* confess about the "lights".' It was the first time she had fully acknowledged their existence – she usually said '*your* lights' or 'those light things' in a mildly disparaging way.

'Why not? I ought to – '

'No.' She paused. 'There are things I must say to you. You must know what they are, but they need saying.'

Tom was a little embarrassed by the sudden intimacy. Like many people who are capable of deep affection, both he and his mother tended to cover up any direct confrontation with each other's feelings by a deliberate cheerfulness. They preferred to share jokes rather than emotions. And this was why the business of the 'lights' caused problems: it was not serious enough, somehow, to be concealed – but it was too serious to be joked about. Tom glanced at the clock above the pine sideboard where his mother kept her best dishes.

'Mum, can't it wait? I must see George first thing, *and* I don't want to be late on the last day of term.'

'There's plenty of time, Tom. Now listen. I'm not going to labour this. I'll say it once and that'll be the end of it.' She stood up and began stacking the dirty breakfast dishes, as if the activity helped her to talk.

'It's impossible for you to understand, Tommy,' she began, 'how important it is for me just being here. Not only in our beautiful home, but in Bloxbury . . .' She carried the dishes over to the sink and ran hot water over them. Tom examined a flaw in the surface of the table.

'You see, as long as your father was alive I didn't mind living in London. But after the heart-attack and watching his life drain away in that ghastly hospital, there was nothing but the terrible emptiness, the poky little flat, the struggle to make ends meet and, all around, the un-friendliness. If you hadn't been born so soon afterwards, I think I'd have gone mad. As it was, I just wanted to run back to my own mother and father, but how could I? They'd never wanted me to marry a man so much older than myself in the first place. And I was proud and stubborn, I couldn't admit defeat. My father did send me money from time to time, but he had no idea how homesick I was. Just as well, perhaps, because I wasn't really homesick for him, as it were, just for Bloxbury.'

She couldn't convey the extent of her desolation, the exile's deep yearning for a lost homeland. Knowing that her parents' cottage, like most of the village, was tied to the Abbey, she had despaired of ever being able to return. 'I thought we'd never get out, never get back. Even my faith began to desert me. D'you remember that restaurant I worked in? I used to pray – I was so tired – I used to stand in that vast deafening kitchen with everybody bustling and shouting and I'd pray "O God,

God, please do something!"' She clattered a plate self-consciously on to the draining-board. 'I'd never have got through it without you.' They exchanged a brief smile.

'Then grandpa died,' said Tom.

'Yes. And grandma, too, within a fortnight – poor old things – and I came back for the funeral. Then afterwards, when Eugene – Doctor Kelly – drew me aside and said that the Abbot wanted to see me, I felt deep down that our lives were about to begin again . . .' She crossed the kitchen and sat down opposite her son. 'Sure enough, Brother Ambrose did everything he could to make us feel accepted and wanted – you got your scholarship to the school, I got my home back and, well, here we are.' She sighed, gazing out of the window and down the neat little garden. Birds were singing in the old cherry tree which grew nearly as high as the roof. 'Yes,' she mused, 'one way or another Brother Ambrose has been a bit of a guardian angel.'

Tom had never quite looked at him like that, but he saw her point and said nothing. His mother's eyes lit up.

'And the things he used to tell me . . . all the doubts I used to have about the Church . . . he made it seem so simple. You know, he practically revised all my views about – ' she stopped herself short. 'Anyway that's not the point. The real point is this: the day you came to me and said, quite casually, that you'd been talking to Brother Joachim, and that you'd thought it over and that you wanted to be a monk – that day I nearly wept on the spot. Ever since I've known Brother Ambrose and realised how, in a sense, *worthless* any life must be that isn't dedicated to God wholeheartedly – ever since then I've dreamt that you might want to join the Order. And now you are. In a few weeks' time you'll be a novice. Just think of it!'

Elizabeth stretched across the table and took one of Tom's hands. She gazed urgently into his eyes. 'Nothing must jeopardise that moment, Tommy. Your – my – whole life is at stake. That's why there must be no mention – not a whisper – of this silly "lights" business . . . all right, sorry. It's not silly. But you know how strict, how . . . adamant Brother Ambrose is. He wouldn't understand as I do. Besides, you'll grow out of it. You're bound to. You'll be much too busy to worry about people's "lights"! Promise me, Tommy. Promise me you won't say a word?'

For a second, Tom was completely detached from his mother. He saw a rather sad, middle-aged woman with slightly dishevelled hair fervently asking him to promise something easy. He was touched.

'I won't say anything, Mum. Don't worry. It's a pretty harmless talent in any case. And who knows? Maybe God gave it to me!'

His mother smiled, out of relief, but also out of the love she felt for her son at that moment.

Tom's brow creased slightly. 'But I can't promise not to see lights. I mean, half the time they just appear. Like the sun coming out. I can't control that.'

'Of course not, Tom. I'm not asking you to stop seeing them. God knows why you've got this odd gift, but you have. And that's that. Just don't . . . *work* on it, O.K.?'

'O.K.'

'Now you really will be late if you don't hurry. Just think! All the lovely holidays ahead of us . . . and the Pope coming and everything. It'll be marvellous. Be sure to give my love to George, poor boy. I hope his ceremony wasn't too gruelling!'

Tom ran upstairs to his room to collect his school bag. He felt exhilarated after the long confidential talk with his mother. Quickly he took off his jacket, slung the bag high up over his left shoulder and put on the jacket again. He looked in the mirror and was pleased with the hunchbacked effect. After a little experimentation, he adopted a withered arm in preference to an ape-like, dangling-arm position and loped down the stairs. He burst into the kitchen.

'I'm off, Mum. Be late back. Going up to Brother Joachim's to help with the crucifix, if he'll let me.'

His mother turned and let out a high-pitched giggle. 'All right, Quasimodo. See you later.'

Tom kissed her on the cheek, gave a blood-curdling laugh and scuttled towards the back door. He paused, straightened up and said, 'It's a funny thing, Mum, but whenever I've tried to have a look at the lights of the other monks – apart from Joachim, that is – I've never been able to see a thing. It's as if . . . as if they were protected by invisible shields. They just stay the same. Just ordinary bodies – ' and before his mother could reply, he was gone.

8

Hannah van Neef strode past the terraced cottages which lined Bloxbury's narrow main street. It was usually empty of traffic but today a number of cars streamed towards the Abbey, forcing her to press close to the walls. As she came to the last house, which was detached from the others and set back from the road, a boy jumped over the low hedge and landed in front of her. She brandished her knobbly walking stick in mock anger. He looked so amazed and, as ever, so disorganised with his dark red hair sticking up, his shirt-tail hanging out and his bag half round his neck, that she burst out laughing.

Frowning to conceal his embarrassment, Tom stared past Miss van Neef's laughing face. Her hearty good humour always made him nervous, largely because he suspected that it was a cover-up for her acute intelligence – he'd seen the way she observed people. Also, there was something intimidating about a creature of such strict habit that she went for the same walk at the same time every morning. He knew her route by heart: a full circle from the hotel, down through the village, and back by the high ridge of woods.

'Excuse me,' he murmured.

'Certainly,' she replied with disconcerting directness. Then, as though she were simply resuming an interrupted conversation, she said, 'Your headmaster is not an easy man to get around, is he? He seems utterly oblivious of a woman's wiles.' She patted her scraped back hair, rolled her eyes and pouted in a comic impersonation of a *femme fatale*. 'Ah,' she sighed tragically, 'these godly men. They have no heart.'

Tom could not help smiling. 'You've been to see Brother Ambrose,' he said shyly.

'Indeed I have, I have,' Hannah replied emphatically. 'But it was quite, quite useless. He refused to let me see his precious Ring – although I begged him. He takes me for a vandal. Be honest, Mr Reardon, do I look like a vandal?'

Tom laughed and shook his head. He couldn't detect any irony in her calling him 'Mr Reardon'; he was rather flattered.

'Ah, you laugh, Mr Reardon, but this is no laughing matter. Bloxbury Ring means a great deal to me. Perhaps as much as a whole chapter!'

Tom knew by hearsay that Miss van Neef had come all the way from the Netherlands to investigate local prehistoric landmarks. This was generally considered an eccentric but harmless pastime – the villagers regarded the numerous banks, barrows and standing stones simply as obstacles in the way of the plough or as a waste of good land. But Tom suddenly saw a golden opportunity: if she knew all about these things, maybe she could throw light on the Ring ceremony . . .

'I'm afraid everyone's forbidden to visit the Ring,' he said cautiously. 'I've seen it, but ages ago of course.' He blushed slightly at the untruth and added quickly, 'And please call me Tom.'

'You have seen it, Tom?' Hannah opened her eyes wide in mock disbelief. Tom laughed again. 'Well now. That is most interesting. I have heard that it contains a burial mound. Can this be true?'

'Oh yes,' said Tom. 'As far as I can remember. And there's a stone on top of the mound.' Hannah van Neef narrowed her eyes.

'What sort of stone?' There was no trace of jokiness in her voice this time.

Tom thought for a moment. 'Just an ordinary stone. Shaped like a pillar, but sort of square. About this high –'

he raised his hand above his head and stood on tiptoe to indicate a height of about six and a half feet.

'Is it granite? Limestone? Or what?'

Tom was a bit taken aback by the staccato questions. 'I don't remember,' he said lamely.

'What colour is it?'

'Colour? I don't know. Just sort of . . . grey, I think.'

'Hm. Well, this is most interesting news . . . most interesting.' Hannah van Neef appeared to be deep in thought.

Tom was intrigued. 'What exactly is so interesting, Miss van Neef? If you wouldn't mind telling me?' he said politely.

'Of course I don't mind, Tom. And call me Hannah. No, it is interesting because it is most unusual to find a Ring enclosing a mound. But to find a standing stone on *top* of the mound – now that is practically unique. I know of only two others like that in the whole of Europe. Let me see, is it possible that the stone might go *through* the top of the mound? Instead of just sitting on top?'

'Er . . . yes . . . *yes*,' said Tom, finding Hannah's evident excitement infectious. 'It definitely could have been coming out through the top – but it would have to be extremely tall.'

'About five metres,' said Hannah, half to herself. 'Perhaps more if the inside of the mound is sunk below ground level . . .' She beamed at Tom. 'I see you are becoming interested. That is splendid! We must have some more talking – sorry, my English! I mean that we must speak again soon.'

'I'd like that very much,' said Tom more eagerly than he intended.

'Good, good,' Hannah said warmly. 'Then it is settled, Tom. I always have coffee at half-past four – I do not understand your English obsession with tea! Please come on any day. You know where I am?'

'At the hotel, yes. Thank you. I must go now. I have to

meet a friend of mine who's just joined the Order. It's the last day of term, you know.'

'Poor fellow.' Hannah clucked sympathetically. 'Well, I shall miss seeing you on my daily walk, Tom. Oh . . . if you see your headmaster I hope you will put in a good word for me about the Ring!'

The Little Brothers of the Apostles were traditionally lenient on the last day of term and their pupils were not slow to take advantage of the fact. The noise in the cloisters was deafening. Shouts of greeting, peals of laughter and loud curses mingled with the clatter of feet and the crash of heavy trunks. In the midst of the jostling, rejoicing boys Tom stood and stared in a kind of reverie at the low arched doorway through which a stone staircase led up to the monks' cells. No boy was allowed through it; it marked the boundary of that otherworldly domain where the Little Brothers ceased to be school-masters and came into their own. Tom realised how little he knew about this private existence, part of which (it still seemed incredible) was centred around a Stone Age burial mound. Had George already passed through the small doorway and out of reach? With sudden urgency he pushed past some younger boys who were playing a violent improvised game of football and headed for George's room. Behind and beyond the din, he seemed to hear the ancient grey silence, six feet thick, of the cloisters' stones.

George was not there. Tom closed the door behind him and sat down on the bed. He had in the past been made to feel uneasy by his friend's obsessive tidiness – the exact square of a folded blanket, books ordered by size on the shelves, precise rows of pens on the desk. He was even more disturbed now by signs, however slight, of carelessness. The white surplice on the floor and the open cupboard brought a sudden dryness to his mouth. The bedside table was bare except for a reading lamp. Surely there'd been a photo . . . He remembered the smart dark-eyed woman, and the trees heavy with oranges. Where was the photograph now?

He sprang up and looked into the cupboard. George kept a travelling bag on the shelf above the hanging space. It was gone. He went to the bed and lifted the pillow. George's pyjamas were missing. He had seen enough. Behind him, he heard the door open. The relieved question had already formed as he turned.

'Where the *hell* – ' The sentence was cut short. It was not George who stood in the doorway. It was Brother Anselm. The kindly old man looked unusually severe.

'What is your business here, Reardon?'

Tom immediately felt as guilty as if he had been doing something wrong. 'I . . . I was looking for Woodward. He's not here.'

'Clearly. You will leave now.' The monk's eyes were hard. He turned and began to shuffle away.

Tom was more than surprised at the change which had overtaken the old man. He hurried after him. 'Brother Anselm! Wait. Please. Do you know where George is?'

It was not the answer which shocked Tom so much as the tone in which it was delivered.

'I do not.'

The three little words stopped Tom in his tracks. They had been spoken with such finality, such complete indifference that, instead of being Anselm's special pupil for an entire year, George might have been a total stranger. The usually genial old monk apparently neither knew nor cared whether George even existed. He receded slowly down the corridor and disappeared. Tom's heart beat faster. There was something terribly wrong. He could only think of one thing to do: tell Joachim immediately – he would know where George was, or at least be able to find out.

The powerful light shone directly on to the crude mass of uncarved wood above the neck. Tom was reminded of a car-crash victim: the body untouched while the head was reduced to a shapeless pulp. He called out again, louder this time.

'Brother Joachim!'

He had never seen the crucifix uncovered before. He forgot his errand, lost in contemplation of the torso. It was boldly executed in strong, angular lines like an Eastern icon. The rib cage was stylised, sharply defined above the smooth musculature of the abdomen. A jagged hole had been left uncarved in the side. The arms were thin and sinewy, straining outwards along the crossbar; the hands did not sag beyond the wicked nails driven through the wrists, but were pressed against the wood, fingers splayed strongly. He was in the middle of examining the folds of the loincloth hanging loosely around the hips, when he was interrupted by a sound at the back of the workshop. Joachim was standing at the foot of the wooden stairs which climbed to his single living room.

'Hardly a work of art I'm afraid,' he said. 'But it's meant well, if that counts for anything. Come to give me a hand?'

'Yes. No. Brother Joachim, it's George. He's gone.' Tom made no attempt to hide his agitation.

'Gone? Ambrose never mentioned – ' The monk stopped, puzzled. 'What do you mean "gone"?'

'He's disappeared. I went to his room – '

'Of course he hasn't disappeared. Have you forgotten? He's a Little Brother now. He can't be expected to stay in his old room!'

'But his bag has gone. His pyjamas, photo – everything except his clothes.'

Joachim thought for a moment. 'Well, he's obviously gone to visit his father in London. A few days' holiday will do him good. He's had a tough time – '

'Yes, yes but both his parents are at home at the moment. In Italy. He told me. And he'd *never* just leave without saying anything . . .' He looked anxiously at Joachim who began to pace up and down.

After a while, he said decisively, 'Look, Tom. There's nothing to get excited about. I'll find out what George is up to – just as soon as I have a word with Brother Ambrose. You'll leave it to me?' Tom smiled and nodded. 'Good. Now, I've got work to do. Are you staying or going?'

'Staying,' said Tom. 'If that's O.K.?'

Joachim handed him a tin of varnish and a fine brush, and pointed to the left arm of the cross.

Crucifixion. The agony of vicious nails severing the nerves. The terrible weight of your own body. The sinews slowly tearing. The blood seeping away. A frog splayed and pegged to a dissecting board died quicker. The long-drawn-out anguish. If you were lucky, your legs were broken – the body jolting down, the intolerable pressure on the chest, the relief of suffocation. If you were lucky.

Tom tried to realise the torment – and failed. It was not imaginable. He was not being morbid; it was his duty, he felt, to meditate on this form of execution, to try to penetrate both the horror and the obscenity. The attempt alone was a chastening experience. He spoke his thoughts out loud, conscious of the almost visible effect of his question as it rippled across the calm oasis of the workshop.

'Are you prepared to die like that, Brother Joachim? Nailed to a cross?' Surprised at the boy's seriousness, the monk looked up from his work.

'Crucifixion is not something one can prepare for. But we all have to prepare for death. One way or another.'

'But to be a monk you have to try and imitate Christ, don't you?'

'You have to become perfect, certainly. As Christ was perfect.'

'Doesn't that make it worse? A perfect man dying so horribly? I know it was necessary . . . that he should die for our sins, and so on. But, all the same – '

70

'Being perfect means that one can never die.'

The simple enigmatic statement was like a full stop to the conversation. Tom grappled with it for a moment in silence.

'What do you mean?' he persisted. 'If you're talking about the Resurrection, that's cheating! You still have to die before you can be resurrected . . .'

'I'm not talking about resurrection.'

Tom looked at him helplessly. But Joachim did not seem inclined to explain himself. He was lost in concentration on his carving.

'I don't know what you mean,' said Tom finally.

The hand holding the chisel hesitated in mid-air. The monk put the tool down, walked across to the door and opened it. He looked to left and right, and closed it again firmly. The obviously dramatic display made Tom nervous. It was not like Joachim.

The monk returned to the workbench and took up his chisel again. His face was as still as a sphinx's, the eyes fixed on a far horizon. Only the dark clouds gathering behind them gave any indication that he was thinking. Tom smiled at him apprehensively.

'What's the matter?'

'I've decided to tell you what we believe,' the monk said softly. 'It's a thing that I, as your tutor, would be telling you anyway. Eventually. But I'll tell you now because I think you're ready for it and because . . . we may not have much time.'

The dreadful words rang in Tom's ears. His voice wavered.

'What do you mean "not much time"? You're not *leaving*. Are you?'

Joachim looked with concern at the stricken boy. 'You know I won't be here for ever. You must be ready to face up to it. Don't forget you're going to be a monk. That means setting your face against the whole world, if necessary. Standing alone before God. I won't pretend to you there isn't terrible desolation . . .' He smiled sadly.

'But there is glory as well. Besides, you don't want to stay tied to my apron strings, do you?'

Tom shook his head manfully.

Joachim continued more lightly. 'Good. In any case, I was thinking of the immediate future. I'm afraid we'll have to see less of each other – I have to devote all my time to preparing for the Holy Father's visit.'

'But I help you, don't I?' Tom protested, waving the varnish brush.

Joachim laughed. 'You do, Tom. And if I were a free agent . . .' he made a helpless gesture and went on, choosing his words carefully, 'It has been . . . suggested that you come here too often. It is thought that this is not a good thing at the moment. So, you must do as I say. Agreed?'

Tom had no need to ask who had made the 'suggestion' – Ambrose's suggestions were always final.

'I suppose so,' he said rather peevishly. 'Though I don't see what Ambrose has to do with it.'

'Brother Ambrose has everything to do with it.' The weary patience in Joachim's voice was worse than a reproach. 'It's about time you understood once and for all that the Order's strength and unity depend on the single authority of the Abbot. Don't imagine that he's appointed randomly – Brother Ambrose was nominated by his predecessor, approved by the Brothers and affirmed by the Holy Spirit. You may think of him now as just a headmaster. But that's only a tiny part of his duties. Above all, he's responsible for interpreting God's will in relation to the Order. Not an easy task. In return, the Brothers freely bind themselves to obey him in all things. Obedience guarantees the cohesion of the Brothers under God; it's also the outward sign of their humility, a sign that no one feels he's above the Order that sustains him. The greater the soul is – and the Order has known many great souls – the deeper the need for obedience.' The monk smiled kindly at the boy whose cheeks were flushed red with shame.

'I'm sorry, Brother Joachim. I wasn't thinking.'

'Very well. You've plenty of time to think between now and your first vows. Remember the oath you'll be taking before the Brothers – and before God: to put yourself entirely at the disposal of the Order. It requires courage to take such an oath. Do you still want to go through with it?'

'More than anything.'

'I'm glad. I've got a lot of faith in you, Tom.' The boy's cheeks turned red again, for different reasons. 'And that's why I'm going to entrust you with the secret. Are you willing to hear it? To share the burden of knowledge? Make no mistake, Tom, knowledge can be a thing of terror, to be taken up like a sword. There's no going back.'

Unthinkingly Tom grasped the left arm of the crucifix, as if to brace himself for a blow.

'Yes. I'm ready.'

Joachim spoke gravely and with great deliberation. 'First you must swear not to tell a living soul what I am about to tell you, which is a secret passed down through the centuries from the time of Christ.'

Tom was pale but resolute. The words came out in little more than a whisper.

'I swear.'

9

Cardinal Benetti, who was trying to cut down on smoking, stubbed out his tenth cigarette of the day and stood up from behind the desk in his office.

'So it has become a teaching Order only in the last century or so?' he asked, indicating that his companion should sit down in a large leather armchair. He himself preferred to lean on the edge of the desk. The two men could not have been more dissimilar to look at. The tall saturnine figure of the Cardinal towered over the plump myopic priest, like Don Quixote over Sancho Panza.

'That's right, Eminence,' replied Father Vittorio. 'There are many favourable reports of the Order's teaching activities. They form the bulk of what has been written about the Order. I even have a school prospectus . . . Bloxbury Abbey sounds a pleasant place with excellent facilities.'

The Cardinal could not help smiling. The little priest looked so owlish with his round spectacles and eyebrows which arched naturally to give him a permanent expression of surprise. He was so earnest and precise too – it was impossible not to like him. The Cardinal smothered the smile with an attempt at seriousness.

'But you say that the first extant reference to the Little Brothers of the Apostles dates from the beginning of the fourteenth century?'

'Yes. The Order was fully organised by that time, which suggests that it was probably founded a good deal earlier. There is an amusing legend about the Abbots of the Order . . .' His startled eyes twinkled mischievously behind his glasses. 'They are supposed to be in possession of a treasure which has been passed down secretly from the founder, whose identity is not known . . .'

Vittorio glanced at the Cardinal to see if his interest was kindled. The priest was particularly proud of his detective work. It had taken him most of the night and he was unwilling to squander his results too quickly.

'What is the treasure?' asked the Cardinal, both entertained and intrigued by the priest's obvious enjoyment in telling the tale.

'One source suggests that it is nothing less than the Holy Grail. Another asserts that it is simply a nail from the Cross.'

'That would make about two dozen nails currently in circulation,' the Cardinal remarked wryly.

'More, I think,' Vittorio said seriously.

Cardinal Benetti smiled. 'What is your opinion, Father?'

'I think that it is more likely to have been a valuable recipe for strong drink. Like Benedictine.' The Cardinal laughed. 'But whatever it is, it must have helped them to retain their popularity.'

'Why?'

'Well, Eminence, nearly every ecclesiastical institution I can think of has suffered rebelliousness from the laity at some time or other . . . when it has accumulated too much land for instance, or become too greedy, or even' – he demurred slightly – 'when its members have fathered too many children. But these Little Brothers have apparently never suffered from complaints – a remarkable circumstance in a largely Protestant country! In fact, they were even protected by the laity during the Reformation, and subsequently re-instated by popular demand.'

'Remarkable indeed. Why then are they not more widely known?'

'I imagine it is merely a question of numbers. They

have always limited themselves to twelve members. But it seems, too, that they have never sought what one might call "publicity". They are a deeply ascetic Order, and their conduct in the immediate community seems to have been both practical and exemplary.'

Cardinal Benetti looked up sharply. 'No suspicion of Protestantism, I trust?'

'Apparently not. They observe all the forms of the Church with great conscientiousness.'

'Hmm. You know I have been in touch with the Abbot? A . . .' He reached for a piece of paper behind him. 'A Brother Ambrose. Seems a worthy man. And surprisingly level-headed – ' he was going to say 'for a monk', but managed to suppress it. He went on, 'I must say that I was inclined to oppose the Holy Father's wish to visit the . . . er . . . Little Brothers of the Apostles. But I see now that he was, as usual, right. If any Order deserved recognition, this one does. It is heartening to see that the monastic life – even in the twentieth century – can still do so much to preserve the precious lifeblood of the Church, eh Father? Have you never been tempted to enter an Order yourself?'

'I considered it, Eminence. Once.' Vittorio shifted uncomfortably in his chair.

The Cardinal mistook the source of his discomfort. 'Bit too spartan perhaps?' He smiled down at the priest.

'Perhaps.'

'Well, there are many mansions, Father. Fortunately for us.'

'Yes. Fortunately.'

'Well. I assume that all you have said is in your notes? Good. I shall pass them on. Now, is there anything else of importance?'

'Not of importance, Eminence. Of interest perhaps.' Vittorio could not resist showing off the thoroughness of his researches. 'I thought it might be worth mentioning that, until quite recently, there was another Order of the same name situated in the Balkans.'

'Oh?'

'Yes. It was only after I'd spent a good hour on the Little Brothers that I discovered they were the wrong ones!'

'A coincidence, I presume.'

'Oh yes. There's nothing to connect them except perhaps . . .'

'Perhaps what?'

'Just an intuition of mine. The Balkan Order was, in fact, the better known of the two. That's why I came across it first. The founders – there are rumoured to be at least two of them – were extraordinary characters by all accounts. Famous for their powers of healing, casting out of devils, and so forth. These . . . skills seem to have been handed down. No less than six members of the Order have been nominated over the years for canonisation – the usual miracles are claimed.'

'Then why haven't we heard of a Saint Jaroslav – or whatever they call themselves?' The Cardinal was indignant. 'Or perhaps you have?'

'No, Eminence. That's the point. The nominations were all quashed by the Order itself. No reason given.'

'Good Lord!' exclaimed Cardinal Benetti. 'Such humility! Was there no investigation at all into the alleged miracles?'

'It was impossible without the co-operation of the Order. And, as you know, the testimony of an enthusiastic flock is not enough . . .'

'I see what you mean,' said the Cardinal thoughtfully. 'About the similarity. The reticence of both these Orders is highly unusual. Most refreshing . . .' He absentmindedly took a cigarette out of its packet and lit it. 'Many thanks, Father Vittorio. If you're still interested, I shall relay to you any further news from our Brother Ambrose. I think the Holy Father will find his visit most profitable.'

To his amazement, Joachim's stern face broke into a smile. He gave a brief laugh.

'Actually, Tom, all this mysteriousness is just part of the ritual. The secret isn't really secret at all. Lots of people know about it. But they don't believe it.' The monk grew serious again and leant forward earnestly. 'The real secret is, that it is the Truth. As a rule people don't like too much Truth – *you* may not like it – but I will tell you this Truth now and you will hold it fast, in silence, until it becomes a part of you.'

He gestured peremptorily towards a chair. Tom sat down.

'First of all, Jesus was not resurrected,' said Joachim, 'simply because He did not die.' He paused to let the full force of his words sink in. Tom sat absolutely still. 'He did not die, because He was the Christ, the Anointed One, the Son of God – in short He was, and is, pure eternal spirit. This is what is meant by perfection. Nothing that is born and dies can be perfect. As long as the spirit is shut up in this ugly, corruptible prison we call the body, it is imperfect. God has buried His divine spark in blood and bone and excrement; but He has given us the means of nurturing it, fanning its weak flame until it consumes our flesh with holy fire and we become whole, a spiritual body of light. He sent his Son to us as the Example. But our dull eyes cannot see pure spirit; they are blinded by the light. So Christ came under the appearance of an ordinary man – a necessary illusion. In reality, He was incapable of sin, immune to bodily affliction, altogether far removed from this world of matter ruled over by Satan. That is why He did not die, *could* not die. They could no more nail Him to a cross than catch water in a net.' Joachim sighed wearily. 'Still, He chose the illusion. We must preserve it,' – he waved a dismissive hand towards the crucifix – 'but one day the whole world will know, and understand, this Truth. Then, whatever we monks have begun, the people will bring to fruition. We are merely the forerunners of a New Order, an Order which will bring transfiguration to everyone. Why do we fast, pray, mortify the flesh . . . ? We are God's prospectors, Tom, panning for gold. The

78

dross of our bodies shall be washed away by the pure waters of our dedicated lives, until only the golden nuggets of God remain!'

In the small hours of the morning, Tom jerked awake from a deep sleep. The pitch-black room prickled with tiny fragments of brightly-coloured dream which receded beyond his reach at the speed of light. He sat up and switched on his bedside lamp. The darkness swirled away and hid in the corners of his room. His head was ringing with Joachim's description of the fantastic Spirit-Christ. He clearly remembered all the words, but without his friend actually there to speak them they conjured up a different image – an image of angels.

He had never been quite certain about angels. He pictured them as beautiful, pristine beings of pure intelligence who stared down on mankind's muddle and suffering with curiosity and indifference. They were as flawless, and as cold, as crystal. The image troubled him.

He stumbled out of bed and began to rummage through his cupboard until he found the little booklet entitled *A Catechism of Christian Doctrine*. He hadn't looked at it for years. There'd been no need: the Little Brothers were strong on the New Testament but never bothered much about official Roman Catholic doctrine. How did it compare with Brother Joachim's inside information? He flicked through the pages.

What do you mean by the Incarnation? the Catechism asked sternly.

I mean by the Incarnation that God the Son took to himself the nature of man: 'the Word was made Flesh'.

It sent shivers through you to know that the Church was deceived. God the Son had glided over the surface of the world's swamp; the Word had never sunk into Flesh.

Why is Jesus Christ called our Redeemer?

Jesus Christ, came the pat reply, *is called our Redeemer because his precious blood is the price by which we were ransomed.*

There was an illicit thrill in knowing that, in fact, the angelic Spirit had never suffered, bled or died. But you had to accept, too, that its Power hadn't sacrificed itself out of love for the world. Your sins weren't paid for. The bread and wine were empty, after all. Without the saving grace of the Redeemer, you had to overcome alone the force of gravity and, all alone, will yourself across the vastness of space. It was difficult not to feel daunted and (you had to admit it) a bit betrayed.

10

Peering over the balustrade, Hannah was just in time to see Mrs. K. scuttle across the wide hall and leave by the front door, slamming it behind her. Everyone knew her as Mrs. K. Her full name seemed to have died, along with her husband, at least fifteen years before. She was a large shambles of a woman who appeared to Hannah as having been battered out of shape by life's blunt instrument. She carried out the day-to-day running of her hotel with an air of martyrdom. Rarely seen on the premises, she spent as much time as possible with her equally widowed, equally shapeless sister down in the village.

Hannah was her only guest and it suited her down to the ground. Both parties had quickly struck a silent bargain to disturb each other as little as possible. Hannah scarcely even troubled Mrs. K. for meals and, in return, she was given the run of the place.

The hotel had once been a small manor house built more than two-thirds of the way up the hill, at the very edge of the woods. Indeed, three sides of the building were surrounded by spruces, beeches and firs, including the front which faced the narrow track that meandered down to the main street. The north wing alone had an uninterrupted view across the valley to the Abbey on the opposite hill. As a result, the hotel was dark and damp; the old prints on the walls, the open fires, even the collection of decaying tennis racquets under the stuffed head of a wild boar in the hall, all helped to make it more like an old family house.

Hannah's room was one of nine principal bedrooms – large but low-ceilinged, with small leaded windows – which gave off the dark, wood-panelled gallery. She went down the wide creaky staircase, crossed the hall and entered the large drawing-room, which was equipped for a more gracious age when guests had actually used the French writing-desks, the spindly card-tables, the magnificent grand piano. On her own, Hannah divided her time between the comfortable sofa and armchairs drawn up to the fire at one end, and her embroidery stand set up in front of the bay window at the other.

Her embroidery was no mere hobby; it was a passion, and she worked on it every day. She loved the ritual of choosing the brightly coloured silks and watching the pattern come to life under her skilful stitches. She had no patience with still lifes of flowers or sentimental portraits of animals, preferring abstract patterns based on esoteric designs or strange geometries.

At present she was on the point of finishing a Buddhist mandala, traced from a photograph of the original which was painted on the wall of a Tibetan monastery. The intricately decorated circles and crenellated squares, resembling the blue-print for some fantastic mosque, glowed like an illuminated manuscript. Hannah touched her handiwork affectionately. It was time to keep her eye open for a new design.

She turned towards the window and looked out, over the roof of the doctor's house, to the valley below. Her gaze was arrested by two figures standing at the foot of the avenue which wound up to the Abbey. At that distance they were just small black patches, like holes punched in the landscape. They were bound to be the Abbot and that other monk. She had seen them more than once in the course of her daily walk. Yesterday they had been up at the farm at the end of the village, nearest the by-pass. Judging by their serious expressions and purposeful strides, they had not been out walking for

82

pleasure. They were probably on their way to chastise the farmer for not going to church regularly.

She regarded them with mild distaste. Why didn't they leave people alone? Hannah's own beliefs centred around a deep reverence for Nature and an absolute respect for other human beings. If pressed for her views on the Deity, she would come down firmly on the side of the lusty old pagan gods – gods of the sky, wind, sea, corn and wine. She felt nothing but aversion for those bloodless holy men who lived by rules, reviled their own natures and worshipped their one tyrannical God.

She was startled by a sudden footfall behind her. She turned abruptly. A smile of genuine pleasure lit up her good-natured face.

'Well, Tom. I'm delighted you have come.'

Wrapped in their own silence, heavy with a single purpose, the two monks were as oblivious of the brightness of the day as stones in clear water. Their black boots rang dully on the tarmac as they trod down the drive of Bloxbury Abbey. The sharp edge to the weather, which had sent ordinary men reaching for warm coats, was lost on them; their dark-blue habits were the same ones they wore winter and summer. As they approached the gates, the taller of the two, who had been walking subserviently a step or two behind, drew level with his companion. The Abbot glanced at him questioningly.

'Brother Ambrose, I must ask you once again about Woodward's initiation.' The sentence hung between them in the calm mist of his breath.

'Must you, Joachim?' the Abbot replied. He was looking distractedly at the woodland on the far side of the valley. 'I should have thought you had enough on your mind without worrying about a novice who proved inadequate to the demands of the Order.'

'Nevertheless, he's gone and I'd like to know what's become of him.'

The blue protruding vein on the side of the Abbot's

83

large head rippled once. 'He returned home to his parents.'

They had reached the gates. By tacit and mutual consent they stopped. It was almost as if they were drawing in a last breath from the rarefied air of their domain before plunging into the outside world. Ambrose continued to stare straight ahead.

Joachim persisted, 'How can you be confident that he will remain silent?'

Ambrose clenched and unclenched his fist. Then, with studied patience, he said, 'To begin with, Woodward was highly overwrought, even at the outset of the rite. He was further disoriented by the demonstration of the power. As a result, I doubt that he absorbed anything of what he was subsequently told concerning our mission. If he does remember, he knows that his vows are still binding; and if by any chance he ever decides to dishonour them, it'll be too late – the Vatican visit will be over. Who will listen to him then?'

'I have your assurance, then, that he has come to no harm?'

Ambrose turned to face him, his expression no longer neutral, but fixed and inscrutable.

'I'm not used to giving assurances, Joachim. Nor am I required to.'

The monk did not waver under his superior's slow glare. He said harshly, 'I have a right to know –'

'A *right*?' The word scythed through the air on a sudden gust of wind. 'You're mistaken. You have a single duty and you will perform it. God knows I don't interfere with your spiritual preparation, so why do you make my task more difficult? We're both bound, in our separate ways, to serve the sacred mission of the Order. But ultimately, Joachim – ' he lowered his voice – 'ultimately the responsibility is mine alone.' He shot a piercing glance towards his companion and continued softly, 'Perhaps it is time I reminded you of your dying master's wish . . . ?'

For the first time, Joachim appeared uneasy. He lowered his eyes and muttered, 'There's no need, Brother Ambrose.'

'I think there is,' he said calmly. 'Whom did he tell you to obey?'

'You.'

'Why?'

'Because you are the Guardian.'

'Yes . . .' The Abbot gazed serenely into the distance. 'I am the Guardian.' There was a moment's silence before he recollected himself. 'Time is too short,' he said briskly, 'for all this sentiment over one unsuitable child. You'll do well to forget him and apply yourself to more important things.' He turned and walked through the gates.

Brother Joachim followed him with his eyes for a moment and then, more slowly, walked after him.

'Long barrows are just old tombs, aren't they?'

Sitting in front of the fire, eating hot toast and drinking Hannah's strong coffee, Tom hoped to steer her unobtrusively on to the subject of the mound in Bloxbury Ring. He had called at the hotel on an impulse. Since George had gone and Joachim was inaccessible, the holidays had begun badly. He would have visited Hannah earlier, but he had not been sure how sincere her invitation had been. In the end his boredom had overcome his shyness. But he need not have worried – the Dutch lady's pleasure at seeing him had been unmistakably real.

'Most people think so, Tom. But they are not really tombs in the way that graves are. They have often been found empty. If human remains are discovered inside, they have usually been put there at a much later date – by people who did not know or had forgotten the original purpose of the long barrow.'

Tom liked the way that Hannah always answered his questions seriously, even if he did not entirely understand her. She had even confided how important her treasured embroidery was to her.

85

'What were they for then – originally, I mean?'

'The best guess is that they were used for death and rebirth rites. The tunnel that leads to the central burial chamber symbolises the passage through death into the underworld. Don't by misled by the word "symbolise". The rites had a real effect. The initiate was subjected to severe hardship and training for a long time. The priests would appear and, with great drama, instruct him in the secret lore of the tribe. There may have been a mock sacrifice. It was a tough ceremony all right. But when he finally emerged, of course, the initiate really was reborn . . . renewed. He had passed the test of death.'

'Did everyone do this . . . this rite?'

'Unlikely. Most people performed some similar rite. Just as they do in your Church.'

'What do you mean?'

'Baptism. Early Christians – and some sects today – used total submersion in water to symbolise a dying away from the body and the material world, and a rebirth into the spirit and the Church. You Catholics could do with a bit more of that these days – dabbing babies with water isn't quite the same!' Hannah paused to glance at Tom, wondering if she had gone too far. She saw he was not in the least offended and went on:

'The full rite – like the one I described – was reserved for the chosen few . . . for those men who were to become priests. It wasn't just a token ordination. Far from it. The priests in those days were not like ours. They were divinely ordained to become leaders of men. They had to rule. And, to rule, you have to have real power. The rite was a tremendously powerful thing – it transformed the initiate into an adept, a master over natural forces, a lord of the occult.' Hannah inserted a piece of bread on to a long toasting fork and held it in front of the fire. Tom watched her in silence. Her brief sketch of the ancient rites made him uneasy.

'What about the barrow in Bloxbury Ring? That stone on the top – what's so special about it?'

Hannah did not answer immediately, but started to butter the toast with exaggerated care. Finally, she said, 'It's just a hypothesis of mine. There's no real evidence.'

Tom's curiosity was aroused. 'Evidence for what?'

'You promise to tell no one?' Hannah smiled and gave him a mysterious look. 'I should be saving up my speculations for the new book. But I'll try and explain some of it to you.' She settled back in her chair.

'The easiest place to start is in ancient Egypt. I believe that the pyramids were not tombs as is commonly thought, but – like our long barrow – they were temples in which the Mysteries were celebrated.'

'What were they?' Tom interrupted.

'The Mysteries of the Cult of the Dead. They were the usual death and rebirth rites, but highly sophisticated – and highly dangerous. The general pattern seems to have been that the adept would enter the burial chamber for seven days, and was probably required to venture very close to physical death. But that's not strictly relevant. The crucial point is the way a pyramid is constructed.'

Tom looked puzzled. Hannah smiled.

'The position and measurements of each pyramid are quite extraordinarily precise. The result is a kind of giant magnifying glass – not for light, but for the Earth's energy. The pyramid, you see, is a living temple that can mobilise the Earth's great natural forces and focus them in an exact spot – usually the burial chamber which lies at the heart of the structure. If an adept can withstand those forces, he can use them to effect a startling change: he can abandon his physical body altogether. Sort of step out of the restrictions of time and space.'

'Do you mean without physically dying? So that his soul remains on earth?'

'Yes – except the word "soul" is rather too Christian. The Egyptians believed in a kind of spiritual body, a counterpart to the physical, which they called a *Ka*. I prefer to call it a spectral body – it has fewer religious associations.'

Tom weighed the idea for a moment. 'What would happen if the body – the physical, that is – died or was killed while the spectral body was roaming around?'

'Good question. It's pretty clear to me that if the adept were killed, his spectral body would die as well. The two bodies, though separate, retain their vital links. Thereafter, your guess is as good as mine. Better perhaps. *You* might say that his soul would go to heaven. Or hell.' Her eyes twinkled, but Tom did not notice.

'But how does this fit in with Bloxbury Ring?'

'Ah yes. I first stumbled across the idea when I discovered certain correspondences between the measurements of the pyramids and those of stone circles in Europe – Stonehenge, for example. It's possible that Bloxbury Ring used to be just such a circle of standing stones and dolmens – I'll be more certain when I get a chance to measure it . . . Anyhow, it doesn't matter because in this case we might have a Centre Stone – '

'The one on top of the long barrow,' Tom supplied helpfully.

'Not on top. If my hunch is correct, the stone was not added on to the barrow but the other way round – the barrow was built around the stone. If I'm right, the stone will plunge deep into the Earth and act as a conductor of energy . . . to tap it and focus it, just like the pyramids. It's very rare. That's why I'm so excitable – I'm sorry, *excited* about it . . . it may never have been properly excavated!'

While Tom was caught up in Hannah's enthusiasm and absorbed by what she said, a part of him abruptly detached itself and observed her distantly, from behind his eyes. A tightness across his chest caused him to breathe out suddenly. The figure of Hannah began to shift and swirl in front of his eyes – to dissolve into a cocoon of light. He remembered his promise to his mother – no lights, unless he could not help it. He mentally shook himself. Hannah rapidly took on shape and form again; but even as she hardened into her familiar outline, Tom glimpsed a cloud of soft amber light – a light almost fragrant in its tangible and mellow beauty. He experienced a rush of warmth towards her.

She had noticed nothing. She was laughing.

'I find it delightfully ironic that such a phenomenon as a Centre Stone should belong to your Little Brothers of the Apostles. If they only knew what they were sitting on!'

Tom picked his way down the steep, narrow track towards the village. The sun had slipped below the horizon and the light was fading fast. When he reached Dr. Kelly's large, solitary house – the only other building, apart from the hotel, in the vicinity – he stopped, wondering if he should drop in for a minute. But there were no lights in the windows and no smoke from the chimney.

On the opposite hill, the modern classroom block loomed darkly, dormant until its inmates returned in the New Year. In contrast, on the other side of the cloisters, the chapel was lit up. The building itself was obscured by the intervening dusk so that its flickering windows seemed to be hovering unsupported above the ground, like a spacecraft on the point of take-off.

The sound of someone stumbling on the track ahead made him strain his eyes through the twilight. He expected to see the heavy rolling form of the doctor returning home. Instead, he made out the shapes of five men. They were carrying something long and heavy, like a massive plank. He stood aside to let them pass. The man holding the top end of the object was John Hooper, instantly recognisable by his long stride and unusual height.

'Evening,' said Tom in the laconic way he had picked up from the local farmers.

John Hooper checked his stride and casually wrapped a wide dustsheet more closely around his load. Then he thrust his craggy face forward and, recognising Tom, nodded amiably. Silently, the other men followed suit as they marched past in step, carrying the concealed object with all the stately care of coffin-bearers. Tom vaguely wondered what it was they were taking to the hotel – unless of course it was something they were dumping in the woods. He shivered and, pulling his coat more tightly around him, broke into a run to stay warm.

11

Dr. Kelly was, as he would say, a little the better for drink. He usually was. Letting himself in through the front door, Tom could hear his voice booming behind the closed door of the dining-room. He paused outside to listen. You could easily tell how far gone the doctor was: the more he drank, the more he reverted to his Irish upbringing. His brogue became stronger and his sentences became laced with the remembered expressions of an orthodox Catholic childhood.

He opened the door to a rush of warm air tinged with the fragrance of whiskey. Dr. Kelly stopped talking in mid-sentence and swung his enormous red face slowly round to look at Tom. He was standing by the fire with one elbow resting on the mantelpiece. His other arm was holding his glass out, with all the feigned reluctance of the genuine alcoholic, while Elizabeth poured him another finger of whiskey. She flashed her son a smile of conspiracy. They were both extremely fond of the doctor. His permanent condition of drunkenness and general outrage was tempered by such boyish charm and basic good humour that it was impossible to be offended by him.

Dr. Kelly regarded Tom heavily. His eyes, though jaundiced and watery, were the purest blue and they gleamed mischievously, contradicting his grave expression. Tom grinned – he knew what was coming and even looked forward to the big man's ritual abuse.

The doctor shook his head despairingly. 'What a

tragedy. What a waste. Look at him. A smart lad like himself . . . his whole life in front of him and what does he do? He falls into the hands of the forces of darkness. A tragedy. I s'pose you've been Up There,' he asked significantly, as if unable to mention the Abbey by name. His dead-pan face was all sincerity. 'There's little enough harm in a priest – at least he can take a drink like a decent Christian man. But your monk is a desperate fellow. He won't stop at fish on Fridays, Tom, you mark my words.'

'Stop it, Eugene,' said Elizabeth, laughing in spite of her indignation. 'Tom knows very well what he's doing, don't you, dear?'

'Yes.' He smiled. 'Besides, I haven't been Up There today,' he added defiantly. The doctor only sighed again and drank lengthily from his glass. With his mass of wiry hair, tufts of which poked out of his ears and nose as well as the top of his open-necked shirt, he looked as though he had grown, out of sheer stubbornness, into a living proof of Darwin's theory of man's common ancestry.

'Anyway,' he grumbled, 'it'll take a darn sight more than Popish hocus-pocush' – the phrase was too ambitious – 'Holy Mother of God, it'll take more than monkery to bail us out if what I saw this afternoon – ' He coughed, and suddenly looked sober. There was an awkward silence.

'What is it, Eugene? What's the matter?' Elizabeth was sufficiently alarmed to pour him another shot of whiskey. The doctor frowned, all his playfulness gone.

'It's probably nothing at all,' he said irritably. 'They shouldn't try to turn me into a cow doctor, that's all.'

'But who's trying to turn you into a "cow doctor"?'

'Powell,' replied the doctor curtly.

'Our neighbour, you mean?' In fact, the farm was half a mile away but since Winston Powell's fields bordered on the cottage, he was considered a neighbour. The Reardons had very little contact with him. He was not a Catholic and had little to do with the Abbey.

'The same. Bloody cows aren't eating.' He looked depressed.

Tom failed to make any sense of this. 'Why . . . I mean, does it matter if they don't eat? For a while?'

Eugene rounded on him. 'It's not that they don't eat – it's the *way* they don't eat. Don't like the look of it. Anyway we're getting in the vet tomorrow. I never was a great one for diagnosing cows.'

Elizabeth moved her hands nervously in her lap. 'What do you think it is?'

'Ah well. Could be any number of things. They put me in mind of some cows I once saw in Kildare, that's all. Long time ago.'

'What was wrong with them?'

'If I tell you, you're to keep it to yourself. I don't want to cause any false alarms. Tom?' Tom nodded. 'Well. I think it could be foot-and-mouth.'

'Foot-and-mouth disease?' said Tom. 'That's bad, isn't it?'

'The worst. In Kildare they slaughtered one herd every day for two weeks. Mind you, they hadn't the proper measures in those days. Still, I hope to God I don't have to live through that again. It'd do very little harm – for a change – if you got your friends Up There to say a few Masses, Tom . . .' The doctor's unique concession to religion underlined the seriousness of his foreboding.

Elizabeth became withdrawn. The lines around her eyes and mouth were more pronounced, making her look older. Tom saw that she was worn out; and he immediately felt fiercely protective towards her in a way that would have been impossible before their recent exchange of confidences.

He had found it hard to accept his mother's version of his upbringing as a time of hard labour and bitter anxiety. It meant abandoning his lingering illusions about her, and accepting that the benevolent god-like being of his childhood was, in reality, vulnerable, uncertain, fearful and *ordinary*. Not that this view could shake the absolute fact of her: she was still the last stronghold. You could commit murder, for crying out loud, and it made no essential difference to a mother. The bond was formed before birth, and long before mere love confirmed it.

Nevertheless, the balance of dependence had shifted. Tom could not give her back the lost years or make them lighter; but he could assume responsibility now, if only in small ways.

'I think it's time you were going, Doctor Kelly,' he said firmly. The doctor looked startled, and glanced at Elizabeth for confirmation of her son's authority. She was smiling gratefully.

'Yes, yes. Quite right, young man,' he said briskly, finishing his drink. 'I only came by to check on your ma's migraines . . . I must be going. See you soon, Elizabeth.'

Tom closed the front door behind him.

High up on the hill, a light was moving erratically among the trees. Hannah stopped short in the middle of a deep breath. She knew from her daily walk that no one lived anywhere near that neck of the woods. Forgetting that she had only stepped out for a spot of fresh air after a long stint at her typewriter, she walked up the track until it petered out in the trees. The light flickered out of sight.

The woods were pitch-black under the starless sky and they exuded a thick smell of decaying vegetation. Hannah hesitated on the threshold, half-inclined to go back to the hotel. She wondered if the light might belong to a newly-settled gipsy camp, until she remembered that the way was too narrow to take a caravan. She took a few steps back and the light reappeared. It seemed quite close and, from its uneven wavering, she realised that it came from a fire reflecting off the branches overhead.

She soon found that distance was difficult to judge in the dark: the fire was further away, and larger, than it looked. It appeared to be burning in a level clearing at the heart of the giant oak wood. As she moved quietly into the hushed presence of the enormous trees, Hannah was struck by the kind of wonder that other people reserve for a Gothic cathedral. Many of the oaks, eroded by disease and ruined by centuries of storms, had long since died; but their branches, like flying buttresses, still supported the colossal trunks and interwove above in a majestic sweeping vault. At the edge of the clearing, the impression of a huge enclosed space was increased by the blaze of the big bonfire which lit up the lower reaches of the trees, but abandoned the ceiling of branches to an obscurity that intimated immense height.

Absorbed in the awesome effect of this natural temple of light, she did not immediately realise that she was not alone. With a sudden jolt of the heart, she saw that a group of people was gathered at a short distance from the roaring fire. They were standing so silently and so still, dressed in funereal clothes, that they might have been mistaken, at a glance, for shadows or the stumps of trees. As her eyes got used to the light, Hannah saw that there were more than she had first thought – about seventy people, a sizeable proportion of Bloxbury's small population. Certain that she had interrupted some archaic pagan festival, Hannah hid behind a tree and watched, wishing she had brought her notebook.

With an air of great solemnity, five men nearest the fire turned in unison to face the crowd. After a respectful pause, the man in the centre who was taller than the others called out with simple dignity, 'It is time to honour the memory of the martyrs who suffered at the hands of the Anti-Christ.'

There was a rumble of murmured response.

'Let us honour their memory.'

The tall man nodded to the two men on his right. They disappeared into the darkness, returning a moment later with a man held between them. He was either drunk or unconscious: his feet dragged along the ground and his head wobbled loosely from side to side.

Hannah grew distinctly uneasy. She didn't like the look of the man's condition and it dawned on her that perhaps she had stumbled on something more sinister than a quaint rural custom. The mention of an Anti-Christ put her in mind of Devil-worship, and she half-expected to see a goat being led to the slaughter. She was quite unprepared for the actual shock: the insensible captive was wearing a long dark-blue robe. His head, which had fallen forward on to his chest, was hidden by a cowl. The crowd came to life and seethed expectantly.

The tall man called out again, almost apologetically. He seemed to be more of a spokesman than a leader.

'Let us pray for the perfect souls of the martyrs.'

The crowd began to pace obediently around the fire, two or three abreast, murmuring a prayer whose words Hannah could not make out. As they moved faster, the prayer started to rise and fall in a kind of moan, like an intense pleading. Whenever they passed the two men holding up the monk, they ducked their heads three times, breaking out from time to time in a low sobbing wail.

This frenzy of lamentation was about to burst out of control when the tall man raised his hand. The villagers instantly fell silent and dropped to their knees. Casually, without hesitating, the two men hoisted the slumped figure off the ground. His robe billowed briefly in the flaming air, and then he crashed on to the apex of the fire.

Hannah was paralysed by the suddenness of the atrocity. She could do nothing but cling to her tree and gaze, transfixed, at the monk lolling among the flames that devoured his legs, his torso and were now leaping up around his head. Then all at once she was bathed in such deep relief that she had to stifle a spasm of hysterical laughter: the man in the fire was made of straw.

She knew that on every November the Fifth the English burnt effigies of Guy Fawkes who had once tried to blow up Parliament, but this 'guy' was dressed as a Little Brother; and it wasn't November the Fifth. The villagers seemed to be commemorating an altogether different event. They remained kneeling, some of the women rocking their bodies to and fro in an ecstasy of sorrow. The praying began again, more subdued this time, as they gravely contemplated the blazing remains of the counterfeit monk. Hannah had no difficulty in recognising the Lord's Prayer, but she had never before heard it uttered with such insistent fervour, as though the words were endowed with magical power. A few heavy raindrops fell on their flushed mournful faces but no one took any notice.

The spokesman gestured to his original four companions who crossed the clearing. Once again the crowd became silent, waiting. Above the roar of the fire more raindrops could be heard pattering on the canopy of branches. The men returned from the shadow of the trees carrying a long piece of wood. As they brought it into the sphere of firelight, Hannah saw that it was a cross. The figure of a dying Christ was fixed to the wood, the dejected head on one side, the arms sagging on the nails. The wounded face was full of pity and pain.

For a long eerie interval, no one moved or made a sound. The tall man stepped forward; his rugged weathered features were contorted by some powerful emotion or, perhaps, by a trick of the dancing light. He ran his eye over the crowd, turned, and spat on the crucifix. The spell was broken: the people surged to their feet and swayed forward, muttering angrily. The black skies opened, unloading a torrent of rain that pelted the trees. The hiss and flare of the bonfire merged with the hubbub of the mob which seized the crucifix and flung it to the ground. Then, with methodical, controlled fury – more frightening than any act of madness – they began to kick and trample on the inanimate cross.

Although she was a long way from being a good Christian, Hannah was appalled. The villagers continued to vent their obscure rage on the image of Christ until, finally, they picked up the cross and flung it with a howl of delight into the fire. Hannah had seen enough; she turned and fled through the shuddering wood, blind to the dangers of the slippery path, deaf to every sound but the violent rain drumming in her head.

Back in her room she locked the door behind her and sat on the bed, too upset to notice the cold water trickling down her neck. After a while she stood up and shook out her hair, as if to shake off, along with the rain, the memory of what she had seen. The last thing she wanted was to get involved in the sordid little ritual or let it interfere with her work. She decided to forget it at all costs – and clear out of Bloxbury just as soon as she could.

12

Although the face was hidden by the hood of the deep-blue robe, Tom had an idea it was Joachim. The monk detached a miniature crucifix from the many hanging from the cord around his waist and held it out. Tom's heart began to pump. He knew the crucifix belonged solely to him; but it had been kept from him all his life. He also knew the face of the Christ was an image of His real face. The honour of being allowed to look upon it shook him. But when he managed to focus on the face he saw that someone had botched the carving. The whole head was a mess.

The monk was shaking all over, as if with silent laughter. It was not Joachim after all, but George. He tried to show George the botched crucifix but his friend was not interested. He kept pointing to the wall behind him. It was entirely composed of shelves crammed with books of different shapes and sizes, glowing in beautiful colours. Part of the wall of books was a secret door, which slid open to reveal stone steps sloping sharply downwards. Tom imagined that they led to an old vault or crypt – they always did. George shook his head and smiled. He put another, wholly unexpected thought into Tom's mind: 'The steps lead to the centre of the earth. There, all the lights merge to become one light.' And indeed the steps were illuminated by a powerful glow, pulsing out of the depths. George began the descent. Tom wanted to stop him but found himself rooted to the spot. The secret door began to slide shut. George's head was level with the threshold. He turned briefly and shrugged; he seemed to be saying, 'Well, I haven't done *this* before.' His face was very big and luminous, and a little sad. The door closed.

Tom woke with the larger-than-life image of George's face still floating in front of his eyes. He dressed hurriedly. The face faded, leaving a nagging vacuum. The dream was some kind of demand, a reminder perhaps of neglected duties. A glance at the weather prompted him to put on his anorak. He opened the window and swung himself out into the branches of the cherry tree. It was quicker that way, and he did not want to disturb his mother.

The air was damp and lethargic under a lid of grey cloud. The street was virtually deserted, with many of the cottages still blinded by drawn curtains. Two men were talking in the middle of the street in low, rapid voices. Tom recognised them as local farmers. He bid them good morning as he passed, but they ignored him. The stone walls of the Abbey loomed to his right. A train of images broke surface like bubbles in Tom's half-dreaming mind.

The first two were familiar to him. They were the adjoining circles, composed of imaginary lines of force, which bounded his world. On one side there was the village circle, shining with its attendant spirits of brightness, and his home – freedom – was at the heart of it, a deep and glowing centre. On the other side was the school circle with the Abbey at its centre. He inhabited that circle, too; but it was grey and it moved forever downwards from the top of the hill, like contour lines moving on a map. It intersected the village circle in his mind as it did in fact: at the point where the grey stone wall met the picturesque village street. Tom had the curious sensation of seeing himself as a bright dot moving along the boundary of the two circles as he walked alongside the wall. He could move from one circle to another as easily as exchanging his jeans for his school uniform, as smoothly as passing through the Abbey gates. Such was the mental sketch map of his world: the bright against the grey, his mother and his past against the present and the school, the private and the public. The two circles.

Ever since the Ring ceremony his inner landscape had undergone, unnoticed until now, a transformation. Behind and within the school circle, pushing outwards, displacing it – dissolving it – was the older, shadowy circle of the Abbey. And behind the Abbey circle – circles within circles – stood a darker circle still, Bloxbury Ring, pushing the Abbey circle inexorably outwards so that its perimeter shifted like a smoke ring.

The Abbey circle was really defined by events. On the blurred expanding edge the Little Brothers struck strange poses – standing in rows in front of the long barrow or sitting in a semicircle at Mass; Brother Paul before the Centre Stone; Anselm's curt dismissal of George. The images did not hang together. It was like watching a game through a lighted window: you could not grasp the rules, you were out in the dark.

Even Joachim was part of the shadowy grey Abbey circle – his miraculous act of healing, his sudden confidences. But then, even as he revealed things, he seemed to be concealing more. He had retreated into the distant, silent realm that surrounded Ambrose. Tom felt helpless in the face of it, like a child listening to grown-ups talk about sex: you felt its importance and weight in every glance, every oblique reference, but you did not know what the mystery was.

And now the bright village was being tarnished by yet another circle, even less distinct than the last. It bore down from the future. It was in the doctor's voice, in the lined faces of the two farmers; it was in the air. It had already begun to take on shape in the rumours of foot-and-mouth disease. Tom could see them closing in, the cloudy circles. They filled his mind, shutting out the light.

He felt dizzy and slightly nauseous. The air was cloying, difficult to breathe. His clothes were sticky. If only he were a monk now, if only his novitiate had begun, he could be part of the pattern. He could travel in a straight line back to the centre of the circles. For the moment the only way out of the miasma was to follow the luminous image of George.

He hurried to Joachim's workshop. If he could find out where George was, and why, he would hold the key to the code. The pattern would fall into place. New, brighter circles could be constructed.

He decided to cut his walk shorter by scrambling over the wall and making his way through the fields and copses, behind the Abbey to Joachim's workshop. It struck him that a brighter circle already existed. It also bore down on Bloxbury from the future. It glinted on the horizon, getting nearer every day. He thought of it as the Pope's circle.

Tom had no illusions about the Church. Whereas the eternal Light shone like the sun on good and bad alike, there were those who blocked the Light and cast a long shadow. The stately procession of the Church through time had often hurled its darkness ahead of it; and, like children at play in a great cathedral's precincts, men and women had stopped in the sudden chill, looking up to find themselves cut off from the sun. But there were others, too. Those who had become transparent to the Light. Like crystal prisms, they illuminated the world with the glory of rainbows.

Surely the Pope was such a man. He was the centre of a circle that girdled the Earth, centre – and circumference. For he had been touched with the wind of the Holy Spirit. Eternity had stepped down from its throne and crowned him God's representative on Earth.

Joachim was such a man. No Light had been conferred upon him from above. He had striven for it within, suffering the hard tests of faith, battling against the insurrections of the flesh.

And what if they were to meet, these mirror images? (Tom pictured them at dusk, on a lonely country cross-roads, shaking hands.) Would the circuit of Light then be complete? Would eternity descend in a lightning flash?

Tom wondered if, at a deeper level, there really could be any meeting. The two men embodied a clash of opposites as irreconcilable as light and dark. Their authority and doctrine rested on conflicting images of Christ: the Pope's failed, abandoned, dying Christ hung at the opposite pole from Joachim's effulgent and all-conquering Spirit. Although only one of these images was the true one, Tom felt them exerting equal pressure, pulling his soul apart. He knew it was weak of him to shy away from the challenge of the powerful Spirit – worse still, it was disloyal to his friend and master. Yet he couldn't help feeling inexorably drawn towards the crucified Saviour, as if He really had died for the sins of the world.

Tom hurried on through the copse where the magical badger's sett was. Its entrance was covered up in leaves. He wouldn't see it again until the spring.

At the edge of the open field the yew-lined parapet of the Ring rose out of the mist to greet him. He turned his eyes away and broke into a run.

Tom burst into the workshop without knocking. Joachim was sitting in his straight, hard-backed chair. He looked thinner and somehow older. His eyes were closed in meditation or pain. He opened them and stood up quickly. Tom had the impression he was expecting someone else.

'Oh. Hallo, Tom.' His brow creased in a slight frown, his voice was cautious.

Tom was wrong-footed; he was no longer quite certain of what he wanted to say. 'I had to come, Brother Joachim . . . sorry. Is there any news of George? It's been days . . . you promised . . . I thought you might have forgotten.'

The frown intensified. The monk's gaze shifted from Tom's face to the fireplace, to the door. He seemed about to say something, but changed his mind. He lifted his right arm and then let it drop again in a gesture of frustration.

Tom grew impatient. 'Look. I realise you're busy . . . and so on. Don't worry. I'll have a word with Brother Ambrose myself – '

'Stay *away* from Ambrose.' Joachim was embarrassed by his own vehemence. 'Sorry. Just stay out of Ambrose's way, Tom,' he said more calmly. 'O.K.?'

'But I just want to know. That's all. I *must* know. I can't explain . . . I had a dream . . . everything's mixed up. George wouldn't have left without telling anyone. He could be . . . anywhere.'

'You exaggerate.' The words were not Joachim's. They were fired from the doorway. Tom turned to see the squat figure of the Abbot standing there and rocking gently on his heels.

'Woodward is not "anywhere", as you put it. He is at home. In Italy.' Ambrose walked smoothly into the room and went up to Tom. He had never been so close to him before. Moreover he stood perhaps an inch or two closer than any other person would have stood. The effect was intimidating. Tom's instinct was to step back; but he stood his ground.

'Can you tell me when he's coming back please, Brother Ambrose?'

'He is not coming back, Reardon.' The Abbot's eyelids drooped. 'Woodward decided not to join the Order. And we, naturally, respected his decision – we are not tyrants, you know.' He drew his lips away from his teeth in a smile. 'I imagine he is even now discussing a new future for himself with his mother and father. We are praying for him, of course. Is that all?'

It was not quite all. Tom stared unhappily at the ground, finding it difficult to think in the loaded presence of the Abbot.

'Why didn't he let me know?' he said in a small voice.

Ambrose regarded him with pity. 'I'm not sure, Reardon. I cannot judge the nature of your friendship. But if it's of any use, I do know that his decision was reached quite suddenly. The monastic life, it turned out, held too many terrors for him – I don't imagine they will trouble you,' he added. Tom's pride was touched.

'I would also guess,' he continued, 'that young Woodward was a little ashamed. It cannot be easy to admit to yourself that you are not . . . how shall I put it? Up to the mark. It might be something you wouldn't want to admit to your friends even though we do not judge him, of course.'

Tom was flattered to be included in the Abbot's 'we'.

'Now, is that all?'

Tom could not, for a moment, think of anything else. He nodded.

'Good. Then let us wish young Woodward well and carry on with our own lives. Would you be willing to do me a small service?'

Tom nodded again, more eagerly. The Abbot's courtesy was unlooked for.

'Thank you. Quite simply, Woodward had no time to attend to his belongings. Perhaps you would pack them for him so that we can send them off?'

'Yes, Brother Ambrose. Of course. I'll do it now.'

The Abbot inclined his head and blinked slowly, like a lizard. Tom headed for the door, pausing only to glance at Joachim. The monk was standing quite still, legs a little apart, staring hard at Ambrose.

As the sound of Tom's footsteps receded into the distance, the Abbot strolled over to the window and looked out. He hummed thoughtfully to himself for a moment before speaking:

'I thought we'd agreed that Reardon shouldn't disturb you, Joachim.'

'As you could see,' the monk replied coldly, 'he was

upset – not unnaturally – by Woodward's sudden departure. I would have liked to have reassured him on that score.'

'Well, I'm glad I was able to do it for you,' said Ambrose mildly. He hummed a few more notes. 'You realise, of course, what a unique position young Reardon holds? He will be the first of the New Order.'

'It's too early to give him any idea of that,' said Joachim sharply. 'His mind and will are very much his own. He must be led gently in the right direction.'

'But he has responded well to the doctrine . . . ?'

'So far, yes. But we've hardly begun. It could be fatal to rush him.'

'Do you doubt his vocation?'

'No . . . No, I don't.'

'Good. Then what I have in mind can't constitute any threat to his future. Quite the reverse . . . It's a singular honour which will only serve to confirm his faith.'

'What "honour" is that, Brother Ambrose?' The monk was suspicious.

Ambrose turned suavely towards him. 'Oh, quite simply, I've decided that Tom Reardon will be the one to represent the believers when our Vatican friend comes to consecrate the chapel.' He smiled slightly as if he had just recalled a private joke. 'He will receive the blessing.'

'But he hasn't taken the vows of a believer,' Joachim interjected.

'I hardly think it matters. He'll shortly be far more than that. You must see that a prospective novice is the ideal symbol of renewal – both a link between the lay community and the Little Brothers, and a testimony to the living continuity of the Order. He even embodies all the innocence and promise of youth . . .'

'I don't think he's ready.'

'Nonsense. I should've thought you'd be delighted in view of your own prominence at the ceremony – '

'That's not certain,' interrupted Joachim curtly. 'You underestimate the hazards.'

'I can't afford to estimate the hazards at all, Joachim. We will be successful. That's all. Meanwhile, you don't want to stand in the boy's way, do you?'

Joachim hesitated, then shook his head. As if surprised to find himself agreeing with his Abbot, he crossed the room to where Ambrose stood, and together they turned to look out of the window.

Side by side and, for the moment, reconciled, a kind of complicity sprang up between the two monks. Neither of them moved their eyes from the view outside, but in their brief exchange they spoke like sleepwalkers who are perfectly attuned to each other's thoughts:

'He will be an asset in the future.' The tiniest tremor of excitement underlay Joachim's casual remark.

'Yes. When the Church is purged of its corruption . . .'

'Yes. When it is steered safely again, by true Christians.'

'Yes. It's getting closer, Joachim. The day . . .'

Then all at once, like soldiers caught slacking on guard duty, they straightened up and resumed control.

'I'm returning to the Abbey,' said Ambrose with his old authority. 'I shall see Reardon personally.'

His head rested heavily and stiffly on the white pillow, his neck rigid. Shoulders, arms, hands – all seemed too heavy to move. His body was dammed up, containing the fever that raged inside him. The more it sought to break out, the more the surface hardened and resisted. Only his fingertips moved. Like tiny outlets through which the fever could leak, they plucked weakly at the crisp sheet. He was being steadily eroded from within. His eyes had withdrawn deep inside their sockets, his cheeks had caved in. His whole face was stretched and gaunt and except for two red patches on his cheekbones, as pale as marble.

Whatever was left of George lived behind his eyes. They alone were free of petrification. They swivelled from side to side, sometimes rolling wildly, showing white. Each time, another word was physically expelled from between his lips. It gave the words peculiar emphasis. They seemed to arrive from a great distance, from a region beyond his mere speech apparatus which lay like a hard lump inside his inert neck. Sometimes the words were so guttural and low they were indistinguishable from grunts. Or else they were buried in the shallow wheezing breaths which he squeezed, with obvious pain, from his hot boulder of a body.

'Eyes . . . his . . . *eyes* . . . the knife . . . oh . . . oh . . . stop . . .'

Cecilia Woodward bent over her son. Her handsome face was ravaged by worry and sleeplessness. Resembling her son's to begin with, it grew sympathetically more like his traumatic mask every minute.

'Don't try to speak, Giorgio. Darling. You're safe now.' There was no sign that the boy could hear anything above the internal crackle of his delirium. His eyes rolled.

'Help . . . oh . . . father.'

'Your father's coming soon, darling. Be calm. Just lie still.' The request was superfluous; and yet it was true that the power of movement in his eyes suggested a bodily thrashing from side to side. Cecilia could almost see the dry heat shimmering around him, distorting his features.

'Help . . . the . . . Ho . . . ly . . . Fa –' He could not finish. His breathing was frantic. His eyes grew wide with fright. '. . . Stop . . .' His swollen lips continued to move, but without a sound. Cecilia poured a trickle of water between them. He could not swallow. The water ran uselessly out of the sides of his mouth. She took his hand, just feeling the fingertips brush against her palm, and sat in silence for a long time.

The windows were open but the shutters were closed. The gentle sunlight which slanted through the slatted vents, gathering warmth from the aromatic orange trees, was cut off by clouds. The dappled patterns on the white sheet grew faint. The semi-darkness of the room deepened to a cavern of pain whose silence was broken only by

108

the rustle of George's renewed whispering. Cecilia strained to make sense of the words, her face clenched in concentration.

'. . . dark . . . oh . . . so . . . *stop* . . . oh . . .' The meaningless syllables broke from his dry lips. She could neither understand nor make him understand that he must cease to torture himself. She moistened a cloth for the thousandth time and laid it across his forehead. She looked into his eyes, desperately trying to read his meaning there. But although they moved and moved, his eyes saw nothing unless some violent images locked inside the burning head.

Then George spoke. His voice was quiet, but virtually normal. Cecilia's heart fluttered; she put both hands to her mouth, stifling her cry of relief. He said, 'Mother . . . Pray for us . . . now, and at the hour of – ' His lips trembled; the rest of the sentence was lost.

Cecilia bent over him excitedly. The red spots on his cheeks were disappearing. His eyes had stopped moving. His breathing was faint. The inner fire had retreated, or broken through to the core. Cecilia saw that her quick hope of a reprieve had been false and baseless. The voice had merely been the final and bitter irony of the dying.

She stood up shakily and, with hurried nervous steps, crossed the room to the door. Opening it, she spoke to someone in a low and urgent voice. He replied in rapid Italian. The door swung open and a priest appeared out of the darkness. He was carrying the paraphernalia of the last rites. He sat down on the edge of the bed. Then quietly and without fuss, he began to administer the sacrament of extreme unction, absolving George for the last time of his sins.

13

The trunk had been put ready in his room. It sat smugly
on the floor, assuming somehow that a person's past life
could be neatly packed away and forgotten. Tom was
saddened that all the hard work, all those long hours,
should have come down to an empty trunk. George had
been so dedicated – perhaps too dedicated (Tom vividly
remembered the pallor of his face, the chewing of his lip).
Had his nerve failed at the crucial moment? The initiation
should have been the proud climax of his life. What
terrible loss of resolve or faith had made him turn and
run?

Tom began to fill the trunk, putting books at the
bottom and clothes on top of them. At the back of the
cupboard he found – startling discovery – a teddy bear. It
was so old that it had no fur left, and only one eye and
ear. Tom felt the kind of sympathy towards it as two
strangers must feel when they are both abandoned by the
same close friend. He tucked it carefully into the clothes
and turned away from its reproachful eye to empty the
desk.

Pulling out the drawers, he tipped all the loose articles
into a heap – pens, notepads, a pocket calculator, a
rosary, paper clips, a Teach-Yourself-Sanskrit book, a
yo-yo (a yo-yo?), envelopes, a broken watch, and so on.
He put everything into plastic bags and stuffed them into
the trunk. Then he took a blank piece of paper and,
smiling to himself, wrote: 'First-class packing by courtesy
of T. Reardon. P.S. What's the big idea? Let me know

what you're doing. P.P.S. I like the bear!' The note would be a surprise. On second thoughts, he crossed out the P.P.S. in case George was embarrassed at having his secret bear revealed.

Fitting the drawers back in the desk, he found that no matter how he juggled with it, the bottom one would not settle in place. He pulled it out again and looked into the space. There was a book lodged at the back. He fished it out and opened it. NOT TO BE REMOVED in red lettering. He smiled again. George had actually broken a rule! A big one, too – George was obsessive about books. He thought of them as people. If you abused one in his presence, he was liable to take it as an act of immorality, a personal affront. And here was a book kidnapped by him.

Tom idly turned over another page. He caught his breath. The frontispiece was a pattern which fascinated him. More than that, it was charged with significance. It was just like . . . like when you hear a new word for the first time and, hey presto, it appears again (usually twice) within a short time – in a newspaper or book, or someone else uses it. It was as though the word was determined to press itself on you, to be remembered. This time it was circles within circles. There were seven of them slipped inside each other like the wooden Russian dolls. He examined them closely. Goose-pimples rose all over him. The smallest circle, at the centre, was a snake biting its own tail.

It was a coincidence of the first order. Not only were there circles, but one of them was a duplicate of Joachim's ring. Perhaps it wasn't a coincidence. Perhaps it was all part of the mystic law of the circles which put things side by side, without explanation. You had to make all the connections yourself. Eagerly, Tom dipped into the rest of the book. It was all in Latin – how typical of George – and would take ages to translate. He flipped over the pages to the end. There were some missing, torn out by the look of it. George was incapable of defacing a book, so who had? It might be an indigestible piece of work but it didn't deserve to have its pages torn; it was far too handsome for that. He looked at the spine. The title, though faded into the leather, was just legible: *Thesaurus Catharorum*. 'Thesaurus.' Something to do with words . . . a sort of dictionary? The other word meant nothing to him.

He lost interest and turned back to the complicated design. It was highly provocative. Had George left it as a kind of message? Probably not; it was too well hidden. It was only by chance that he had found it. Chance or . . . Providence. He was overwhelmed by a bizarre sensation, like an intense *déjà-vu*, in which he saw his earlier images of the circles as simply a premonition – as if the design had caused the images, as if the images were echoes of the design. He didn't like it, he was getting out of his depth: the book was just a book, solid in his hands. What should he do with it? He would . . . a tiny part of the pattern slotted into place, clean as a piece of jigsaw: the book wasn't meant for him. It was for Hannah. The design was exactly the sort of thing she liked to embroider. It was as clear as a command.

He slammed the trunk shut and, remembering NOT TO BE REMOVED, thrust the book under his anorak and zipped it up. The loose material successfully concealed the hard edges. Casting a last searching glance around the room, he opened the door and made his way through the empty corridors, down the flights of stairs, to the cloisters.

'Come here, boy!'

Tom froze. The barked command twanged off the stone walls so that it was difficult to tell where it had come from. He re-traced the echo of the shout to the foot of the steps which led to the monks' cells. The Gothic archway was filled by a monk. He was standing on the bottom step with his arms lifted and leaning against the stone jambs. He was tall and his head was mostly a mass of untidy black hair and a bushy black beard. Tom relaxed. It was only the Mad Monk, a nickname given to him because of his resemblance to Rasputin.

Tom walked cheerfully towards him. Brother Gregory swung himself effortlessly through the archway and landed in the cloisters. He stood with his arms folded, waiting.

'You wanted me, Brother Gregory?' said Tom.

'What are you doing here, Reardon? What's your business?'

Tom thought at first that his hostility was, as it usually was, mostly put on. But the anger in his tiny eyes made him decide to play it straight.

'I was just packing Ge . . . Woodward's things.'

'Pal of Woodward's?' The black beads glinted suspiciously in their pockets of flesh. 'What were you looking for? Quick! *Speak*.'

'I was – '

Unseen and unheard in his coming, the Abbot had materialised beside them. He spoke: 'Thank you, Brother. The boy was acting on my instructions. You may go.'

Gregory lowered his head, turned and padded off.

Ambrose looked into Tom's white face. 'Large man, isn't he?' The remark drew attention to his own size and, by implication, his authority. He was standing too close again. Tom grew distinctly uneasy. *Stay away from Ambrose*. What had Joachim meant? He wanted to leave. But Ambrose was not someone you simply walked away from. Instead, Tom jittered sideways towards the main entrance like an unbroken colt. Ambrose casually shortened the reins.

'I haven't finished yet.'

His voice was not unpleasant, but there was no appeal against it. It was like the gentle click of a pistol being cocked. And as for Ambrose's eyes . . . it was all right if they weren't trained on you; if they were – Tom stared

113

politely at the vein on the Abbot's head and waited for him to finish.

'It would be . . . unfortunate if I were to see you at Brother Joachim's again. For the time being. He has a great deal to do. I cannot – and will not – allow him to be burdened by every little problem. He is too kind. He has time for everyone. He must be protected from himself. You cannot appreciate how much the Order relies on him. If eventually, and by the grace of God, you are to become a Little Brother, you must begin by recognising that you cannot merely do as you please. And you will be wise to begin now . . .'

The silvery voice spoke for what seemed a long time. Every phrase was hand-picked, every nuance adroitly tuned to evoke a whole range of responses. Tom felt, by turns, menaced, remorseful, guilty, threatened, ashamed, until it was drummed into him how selfish his attachment to Joachim was. Without his friend's actual presence, he grew muddled. He could no longer remember that, in fact, it was trust, affection and respect which united them. He could only see the baseness of his motives, the cynicism of his needs.

If it had been simply a matter of words, Tom might have seen through his confusion. But it was the Abbot who was speaking. Even as he widened the gulf between Tom and Joachim, he drove himself in like a wedge behind the words. As he spun his web of insinuations, he implied that he alone could deliver the struggling boy from the welter of negative emotions. Tom went on nodding and staring at the eloquent bulge of the blue vein until the Abbot had finished. He was numbed, miserable, waiting only for Ambrose to let him go. Then he heard something totally unexpected.

'Tom.' The Christian name was like a caress after a series of blows. 'Brother Joachim has been telling me about you. I am impressed . . .'

Tom could scarcely believe his ears: the Abbot was asking him to represent the village at the Holy

Father's special ceremony of blessing. Out of everyone, he had been chosen as the symbol of friendship, of regeneration. He was being asked if he was equal to the honour.

'Y . . . Yes. Thank you, Brother Ambrose.' The cloud of misery lifted; he felt almost light-headed. At last he would be able to thread his way back to the centre of things. He was not going to be left out in the dark after all. He was virtually a Little Brother already.

'I'm pleased,' said Ambrose. 'You will do us credit. Go to the chapel at nine o'clock tomorrow and Brother Paul will rehearse the procedure with you.' He turned on his heel and walked away.

For one sickening moment, Tom had the impression that he had no will of his own. It had become attached to Ambrose. It was being pulled out of him and stretched like elastic from the region of his stomach. The tension grew acute. Then all at once, there was a sensation of snapping or tearing – like a pulled muscle – and he was released. He recoiled with the shock, swaying backwards two steps. His body was trembling; his mind was numb and uninhabitable. He was driven back into the detached part of himself, the part that lay behind his eyes. It was watching Ambrose walk away.

His heart slowed to a heavy beat, with silences in between. His body grew very still. He knew he had drawn in a long breath some time ago. His chest tightened. He knew then that it was going to happen. He could stop it – now – if he wanted to. But he didn't want to. Not even for his mother's sake. He had to know, for better or worse, what lay behind the bland dark-blue robe, the silky voice, those double-barrelled eyes. He wanted to see the Abbot's light.

His breath came out. He let it blow a clear channel through the intervening mist, let himself be directed by it. He was watching. The grey walls leapt into sharp relief at the edge of his vision. They appeared to curve upward and over to form a tunnel through which the

Abbot was walking in slow and silent motion. Panic whispered deep inside him: what if the light were too bright, what if it burnt out his eyes? He braced himself.

He could hardly believe it. Even though Ambrose was moving farther away from him with every step, the back of the monk's head leapt into sharp focus. Faster than a zoom lens, his eyes could pick out single hairs from the cropped head. He could count the wide pores in the skin of the Abbot's neck. It was like looking down a telescope. As for Ambrose's light – it refused to come on. He was burrowing at the surface of the man, but it was unyielding as the stone walls. Instead, the monk stopped. His head began to swivel.

Tom had the wild idea that Ambrose knew he was being scrutinised; that he could feel the eyes burning the back of his neck. He did not know if he could hold out. He felt cruelly exposed: what if Ambrose could see him as clearly as he was being seen? He couldn't bear the thought of being so close to that face. The head turned. Tom could not risk it. He blinked rapidly and shook himself back to normality. For a split second he was aware of two superimposed images. The Abbot's face was barely inches away – he saw the saliva on his teeth and the black, empty eye-tunnels levelled at him. At the same time the whole man was standing at the end of the cloisters, looking over his shoulder and smiling quizzically.

'Did you find anything, Reardon?' he asked.

'What? I'm sorry, Brother Ambrose . . . ?'

'In Woodward's room. Brother Gregory was asking. Was there anything of interest?'

'Er . . . yes.' He was about to produce the book. But some part of him, unmoved by Ambrose's magnetic field, rebelled. He casually put his hands in his pockets and held the anorak away from him. The book was safely hidden.

'Yes. I found a teddy bear.'

The Abbot's eyebrows went up. Then he walked off towards his study.

Tom was surprised to find Hannah at the hotel. She usually spent the day tramping across the countryside armed with stick, notebook and measuring-tape. Today she was sitting listlessly on the sofa in the drawing-room, staring into the fire. A book lay neglected on her lap. She brightened up when she saw Tom.

'You're lucky to find me in, Tom. I didn't sleep at all well. What is this you have brought me? A book?'

He explained about the pattern of circles. Hannah was delighted, and eager to start sketching an enlargement immediately. He was glad that his discovery seemed to cheer her up. Although she pressed him to stay, he declined – the encounter with Ambrose had left him curiously drained. It was like coming in from a buffeting by high winds.

All the way home he puzzled over the absence of the Abbot's light. He considered the possibility that his gift had deserted him or changed its form, but decided that the difference was more likely to lie with Ambrose. He had the strongest feeling that the light was *there*, but that it had somehow been withdrawn inside the protective shield of the body. After all, the same thing had happened – less dramatically – with the other monks he had tested: they were simply impenetrable to his inner vision.

Tom greeted his mother with the news that he had been chosen for the Pope's special blessing. She was surprised at first, then overwhelmed by Ambrose's kindness and, finally, a little tearful. She was so full of the honour bestowed on her son, that she did not notice his own slightly reserved attitude. While he recognised that his mother reaction was, as it were, the right one – the reaction he should have had – he resented its unquestioning wholeheartedness. He couldn't help feeling more ambivalent. Behind his excitement at being the centre of

117

such an historic event, he experienced a heightening of the obscure tension deep inside him. In some ill-defined way, it seemed that he was being carried on a dark tide towards a choice he was neither ready nor willing to make.

14

The letter was leaning against the cup which Elizabeth
had already filled with coffee. While he drank, Tom
examined the handwriting on the envelope. It was composed of shakily printed block letters.

'You've got time for a piece of toast,' said Elizabeth,
suppressing her curiosity about the letter.

'No, thanks. I'm late for rehearsal as it is.' Tom was
supposed to be at the chapel in twenty minutes to receive
his instructions for the ceremony of the Pope's blessing.

The stamps on the envelope were Italian. It had to be
George. Torn between wanting to read the letter and his
fear of being late, Tom ran to the front door, opening the
envelope as he went. He glanced at the foot of the first
sheet of paper. The signature was familiar.

'It's from George,' he called out to his mother. ' 'Bye!'
He hurried out into the street. 'George,' he said again,
under his breath.

It was difficult enough trying to read the letter as he
ran; it was made impossible by the unsteadiness of the
writing. There was no address at the top and no date. The
letter began abruptly. Tom had to stop by the Abbey wall
to make sense of it. The rehearsal would just have to
wait. He leant against the grey stones and held the paper
close to his eyes:

Dear Tom,
    Sorry I can't write easily so I must be brief (it's hard
to move my hand. Also I have a high temp.) Important:

don't join the Order. Please. V. important. Can't say why. Vows still stand – secret etc. But stay away, esp. Ambrose. He may be mad I don't know they all may be. But don't worry – *I'm* not mad. Just ill. Will explain all later when I'm better. Leave them alone, don't forget. Everything wrong, *wrong* – believe me,

George

The note was cryptic, its message extreme, to say the least. It did not sound at all like George, even if he was sick. But most puzzling was the postscript scrawled under the signature. It read:

NB NB NB
If HE didn't die on the Cross, we are condemned by our sins for ever – but I know my Redeemer liveth.

Two more sheets of paper were enclosed. Covered in writing, they were even more illegible than the first. Tom looked at his watch. It was nearly nine o'clock. There was no time to decipher them now. He stuck the letter into the back pocket of his jeans and hurried towards the Abbey.

'Not a good start, Reardon.'

The young monk tapped his watch. He was standing in one of the arches of the covered colonnade which connected the old cloisters to the chapel. His robe was flapping in the wind.

'Sorry, Brother Paul,' Tom panted. He had run all the way up the drive.

'Never mind.'

He led Tom towards the double doors of the chapel. There was a bundle lying in front of them. Paul picked it up.

'Your cassock and surplice,' he said. 'You'd better try them on.'

Tom took off his anorak, put the black cassock on over

his shirt and jeans and buttoned it up. It fitted well. The while surplice went on top. Brother Paul showed him how to half-fold his arms stiffly in front of him so that they were hidden in the baggy sleeves.

'Good. Now, before we start I am bound to remind you that, although the whole ritual is essentially a simple one, it is nonetheless an occasion of great significance and solemnity for the Order. So you will conduct yourself accordingly. Is that clear?'

'Yes, Brother Paul.'

'Right. First of all, you remember that Mass will be said by the Holy Father for the Little Brothers alone. I have been elected to a symbolic post, which we call the Keeper of the Keys. I lock the doors to remind my fellow Brothers inside that they are set apart from the world in God's service. It also serves to remind those outside that there are times in the lives of God's servants – and that includes the Pope – when they should be allowed to worship in private, to renew their faith and strength.

'While Mass is going on, our friends from the village will assemble here' – he indicated the length of the colonnade – 'to wait until I admit them to the Thanksgiving Ceremony. The Pope's special blessing – your blessing – is the act which will inaugurate the Thanksgiving. Don't worry. It's not complicated, but once again it's highly symbolic. You must make sure that you're standing in front of the villagers, as close as possible to the doors. There'll be no problem – everyone understands the importance of your rôle . . .'

Paul explained the procedure and suggested that they rehearse it. As he turned to enter the chapel, Tom could not help the remark: 'Exciting, isn't it?'

The young monk gave the boy a puzzled look. Then his mouth twisted into a crooked smile. 'Yes,' he said. 'Yes, it is exciting.' He went inside and locked the doors behind him.

Tom waited patiently outside. The wind was surprisingly strong since it was funnelled between the columns by the buildings at either end. He noticed that some words were carved in the stone above the doors. It was low enough for him to reach up and trace the carving with his finger. The words were 'Be ye Perfect . . .' He recognised them as part of a quotation from the New Testament. It went something like: 'Be ye Perfect even as your Father in heaven is perfect.' He supposed that there had not been room for the whole saying. Nevertheless, the short command was formidable enough.

At last he heard Paul's big metal key rattling in the lock. This was the signal.

He knocked three times on the doors and cried out, 'A good Christian seeks entrance to the house of God!'

There was a pause. He heard the key turn and one of the doors swung open. He stepped into the chapel and waited while Paul locked the door behind him.

It was as dark as usual where he stood. The only illumination came from the narrow strips of stained glass which were squeezed between hefty stone mullions; the high ceiling was virtually lost in shadow. But, about three quarters of the way up the chapel, there was a dramatic change. The whole of the far end was a blaze of light. Every candle in the choir stalls which faced inwards at right angles to the pews, was lit. In addition, there were four huge candelabras on the semicircular platform where the altar stood. As Paul walked past he said in a low voice: 'I thought the candles would make it a little more authentic . . .' Tom nodded gratefully and followed him up the aisle. As instructed, he walked with his head respectfully lowered and his hands gripping his forearms inside the sleeves of the surplice. Paul looked over his shoulder and smiled approvingly.

When they reached the three shallow steps which led to the altar, the young monk stopped and said, 'At this point, I turn to the right and join the other Brothers who will be kneeling on either side of the aisle at the edge of the platform. You will approach the Holy Father who'll be standing on the top step here. Say nothing. Just kneel quietly on the bottom step. If he should be gracious enough to offer you his hand, kiss his ring. Otherwise he will lay his hand on your head and pronounce the blessing.

'As soon as he has done so, you will rise, take two steps backwards, turn to the left and take a seat in the front choir stall. Brother Ambrose will then stand and say a few words, thanking His Holiness for blessing you – the Order's newest prospect – and thus for blessing the whole future of the Little Brothers. That's it. I'll return then to the doors and let in the congregation for the general Thanksgiving. Any questions?'

'I can't think of any. Thanks. It seems pretty straight-forward.'

Tom had time now to study the improvements which had been made to the chapel. The walls were entirely panelled in new wood which shone in the light from the candelabras. These were even larger than they had looked from the other end of the aisle. They stood nearly six feet high and each had twelve branches. Two were posted on either side of the altar which was covered in the purple cloth of Advent; the other two were further back, on each side of the huge tapestry which hung down the length of the wall, replacing the old crucifix. Apart from these concessions to decoration, the chapel was relatively plain and bare, a testimony to the self-denial of its owners. But there was something missing.

'Where will Brother Joachim's crucifix go?' Tom asked. 'Here?' He pointed to the expanse of tapestry behind the altar.

The monk smiled his crooked smile. 'Turn around.'

Tom turned to face the entrance. He saw that two narrow wooden galleries had been constructed on each side of it, supported on thin wooden columns. There were four steep tiers of seats, the lowest being some way above the level of the rounded top of the doors. Between the galleries hung Joachim's crucifix. It was much larger than it had looked lying on the workbench. Even taller and wider than the doorway over which it was suspended, it dominated the entire windowless wall at that end of the building. Its arms overlapped the galleries to left and right. The effect was breathtaking. The figure of Christ, far from being tortured or dying, seemed to be stretching its arms to the utmost as though He were flying or about to embrace the whole world. The massive head wore its crown of thorns with kingly pride; the expression on the face was noble and expectant. The eyes, open wide, were the calm eyes of a conqueror.

'Do you think the Carpenter Himself would approve?' said Paul, who was busy snuffing out the candles.

'Oh yes,' said Tom. 'Oh yes, I think He would.'

'Padre . . . Padre Vittorio!'

Father Vittorio tried to block out the shouts of his excitable housekeeper. He had not finished his morning prayers. Kneeling dutifully in front of his plaster statue of the Blessed Virgin Mary, he was asking her as usual to intercede for him. He was asking for some small contact with the living God that his faith might be restored. As usual the bright blue Virgin with the rosy cheeks beamed down at him speechlessly.

'Padre!'

He was fond of the statue for all its cheap vulgarity. A more artistic icon might have been a temptation. He might be moved by its beauty and mistake the feeling for a sign from the Mother of God. The few lire's worth of plaster and paint reminded him that faith was as likely to enfold an open-hearted simpleton as a high-minded aesthete. More likely perhaps.

'Padre. Telefono!'

Vittorio frowned. Who could be phoning him so early? He genuflected hurriedly and went downstairs.

It was Cardinal Benetti. He sounded nervy and his sentences were punctuated with heavy exhalations of tobacco smoke.

'Father, I've had a telephone call from a distant relative

of mine. Her son has just died from an extraordinary fever – apparently the boy became paralysed and virtually unable to speak. Cecilia – my relative – is convinced that he was in some kind of distress other than his illness.' He paused. 'You're wondering what this has to do with you? That's easy. The boy was about to become a novice monk when he was struck down. His Order was in England. It was the Little Brothers of the Apostles. Yes, it is something of a coincidence. Frankly, I was inclined to get on to the Abbot right away to find out the background to the illness and so on, but I hesitated on two counts: firstly, Cecilia is a sensible woman and, even granted the death of her son, she was unusually perturbed. Secondly, the doctors are still unable to agree on the exact nature of the illness . . . So it occurred to me that I should check with you first: did you come across anything out of the ordinary in the course of your research? Anything, shall we say, untoward?'

Vittorio was already mentally reviewing his research. His memory kept snagging on a tiny peculiarity; a single footnote buried in the lengthy books. The name Anthony came to him. Anthony had written a book called . . . called . . .

'Father? Are you there?'

'I beg your pardon, Eminence. I was thinking. There may be something. May I call on you later?'

Vittorio replaced the receiver and walked slowly into the kitchen where his morning coffee was on the table. He had dispensed with a more substantial breakfast three years ago, as a penance. He drank the coffee without sitting down.

Who was Anthony? Obediently his memory whirred and clicked. He was a Little Brother some time in the late seventeenth century. He had left the Order suddenly (why? The footnote did not say.) The book he had written had attained considerable notoriety. It was called . . . *Thesaurus Catharorum*. *'The Treasure of the Cathars'*. The question now was, why had an English monk written a book of that title? What treasure? And why the Cathars? What possible interest could a Little Brother have in a sect of heretics who, at one time, constituted the most severe threat to the Church that it had ever encountered?

The priest's natural curiosity would not be satisfied until he had answered these questions. He put down his coffee cup and rubbed his hands together. The hunt was on.

Outside the chapel, Tom said goodbye to Brother Paul and, pulling out George's letter, sat down on his rolled-up anorak with his back resting against a column.

The rest of the letter had obviously been written later. Some of the words had been left out, some scratched out. The writing was sometimes small and crabbed, sometimes large and wild. George had clearly not been in full control of his hand nor, it seemed, of his mind. His condition appeared to have worsened, not improved as he had hoped.

It took Tom a long time to work out the full message. When he had finished, his eyes were strained and his hands were trembling. The letter read:

Can hardly move, Tom. Sorry. It's coming from the top of my head, it burns *there* where he touched me. Doctors don't know what – so I must tell you now. They put me in the long barrow, hours, days – I don't know – lying there, cold silent dark pressing down. So hungry, so *tired* but it's dangerous to sleep down there with the power all around in the dark. I pray yes I pray to the *SPIRIT* that is light – must *cast off* the body to be free of the dark – but nothing comes, so lonely down there, but this is not what I must tell you . . .

They take me out through the tunnel – it's *bright* bright as day but it's not, it's a fire. They come out of the fire no faces I'm frightened they're all around – so many questions, so much to remember, I can't tell you how much. I kneel on leaves they're all around I

126

remember the answers and the vows, yes, *good*. I swear NOT TO SPEAK of what I see, hear etc. but I MUST speak now. They tell me so many things – I am at the first circle, they say, the circle of death and rebirth, I must be born many times. They say. I will learn to leave the barrow *in the spirit*, I must become perfect, they say, all things are possible even the conquest of death for ever – so many frightening things but they are *not* what I must tell you, Tom, now . . .

At this point the letter became even less coherent. In his delirium George seemed more and more to be re-living the events surrounding his initiation. The sentences became increasingly fragmentary, the words mere signs which pointed to some experience that lay beyond words.

They stand me with the fire on my back, they say I must witness the circle of power – they're chanting chanting singing a mad slicing sound it cuts my ears inside, it's in my head, O God it stops and – look the *Stone* – it's lighting up and something's growing out of the Stone I swear it – it's *him*, he's skimming gliding over the mound, over the ground towards me he's in front of me, *Ambrose*. His face with fire on it shining and his eyes, O God, dark with fire in them – I look into them I can't help it. He shows me a knife he's smiling he's pushing pushing the knife *into his stomach* I can't take my eyes away, they hurt, his eyes burn me – He doesn't mind the knife it sticks out it doesn't hurt he smiles. It's not a dream, it's real *real*. I'm sick, falling, face in the leaves – he's whispering at me I don't understand he says it's all in the serpent's circle – the treasure – it's terrible, scary, outside everything, you won't believe it, Tom, but it's all true – they're only *waiting for the Holy Father*. I must tell you, stop *stop* Pope stop –

The letter ended as abruptly as it had begun. Despite the cold and the ache in his back, Tom hardly dared move. Carried away by the nightmarish stream of words, he sat and stared blankly at the piece of paper fluttering between his trembling fingers. The low whistle of the wind blowing between the columns reminded him where he was. He jumped up guiltily, expecting to find that he was being watched; but, glancing frantically around him, he found that there wasn't a soul in sight. Close to panic, he stuffed the incriminating letter into his pocket, trying desperately to hear himself think above the pounding in his head. There was only one thing to do – it meant disobeying Ambrose and risking his anger, but he had to deliver the letter to the one man he could be sure of.

Cautiously he left the colonnade's half-shelter and began to skirt round the back of the Abbey towards Joachim's workshop. He kept as far away from the cloisters as possible. Their narrow windows, like eyes, followed him along the cliff which plunged to the flood plain below.

Vittorio wiped his spectacles and bent over the diagram again. The craftsmanship of the engraving was exquisite. Every detail was perfectly rendered, right down to the last scale on the serpent in the centre. Each of the seven circles was minutely labelled in Latin. He held his magnifying glass a few inches from the writing. The first label was *Circulum Abstinentiae*, the 'Circle of Abstinence'; the second, *Circulum Purificationis* – the Circle of Purification – and so on through to the sixth circle which was tagged the Circle of Power. The tail-biting serpent was edged with the words *Hic jacet Thesaurus*: Here lies the Treasure. Vittorio did not understand. If the diagram was a treasure map, it certainly did not refer to a geographical location.

He had been right about the footnote. A renegade monk called Brother Anthony had written a book called *The Treasure of the Cathars*. It had been privately published in 1691 by a Jewish bookseller and printer who lived off London's Fleet Street. The scholar who wrote the footnote mentioned the chief cause of the book's brief notoriety: it claimed to reveal the 'secret of immortality'. He had added a sardonic comment: 'I have been unable to locate a copy of the book but, since the so-called Brother Anthony died suddenly before his work had left the bookseller, his claim would seem to have been somewhat exaggerated.'

Vittorio had been confident of succeeding where the scholar had failed. There were very few books, if any, which could not be found in the Vatican archives. They contained the most comprehensive collection of theological documents ever assembled in one place. He was therefore more than surprised when he found that no copy of the book had been placed there. He was not daunted – his sharp brain told him that the book's absence was more significant than its presence. With great ingenuity he managed to track down a copy of the book's frontispiece, which had been commissioned by the former Little Brother. It seemed to be a schematic summary of the book's contents; but, without the book, it was useless. The enigmatic circles gave nothing away.

He was not perturbed. He merely decided to tackle the problem from another angle. Stowing Brother Anthony away in the back of his mind, Vittorio decided to set down what he knew about the Cathars. On the face of it, the facts were straightforward.

The name 'Cathar' derived from the Greek *Katharoi* meaning 'the pure ones' and, subsequently, the 'perfect ones'. By the turn of the thirteenth century, the disease of Catharism was concentrated in the region of Southern France known as Languedoc. Incited by the Cathar leaders who were called *Parfaits*, or Perfect, the people of that area openly defied the Roman Catholic Church. In 1207, Pope Innocent III decided he could no longer tolerate such defiance, which was in danger of spreading. He instigated a crusade – a holy war in which the forces of orthodoxy were offered indulgences, or remission of their sins, if they fought against the heretics. The crusade lasted longer than expected; but in the end the power of the Cathars was essentially broken. Those who escaped death in the war were mostly executed or dispersed by an Inquisition which re-established the absolute authority of the Church. This much Father Vittorio knew.

He also knew, more or less, the particular brand of heresy for which the Cathars were condemned. It was to do (it usually was) with the problem of Evil. The Cathars did not believe in the sovereignty of Good. They did not believe, in the orthodox way, that Evil was a kind of negation of Good – a falling away from God, the ground of all Goodness. They believed that Evil was a positive force in its own right, equal and opposite to Good. The universe was split between God and Satan. God was identified with spirit and light; Satan with matter and darkness.

Satan had created the world, not God. God ruled over some remote spiritual realm; Satan was master of the physical realm and the Lord of Creation. Fundamentally, man was a spiritual being belonging to God. But he inhabited the physical world which belonged to Satan. His soul, a fragment of God's pure spirit, was imprisoned in the work of Satan, namely a body.

One of the crucial outcomes of this conflict between soul and body was the Cathar view of sexuality.

Since the body was a satanic lump of waste matter, any amount of sexual intercourse was theoretically acceptable simply because it had no bearing on the soul. But the consequence of sex was a different matter: the birth of a child meant that another fragment of immortal spirit was trapped in the mire of flesh and blood. In other words, sex was not sinful as long as it was divorced from procreation. In a grotesque reversal of the Roman Catholic view, the Cathars tolerated indiscriminate sex but deplored married love.

In practice, the Cathar élite – the Perfect – regarded sex as a distraction, a waste of energy. Their only remedy for the soul's disease was to renounce the body altogether. They believed that it was their duty to purge the body ruthlessly of its base desires – to root out every instinct – until the soul could be reunited with the pure spirit of God.

Vittorio was barely able to suppress a shudder. He regarded his own ample body with affection. The violence of Cathar beliefs was distasteful. They were not only extreme, but also naive: it was far too cut-and-dried to separate God and Satan, soul and body in that way. God penetrated the entire universe from the largest star to the smallest stone. There was nothing evil in the world but that man made it so. It was tempting at times to believe otherwise – every time, for instance, a single child was run down in the street, it was hard to discern the handiwork of God. Hard, but not impossible. Such acts of destruction were tests of faith.

The priest sighed. It always came down to faith. If there was one Cathar feature that he found attractive, it was their rejection of faith. They wanted nothing to do with it. They claimed instead that devout souls could know God at first hand, leaving no room for doubt.

Vittorio returned to Brother Anthony. If the Little Brothers of the Apostles had discovered that he was writing a book about the Cathars, they probably would have done well to expel him. The trouble was, everyone agreed that Anthony had left of his own accord and then written the cursed book. There was nothing for it but to dig more deeply in Cathar history; and, this time, to dig for treasure.

Father Vittorio hurried down to the labyrinthine archives where the books and manuscripts, like a vast and living memory, stretched back to the dawn of Christianity.

Four hours later he was back at his desk, writing feverishly. He had a great deal to tell the Cardinal. The picture of the Cathars which he was now painting was very different from his original sketchy version. And that was the least of his troubles.

As still as a tree, the solitary monk stood by the stream. Even before his fair hair was ruffled by the wind and he began to stroll towards the willows, Tom knew it was Brother Joachim. In two minutes he had zigzagged down the spur and run to the bend in the stream. The monk turned and watched him approaching. His face was pale and expressionless.

'Tom . . . why?' There was no anger, only weariness.

'This.' Tom handed him the letter.

'Tom, you've been told I must be left alone. You understand that – '

'*Please*. Read it.'

Joachim read the letter. Occasionally Tom helped him to decipher a difficult word and, all the while, watched his expression carefully. It didn't change. Either the monk was unmoved or he was guarding his reactions. Only when he had finished did his breathing betray the faintest hiss of anger.

'Well?' said Tom. 'What do we do?' He already felt easier now that the burden was shared. He was ready to put himself in Joachim's hands. His friend's reply was the last one he expected.

'We'd better pray for him.'

'*What*? But something awful has happened. George is in a terrible state – the initiation, Ambrose, everything. How could they *do* that to him?'

'Calmly now, Tom. Does this sound like the George you know?'

'Well, no. But he's obviously very ill . . .'

'Exactly. He's delirious, raving. Look at the way he's describing things. He's actually seeing them, but that doesn't mean they happened. It's pretty clear to me that they're hallucinations.'

'What . . . you mean even Ambrose and the knife?'

'Especially Ambrose and the knife. Our Abbot is a remarkable man, certainly. But would he go to all the trouble of stabbing himself simply to frighten a boy out of his wits? Come on, Tom. Think. The truth is probably serious enough: George is having some kind of a breakdown which – '

'But the long barrow,' Tom protested. 'Was he imagining that as well?'

'Didn't you know? I always thought it was an open secret that initiation rites were held at the Ring. Of course George wasn't imagining that part. It's a wonderful place for a ceremony – so old and dramatic . . . But it's only a device to impress the initiate, to concentrate his mind. I'm not saying the ceremony isn't a very tough business – as you'll find out – but it's not as serious as all *that* . . .' He smiled and punched Tom playfully on the shoulder. 'George has blown it up out of all proportion. It's not so surprising; put it this way. He has a gruelling year, his resistance is low, he's been fasting for days, very little sleep, he panics at the initiation – poor boy – he runs off home, contracts some kind of virus with high fever and, who knows, hysterical paralysis. On top of all that, he's plagued by a sense of failure and remorse, he goes over it all again and again in his mind, feels persecuted, especially by Brother Ambrose – classic symptom – and wants to implicate everyone in his personal grief. Doesn't he even tell you to avoid the Order?'

He had to admit that what Joachim was saying fitted the facts. In the cold light of his logic, the letter did begin to look like a mass of unbalanced ramblings. Yet Tom was troubled by a touch of glibness in the monk's interpretation. Beneath the cacophony of delirium, he seemed to detect in the letter resonances which echoed his own confusion. They vibrated most clearly in the enigmatic postscript – in George's assertion that his Redeemer lived.

'What about the bit at the end of the first letter? George doesn't seem so ill there. What does it mean? I think he wants me to believe that Jesus isn't immortal in the way that you said . . . I think he means that Jesus *did* die. That he passed *through* death and was resurrected so that he's sort of . . . still alive *inside* people, still redeeming them . . .' He anxiously searched Joachim's face for signs of understanding.

The monk closed his eyes briefly. 'I've told you, Tom. The truth isn't always easy to accept. George wasn't ready for it, after all. Maybe you're not.' He sighed. 'Perhaps I was wrong to tell you – '

'I *am* ready. But how do I *know* that what you said is

true?' He couldn't seem to impress on Brother Joachim how torn he was, how much was at stake.

'You don't know. Not yet. You have to take my word for it – that's what a tutor is for. But if you keep faith with what I've told you, in time you'll know it's true beyond the shadow of a doubt. In time, everyone will know . . .'

'Including the Holy Father?' Tom asked boldly. 'When will you inform *him* of his wrong beliefs? Perhaps George was talking sense and he should be stopped.' He immediately wished he could retract the bitter words, but it was too late – Joachim was regarding him icily.

'I see I've misjudged you, Tom,' he replied distantly. 'It's probably my fault – I've never explained to you properly what it means to be a monk. We have always set ourselves a little apart from the Mother Church which must necessarily be, and always has been, a worldly institution. If occasionally we have to remind the Church of its origins and purpose, we will not flinch from the task. However, this needn't concern you. You're free to opt out. The Little Brothers can't afford the faint-hearted.'

Tom thrust his hands in his pockets and glared out over the meadows. Hearing Joachim speak like that was almost more than he could bear.

'I'm not opting out,' he said fiercely. 'I think serving God is what . . . what I am *for*.' The final words came out in a rush. He felt acutely miserable that the letter had come between him and his friend.

'Actually,' said the monk softly, 'I think so too.'

Tom kept his head turned away in case Joachim should see the grateful, ashamed tears which pricked the backs of his eyes. Fortunately the monk went on, 'I understand your concern about the Pope, Tom. But think of it this way: he himself wants to visit us. Do you think he would take it kindly if he were prevented from seeing his Brothers in Christ?'

Tom shook his head desperately. 'No, but *which* Christ?' he burst out in a last protest. 'That's the whole point. I find it so hard to believe completely in your

Christ, the pure Spirit . . . He's so overpowering and . . . and *dazzling* – not a bit like us, well, like *me*. I know I'm weak but I can't help it.' He swallowed and hung his head, unable to meet Joachim's eyes.

'Tom. Listen. I never said it was easy to believe. God knows, I had my doubts. But that's also the whole point: the divine spark buried deep inside us is strengthened by doubt and struggle. Don't take it so hard. You won't always be in the dark, I promise. Trust me.'

'I do trust you, Brother Joachim,' said Tom. 'I'm sorry. I just need to know more.'

'You will. Be patient. Brother Ambrose has promised me that he'll personally teach you – '

'Ambrose?' Tom was aghast. 'What do you mean? You're my teacher.'

Joachim took him by the arm and led him a little way along the bank of the stream. He appeared to be having difficulty in finding the right words. At last he said, 'I shouldn't be telling you this. But I'm glad in a way that it's come up. I tried to warn you before that I wouldn't be here for ever. Well, I have to leave soon. There's work to be done elsewhere and I've never really fitted in here . . .'

Tom's brain refused to absorb the news. 'But you're my teacher,' he repeated stubbornly.

'Tom!' Joachim said sharply. 'We must both do as we're told . . . go where we're sent.'

'I suppose I'll never see you again,' he said in a hopeless monotone.

'You're being self-indulgent, Tom. Of course you'll see me again – we might even work together . . . as colleagues. We'd make a good team, eh? But it's important, of course, that this stays strictly between us. Do you understand?' His voice trailed off. He was looking up at the cliff. There were three monks standing on the edge of the precipice. The one in the middle was shorter and squarer than the other two.

'Oh Lord. He's seen me,' moaned Tom. 'I'm not supposed to bother you.'

'Don't worry. I intend to speak to our Abbot. He won't say anything to you.' His firmness was reassuring. He held up the letter. 'I'll show him this, if you don't mind. I'd be interested to know what he has to say about it. Go home, Tom, and for heaven's sake, *relax*.' He patted the boy's shoulder and walked away.

After a few steps he paused and half-turned to look back. His expression was suddenly so gentle, yet so melancholy, that it sent a ripple of irrational fear through Tom, almost as if his friend was already lost to him.

Joachim raised his hand once in parting salute and began to climb the hill.

When Tom looked up at the cliff, he saw that the monks had gone.

16

Father Vittorio had soon found that the archives contained virtually no original Cathar documents. Whatever books had preserved their doctrines and secrets had been cast into the flames by the Inquisition seven centuries ago. But the reports of the Inquisition itself had made fascinating reading. They consisted mostly of confessions by Cathar followers and sympathisers, from noblemen and landowners down to tradesmen and peasants. Although the reports were biased, setting out to condemn the confessors in the first place, the simple and often moving testaments of the people shone through. They built up an idea of life in thirteenth century Languedoc which bore no relation to the one Vittorio had imagined.

To begin with, the whole region was entirely separate from the rest of France. As an independent principality, it was free to foster one of the most extraordinary flowerings of culture in the Western world. Men gathered there from every civilised corner of the globe to share their art and science. Greek philosophers, Moorish scholars, Jewish kabbalists, Egyptian magi, alchemists, astronomers and Arab mathematicians – all thronged the luxurious gardens and courts of the great houses, while poets and troubadours sang their unforgettable ballads of courtly love, chivalrous deeds and earthly woe.

Gradually Vittorio had become acquainted with the religion which lay behind this extravagant culture. The Cathar community was divided into two parts: the

Perfect men and women who were the Cathars proper, and the Believers. The vast majority of the testimonies came from the Believers. Without exception, they admired the Perfect who seemed to have been as tolerant towards others as they were strict with themselves. Despite, for instance, their liberal attitude to sex, the Perfect themselves were fiercely ascetic, preaching and practising absolute chastity, prolonged fasting and total non-violence. The Believers, of course, were asked to follow suit; of course they rarely did. But the Perfect were reconciled to the imperfection of their flock. They recognised that the life of a monk or nun was not for everyone. They were compassionate.

But once a Believer entered a Cathar monastery, the lenience ceased. In aspiring towards the state of the Perfect, he was expected to live up to the title. The Inquisitional records brimmed with legends and rumours of the initiation rites which were designed to bring a Cathar monk to perfection. Nothing was certain; the rule of the monasteries was secrecy and silence. There were many tales, too, of the Perfects' superhuman powers. One of them reached such divine illumination that he had to wear a hood over his face in case his radiance blinded his fellow monks; another was seen kneeling in an attitude of prayer sixty feet above the ground with no visible support. Many of them starved themselves to death by way of ultimate purification. In short, all the stories bore the usual signs of imaginative embroidery. But on one point they all agreed. The Perfect had miraculous powers of healing. Practically every ailment from cataracts to cow-pox had been cured at one time or another by the simple laying on of a Perfect's hands.

It was hardly surprising that the Perfect were enormously popular. Too popular for the Catholic clergy who, over the years, had grown lazy, corrupt and dissolute. They often displayed more care in tending to their parishioners' bodies than their souls; or else they were just plain drunk. They could not compete with the Cathars. They had no answer to the exemplary lives of the Perfect, to say nothing of their powers. In the end, the Church of Rome was not so much forced out of Languedoc, as laughed out. The priests and bishops slunk away from the region, or else gave themselves over entirely to running estates and making money.

The Vatican grew frightened. The success of the Cathars and their heretical beliefs threatened to undermine the whole Roman Catholic Church. The wily Pope Innocent III hit on a plan. He made an offer to the noblemen of the comparatively barbarous north of France: in return for a general pardon of their sins, they were to stamp out the Cathars. The northern barons, who were already envious of their southern neighbours' prosperity, were less impressed by the Pope's promise than by the prospect of rich lands and booty. The deal was struck. The loot-hungry warlords swept down on the peaceful region of Languedoc. So began a crusade which lasted nearly forty years. By the time it was over, the whole area was so badly devastated that the effects were said to persist down to the present day.

The first onslaught lasted for about twenty years. The death toll could not be easily assessed – over all, it numbered tens of thousands of men, women and children. One town alone saw the massacre of fifteen thousand inhabitants. Father Vittorio was sickened by the slaughter, and ashamed. He felt implicated in the bloody action of the Church. He was not sorry to discover that, against all the odds, the invasion had failed. The Cathars were able to worship freely again.

The respite was brief. A second invasion, under King Louis VIII, finally succeeded in subduing Languedoc. The righteous agents of the Inquisition were sent in to finish what the soliders had begun. Thousands were interrogated; many of them were burnt at the stake. The remaining Cathars regrouped in the mountain fortress of Montségur – the Mount of Safety or, perhaps, the Mount of Salvation. There, in 1244, they made a last astonishing stand against the invaders.

Vittorio began to feel threatened by his sympathy with the Cathars. He had to remind himself just how dangerous and corrupt their doctrines had been. They struck at the heart of Christianity – the Saviour Himself. They thought that Christ had never become a man because He would never let Himself become embroiled with Satan by assuming a body. So they denied the Incarnation. They denied the sublime paradox: that Christ was both God and man. They claimed instead that He was (as one Believer so eloquently remarked) 'a phantasm' – the bloodless appearance of a man. Their wish to excuse Christ from the indelicacy of a body did Him a great disservice: it made His sacrifice on the Cross meaningless. For in order to wash away the sins of the world, His Blood had to be real, substantial, innocent – and shed. If the Cathars had prevailed, there would have been no Redemption; and, without the fact of Redemption, the whole edifice of the Church would crumble to dust.

Vittorio saw clearly now the need to disinfect France from this pernicious epidemic, however much he regretted the exterminations. However, the dogmatic differences between Cathar and Catholic were not his immediate concern. He had found something which struck a terrible and resonant chord. It was buried in the account of the siege of Montségur. He could no longer ignore the connection that he was half-afraid to make. It was time to see the Cardinal and to talk about treasure.

'When I compared the various accounts of the Cathars' last stand at Montségur, Eminence, I found a great many hints about their treasure. The trouble was that the hints often contradicted each other. In the end, I discarded all the accounts which were not based on hard facts and came up with the only solution which fitted the evidence . . .'

Cardinal Benetti was listening intently to the little

priest who was pacing nervously up and down in front of his desk. The room was thick with cigarette smoke and the blinds were half-drawn against the glare of the evening sun. The rude sound of car horns wafted up from the street. Vittorio's story was drawing to a close. He was uncomfortably aware that all this talk of Cathars, together with the priest's unusual behaviour was beginning to have a similar effect on him. He lit a cigarette.

'It now seems undeniable,' Vittorio was saying, 'that there were two treasures.'

The Cardinal pressed his fingertips together and frowned. The priest hastened to explain. 'You see, Eminence, the Cathars were extremely rich. They had the financial support of all Languedoc. How else could they have lasted so long against the overwhelming numbers of the invaders? Their enormous hoard of gold, silver and coin was stashed away in Montségur. Apart from anything else, the Perfect needed it to maintain their army of mercenaries – you remember, their creed forbade the Cathars themselves to fight.

'Now, imagine if you will the last of the Cathars in their mountain-top stronghold. It was virtually impregnable. The besieging army had no choice but to starve them out. It was a sizeable army – about ten thousand strong – but, even so, it was not large enough to seal off the mountain completely. With the help of sympathisers among the enemy, the Perfect were able to ferry out their entire treasure and store it nearby in a secret place. It has never been found – it has never even been heard of again . . .'

Vittorio paused to wipe his spectacles. There were beads of perspiration on his forehead.

The Cardinal prompted him: 'And you think that our friend Brother Anthony knew something about this treasure and wrote it down in his book?'

'At first, yes. Then I became interested in the persistent rumours of a second treasure – a mystical treasure which had nothing to do with material wealth. Suddenly the tales of untold riches seemed like a gigantic red herring;

the second treasure seemed to be the important one. I also reasoned that if Anthony had stumbled on a hoard of gold, he would not have advertised it. My guess is that he was writing about the more elusive, mystical riches – whatever they were.' He pointed to the diagram of circles on the Cardinal's desk. '*That* may have some connection with it. At any rate, it hasn't anything to do with gold . . .'

'You have evidence that the second treasure really existed?' asked the Cardinal. He was impressed by the intricacy of the diagram, but equally baffled by it. If it were an elaborate piece of hocus-pocus, someone had taken a lot of care over it.

'Oh yes, Eminence. It's in all the history books. We must return to the siege. It ended quite suddenly. On reflection, it is hard to know which side really gave in. There were only around four hundred Cathars left in Montségur – against an army of thousands. Yet the terms of their surrender were astoundingly lenient: the mercenaries and other fighting men were to be given a free pardon, while the *Parfaits* – the Perfect – were also to be let off more or less scot free. They had only to make a token renunciation of their beliefs and to confess a few "sins" to the Inquisition. It amounted to little more than paying lip-service to the besiegers.

'Instead of accepting eagerly, as you might expect, the Cathars asked for a truce to consider the terms and freely offered hostages to guarantee that no one would escape meanwhile. Two weeks passed. No word from the defenders. Around two hundred Perfects were seized and burnt without trial. It only needed one whisper against the Cathar faith for any one of them to save his own life. Every one of them chose to burn . . .

'Meanwhile, unknown to the enemy, four of the Perfect had remained hidden in the fortress. On the night after the truce expired, they made a daring descent down the sheer precipice which formed the western face of the mountain. And they took with them the Treasure of the Cathars.' Father Vittorio paused and slumped into one of the Cardinal's armchairs, waiting for his superior's response. The Cardinal looked thoughtful.

'You have been doing a lot of guessing, Father,' he said with a touch of irony. 'What do you guess the so-called treasure was?'

Vittorio shrugged. 'I don't know, Eminence. A piece of secret doctrine . . . a book perhaps. Something portable, anyway. Something quite out of the ordinary. I naturally would not go so far as to say that it was – er – the "secret of immortality".'

'Naturally,' said the Cardinal.

'That was, you recall, the wild claim attributed to Anthony's book.'

'I remember.'

'I think it possible – likely even – that Anthony discovered the story of the Cathars' treasure and decided to set down his own speculations about it. Rather like myself. And, like me, he probably got carried away.'

Vittorio gave a forced laugh. He did not believe a word he was saying. Of course he had got carried away. That was part of the method, as it were. In the heat of the chase, he could act beyond himself. He could make connections or find new pathways which would normally seem too bizzare or too hazardous. That was what made him different from the usual plodding scholar: he guessed a great deal, and he always knew deep down when his guess was right. Right now, he had guessed his way to the brink of something too catastrophic to contemplate. He had to know more, to find proof. For the moment, he wanted to avoid frightening Cardinal Benetti. He did not relish being written off as a madman.

'Yes, Father. You *did* get rather carried away. Your research has been more creative than usual. Most entertaining. Have you any more speculations?'

'No, Eminence.' It was not the truth; but he could see from the Cardinal's face that he was beginning to make connections of his own.

144

'Of course,' said Cardinal Benetti with studied indifference, 'there was some sort of story about a treasure belonging to the Little Brothers of the Apostles, wasn't there? It would be incredible if . . .'

'Incredible,' agreed Vittorio.

'I mean, it would be fantastic to suggest a link between . . . ?'

'Fantastic, Eminence.' He judged that the moment was ripe for his bombshell. 'Except that . . .' He shrugged.

'Except what?' said the Cardinal sharply.

'It may be nothing at all . . . a coincidence. It's just that when Brother Anthony left the Little Brothers, he fled to his sister. She was a nun. He stayed at her convent, whose records indicate that he was unwell. In fact, he died within eight days of his arrival. During that time, he managed to dictate *The Treasure of the Cathars* to his sister, who regarded it as a dying testament and therefore important enough to publish. The cause of his death was not known. But the symptoms of his disease were described as a fever of unnatural force, coupled with a creeping paralysis from head to toe.'

Neither of the two men moved, nor looked at each other. The talk was over; it was time for action. Cardinal Benetti's first instinct was to book himself on an immediate flight to England. His reason prevailed. He was too headstrong, too ill-informed and, above all, too indispensable to the success of the Holy Father's visit. He needed a man who was subtle, knowledgeable and inconspicuous. Vittorio had followed his thoughts exactly.

'Eminence, I shall need a letter signed by you, in case I have to reveal my identity and call upon the authority of the Vatican.'

'Of course. How do you intend to introduce yourself?'

'I might try bowing three times,' the little priest joked. 'It was the Believers' formal sign of reverence towards the Perfect.'

PART II

Sacrifices

17

The taxi-driver threw his car around the sharp bends of the winding lanes as if he were being pursued by demons. Judging by his relaxed, tuneless whistling, it was his usual way of driving. Father Vittorio wedged himself more tightly into a corner of the back seat and tried to concentrate on the tall hedgerows which flashed past the window. They grew so high in places that they met overhead in leafy tunnels which all but blotted out the last of the fading daylight.

Rounding a particularly tight bend, the taxi emerged on to the first stretch of straight open road for miles. In the middle of the road stood a policeman; beside him was a sign which read BLOXBURY and, behind him, three men were unloading some planks and oil drums, painted yellow, from the back of a battered pick-up truck. The taxi slowed to a halt. The driver wound down his window and shouted to the policeman, who seemed to be a friend of his, 'What's the story then, Harry?'

Vittorio waited anxiously as the young constable, who had very pink cheeks and sticking-out ears, strolled over to the car and bent down to speak through the window.

'Roadblock, Arthur,' he said. 'Now on, nothing goes in, nothing goes out except on special business.' He peered suspiciously into the back of the taxi. 'What's this?'

'Fare for the hotel,' said Arthur. 'What's up? Somebody rob a bank?'

'Don't be daft,' said the policeman. While keeping one

eye on the priest, he pulled a piece of paper from his top pocket and thrust it under the driver's nose. 'Quarantine, see? Ministry orders. Bad case of foot-and-mouth. Nothing goes in – '

'And nothing goes out, Harry,' supplied the driver. 'What about this bloke then?' He jerked his head backwards.

The policeman shrugged. 'Have to take him back to town, Arthur.'

The bloke surprised them both by getting out of the taxi. He was dressed in baggy brown corduroy trousers, a checked shirt and an old tweed jacket with leather patches on the elbows. A tweed hat, set at a rakish angle, completed the outfit. Vittorio was proud of the disguise.

'Thank heavens, I'm just in time. A few minutes more and you would doubtless have completed your road-block. All the same, I quite understand that you can't let this taxi through – ' he smoothly extracted some notes from his wallet and pressed them into the driver's hand – 'but the walk to the hotel will do me good.' He looked at the constable appealingly and added, 'I've come all the way from London, you know.'

The young policeman looked at him carefully for signs of any challenge to his authority, but he was greeted by a pleasant smile and an innocent pair of glasses. He decided to be lenient. Besides, the bloke spoke English much too well to be a native. He was definitely foreign, and probably French. The French could cause any amount of trouble. He turned to the taxi-driver.

'I can let this gentleman through, Arthur. But you'll have to turn round. Can't have you driving in and out. More than my job's worth.'

'Suits me,' said Arthur. He got out, removed Vittorio's suitcase and fishing rod from the boot, returned to his seat and began to reverse his taxi at high speed down the road.

'Right, sir.' The policeman rubbed his hands together.

'Last in, eh? Hope you're not planning on coming and going?'

'Oh no, I'll stay inside the quarantine area. The peace and quiet will be welcome. How bad is the foot-and-mouth disease?'

'Bad enough. One herd gone. The rest under observation. Too soon to tell.'

'I see.' The priest struggled forward with his heavy suitcase.

Hesitating in front of the makeshift barrier, he almost expected another, intangible barrier to prevent him from slipping between the oil drums. The three men had unloaded the last plank and were watching him with blank faces. Were they Cathars? The policeman called out to one of the men:

'Hey, John! Fancy giving this gent a lift to Mrs. K.'s?' The men looked at each other. Then the tallest of them stepped forward and spat noncommittally out of the side of his mouth.

'Might be arranged,' he said.

'I'd be very grateful,' Vittorio admitted.

The man called John took the suitcase out of his hand and swung it easily into the cab of the truck. He nodded towards the passenger seat and climbed in behind the wheel.

They drove in silence. Vittorio was aware of the man's sidelong glances, sizing him up, but he was too tired to care.

Dusk had fallen by the time the truck pulled up in front of the hotel, and a single light showed on the ground floor. It looked neither welcoming nor comfortable. Growing increasingly depressed, the priest remembered to offer the man some money, which was refused. The truck bumped away down the dirt track. Vittorio pushed the front door open on to the dark, chilly hall, and stood there at a loss. There was no one about; perhaps the house was not a hotel at all.

'Hello!' he said. 'Is anybody there?'

151

A door opposite him was flung open and a squarish, formidable woman appeared, framed in the rectangle of light.

'Ah! Mr. de Vere?' she inquired.

'Yes,' said Vittorio. His assumed name sounded strangely on his ears, but he was pleased with it. 'Victor de Vere' was meant to suggest either a classy English name or, in case he had to account for his foreign origins, an equally acceptable French name.

'Mrs. K. warned me of your coming,' the woman went on. 'You might find it odd to be welcomed by another guest. I am Hannah van Neef. Come in by the fire – you must be exhausted . . .'

It was true; he was exhausted. A part of him struggled against it – struggled against the warm welcome of the friendly stranger. Time was desperately short; he had forty-eight hours' grace before the Holy Father arrived. And, apart from that, he had sworn to stay on his guard with everyone the moment he entered the danger zone. But another part of him was too tired and miserable. He hadn't the heart to remain aloof. Grateful as a dog, he found himself thanking Hannah van Neef, sinking down on a sofa in front of a blazing fire, and breathing in the sweet aroma of expensive coffee.

The chimes of Big Ben sounded distantly but clearly through the darkness outside. Cardinal Benetti cast a cold eye over the room which the Archbishop had put at his disposal. It was satisfactory. He hoped the same could be said for the chaplain, Father Dominic, who went with it. The young man was standing by the desk, head lowered, unable to meet the Cardinal's sweeping gaze.

'So you're going to look after me for a couple of days, Father?'

'I'll do my best, Eminence.' The chaplain's face had gone bright red with relief. He added in a rush, 'I was terribly worried that you wouldn't speak English, Eminence. My Italian is frightful.'

152

The Cardinal's mouth twitched. 'I hope I can make myself understood,' he said ironically. 'Well, Father, there's much to do. Unpack this for a start, please.' He humped his heavy briefcase on to the desk and picked up the phone to check that it was working.

'This is the direct line? Good. And it's the number you sent me in Italy? Excellent.'

He had no sooner replaced the receiver than the phone rang. He looked at the chaplain quizzically.

'It's the first time, Eminence. It was only installed this morning.'

Cardinal Benetti answered it. A familiar voice could be heard at the other end.

'Your Eminence, this is Brother Ambrose . . . from Bloxbury?'

'Of course. What can I do for you, Brother Ambrose?' He signalled frantically to Father Dominic for his cigarettes. The priest, clearly disapproving of the habit, passed the packet to him as if it were about to explode. 'No hitch in our arrangements, I hope . . .' He was careful to keep his voice normal.

'In a way, yes,' replied the Abbot. 'I'll come straight to the point: there has been an outbreak of foot-and-mouth disease on one of the farms. The whole village has been placed under quarantine until we can be sure that the incident is an isolated one.' His direct and matter-of-fact tone, tinged with the proper amount of concern, was very much to the Cardinal's taste. He was impressed in spite of himself.

'I see. You have my sympathies.' The Cardinal was thinking quickly. If this was some kind of ploy, what advantage could the Little Brothers gain from it? He could not see any, but it was a unique chance to test the Abbot. 'This puts a different complexion on things, Brother Ambrose. I may have to postpone the Holy Father's visit . . . indefinitely.' He waited for the shocked response. It did not come.

'I quite understand. Naturally, we will be disappointed.

153

But the Holy Father must not be put at any sort of risk.'
There was nothing except genuine concern for the Pope's well-being. Cardinal Benetti was disarmed.

'On the other hand,' he said hastily, 'I am as reluctant to change plans at such short notice as you are. Have any . . . precautions been taken?'

'All the relevant authorities have been informed and I have personally liaised with officials from the Ministries of Health and Agriculture. I need hardly add that the police have sealed off the village and that roadblocks are being manned round the clock by volunteers to reduce any traffic to the minimum.'

The Cardinal was lost for words. He was not used to coming up against people who were as efficient as he was. Especially monks. He made one last attempt to discern a sinister purpose.

'I congratulate you. But if the Holy Father were to visit you as planned, I suppose that you would want to make some adjustments to his arrangements – his entourage, for instance?'

'We wouldn't dream of it, Eminence. But it did occur to me that the quarantine could help us in other ways – it would deter the press, for instance. Just as His Holiness wanted. And I must say that the authorities would be happier if he could be persuaded to use a helicopter . . . we have an excellent field behind the Abbey – '

'I'm afraid not.' The Cardinal sighed. Much as he loved his old friend, Pope John the Twenty-Fifth was a difficult man to organise. It was bad enough that he had wilfully insisted on 'dropping in' on an obscure Order; it was worse that he had insisted on travelling by car. He wanted, of all things, 'to enjoy the English countryside'.

'Never mind, Eminence. I've already arranged for at least three cars to be let in – as well as a full police escort, of course. And I could always arrange for more if you think it necessary . . .'

The Cardinal was again reduced to silence. His idea of an entourage was a Special Branch man inside the Pope's car and a pair of police motorcycles. Speed and secrecy had been the keynote of his security arrangements. He was abashed by the Abbot's elaborate expectations.

'The Holy Father would be keeping, er, a much lower profile than that, Brother Ambrose. He is looking forward to visiting you and your Order. I think we can safely go ahead as planned – providing there's no danger to him personally?'

'None whatever, Eminence. His car will have to be disinfected when it enters, and again – more thoroughly – when it leaves. That's all.'

'Well, that's settled then. Thank you for phoning. My chaplain will contact you on the day to confirm the exact time of arrival. Goodbye, Brother Ambrose.' He rang off, slamming the receiver down.

'Is everything all right, Eminence?' asked Father Dominic. When he was nervous he sank his head between his shoulders and moved it from side to side. This idiosyncrasy set the Cardinal's nerves even more on edge.

'Everything's just fine, Father,' he snapped. But he was angry with himself, not his chaplain. He should not have let himself be drawn into Vittorio's brainstorm. If ever the Little Brothers (after centuries of self-effacing good works) found out that he had sent someone to spy on them, he would be put deeply to shame. He could only hope that the priest had already failed to cross the roadblocks and that his wild-goose chase had been brought to a premature end.

Ambrose pushed the telephone away and allowed himself the luxury of basking a moment in the light of his triumph. Suddenly the study door was flung open and Joachim was marching towards him, wearing his anger around him almost visibly, like a cloak. He leant across the wide desk and banged some sheets of paper down in front of his superior.

'Look at this letter. You'll be pleased with your

handiwork. Woodward hasn't got a hope in hell.' The cold, stinging words matched the hard, narrow face. The Abbot looked briefly into the monk's implacable visor of rage and flinched, averting his head.

'Damn you, Ambrose.' Years of self-restraint lent the curse a peculiar force.

Ambrose hunched himself in his chair, compressing his body like a steel spring. 'Anyone would think I had a choice, Joachim,' he said quietly. 'I couldn't risk everything for the sake of a single wretched boy. You know that.'

'There's always a choice. Once you start to murder the innocent, who knows where it will end? You have conveniently forgotten that the power is not yours to dispose of – it's given by God. You're not fit to hold authority. This abuse is . . . an *abomination*.'

'Oh, Joachim,' the Abbot said wearily. 'Do you think that we've been given the power merely to act like emasculated parish priests? We have been appointed the instruments of God's will on Earth and you come in here, flapping your scruples like a nun's skirts . . . For God's sake, man,' he hissed, 'we've been preparing seven hundred years for the Anti-Christ to set foot inside the Abbey and you suggest we throw it all away for a weak child. Can't you see he destroyed himself? Anyone who stands in the way of history is liable to be crushed . . . *Anyone*.'

Joachim was completely unmoved. The knuckles of his large hands showed white as he gripped the edge of the desk.

'So you think you can commit any crime as long as it's in the name of "history" – don't delude yourself, Ambrose: the moment you start using force, you debase yourself to the level of the enemy. The sacred law stands – *any* act of violence is, and always will be, anathema to the Order. Even you are not above the law.'

Ambrose's arm jerked up with the dreadful detachment of some mechanical thing. For a second, he seemed

156

about to strike the defiant monk. Joachim remained impassive and unblinking.

'*Hypocrite.*' The Abbot brought the flat of his hand down on the desk. 'You're about to take part in an act that makes murder look like a white lie – and you dare to preach to me about non-violence! What about our Brothers, hideously burnt at the stake in their thousands? How impressed would they be with your pious prattle?' Ambrose pushed back his chair violently and stood up. There were white flecks at the corners of his mouth. 'I am ready to avenge those innocent deaths, Joachim. Are you? The time has come full circle. It's our turn now. We're ready to complete God's purpose and we will have our revenge!'

Joachim gazed at him with mingled pity and scorn.

'Revenge? Haven't you put such primitive passions behind you? Our mission has one purpose and *only* one: to restore the true faith. By the grace of God, the Church will begin – through us – a new and glorious age. A renaissance of the faith can't be built on obsessions with *revenge.*'

The Abbot stood in silence, breathing hard. When at last he spoke, his voice was as soft as a knife leaving its sheath.

'Be very careful, Joachim. I won't see the work of a lifetime wrecked by your weakness. God alone knows why you are the chosen one, but as long as you are you will be accorded a certain respect. But don't make the mistake of thinking that because you wear the snake-ring you can overturn the will of the Order . . . *my* will. While I am the Guardian, my word shall be law. I am indispensable; you might find that *you* are not. There are others who can wear that ring.'

'Ambrose, you're a fool – a fool to think that the snake-ring can guarantee the seventh circle. Can't you see that nothing guarantees that leap into the unknown? The ring is no more than an aid, a companion to the task.'

'That may, or may not be so. We've only one way of finding out, haven't we? One chance. For the first and last time.'

'Yes. Meanwhile, there will be no more violence.'

'I warn you, Joachim – '

'No! I'm warning *you*. Swear, Ambrose, *swear* that no innocent person will be harmed.'

The two Brothers faced each other, locked in silent combat. Ambrose was the first to give way. His back seemed to bend slightly under the pressure; his body relaxed. He moistened his lips and stretched them into a thin smile.

'If you insist . . .'

'Swear by the perfect souls of our slaughtered Brothers.'

'I . . . swear by their souls,' said Ambrose, and added with a half-sneer: 'A shade melodramatic for you, Joachim.'

The monk merely pointed his finger at the Abbot's head.

'Remember,' he said.

18

As he walked past the pretty cottages, it seemed to him that the village was unnaturally quiet. A comparable village at home would be up and humming by this time of the morning. Maybe it was the effect of the foul weather; or perhaps, with the coming of the epidemic, the villagers had lost heart. Except for the occasional twitch of net curtains as he passed, he could have been in a ghost town.

He pushed open the gate of the last house and rang the bell. The door was opened by a middle-aged, attractive, but harassed-looking woman.

'Mrs. Reardon?' He gallantly doffed his hat.

'Yes . . . yes.'

'My name is Victor de Vere. May I have a word with you?'

The woman seemed to focus on him for the first time. 'What? If you're selling something . . .'

'No, no. Nothing like that. Actually it's your son I really wanted to see. I'm . . . an old friend of Giorgio's parents. Giorgio Woodward.'

Her face lost its preoccupied air and lit up with a smile. 'George? You're a friend of George's? Come in, please. Tom will be delighted.' Flustered, Elizabeth ushered him into the drawing-room, taking off her apron at the same time. 'I'll just go upstairs and get him. He's in his room. He's . . . well, he hasn't been himself lately.'

'Oh?' The priest adjusted his glasses sympathetically.

'You know . . . boys of that age. Says he has trouble sleeping.' She forced out a laugh and left the room.

Vittorio studied his surroundings and, finding nothing out of the ordinary, sat down to wait.

But it was difficult to sit still. There was so little time – a day at most before the Holy Father blithely left London for Bloxbury. The Cardinal needed his verdict that night. At the same time a careless remark, a false step, could be fatal. If he could win the confidence of Giorgio's best friend, he might find out all he needed to know. Who could tell how deeply Tom Reardon was already ensnared and indoctrinated? With luck, he was still too young to form part of the conspiracy, yet old enough to have absorbed an idea of the Order's teachings. At any rate, he must not be rushed. According to Hannah, he was not a boy to respond to bullying or shock tactics. Hannah! what a Godsend the woman was, what an ally . . . At first she had seemed tiresome – trying to interest him in her embroidery! But, once steered on to the right subject, she had revealed unsuspected talents. Although, like himself, she was an outsider, she knew nearly as much about Bloxbury and its inhabitants as she did about dolmens, barrows and stone circles. He had been sorely tempted to tell her a few things she didn't know . . .

Mrs. Reardon re-appeared with her son. He was bigger than Vittorio had expected – not so much tall, as broad and strongly built. His careless appearance marked him out as free from the vanities of adolescence. His face, amiable and strong-boned rather than handsome, was drawn, almost gaunt; and there were black circles under his eyes.

'This is my son – Tom,' said Mrs. Reardon, affectionately ruffling his striking red hair. Embarrassed, he moved his head away a shade irritably.

'Hello, Tom. I'm Victor de Vere. Giorgio – George – might have mentioned me . . . ? No? Well his parents are old friends of mine.' It was frightening how smoothly the lies popped out.

Tom was far from being a nervous person, yet his sleep had been fitful lately and troubled by grotesque dreams.

160

When he woke, dull and unrefreshed, they continued to plague him as a welter of fearful images which ran through his mind with a life of their own, growing more vivid for his lack of rest. The killing of Winston Powell's cattle played a large part. He had not seen the massacre, but he'd heard it. It was impossible to banish the plaintive bellowing of the infected beasts from his mind. The sound continued to haunt him, like a helpless cry of protest against the fact of death, until it became some-how bound up with George's apparent suffering and, in the end, with the whole idea of innocent sacrifice. He had become prey to a kind of superstitious belief that the disease – the pestilence – was like a boil on the face of the community, an inkling of a sickness that went beyond the physical.

When his mother came into his room, Tom was staring listlessly out of the window, through the branches of the cherry tree to the fields beyond. They were empty. A friend of George's had come to see him. A few days before his heart would have leapt. Now, he reacted cautiously: news had a way of not always being good. But the neat, fattish little man in the drawing-room looked pretty harmless. Despite his usual awkwardness in the presence of strangers, Tom was able to blurt out: 'Is George all right?'

'He's at home – in Italy, you know.'

'Yes. I know. I got a letter from him.'

Mr. de Vere smiled at Elizabeth, who immediately realised that she was not wanted.

'I'll go and make some coffee,' she said tactfully.

'That would be nice,' said Mr. de Vere, watching her leave the room. Then, turning to Tom, he went on, 'A letter, you say? How did he seem to you?'

'Bad. He could hardly write. It was an awful fever with . . . hallucinations and things.'

'What sort of hallucinations?' Mr. de Vere was watching him keenly from behind his glasses. Tom did not like it.

'Just stuff about the Little Brothers . . . His initiation

and so on.' Why didn't the man get to the point? Who *was* he anyway? Mr. de Vere seemed in no hurry.

'Ah yes, his initiation. It can't have helped. Poor George must have been under a lot of strain . . . ?'

'Yes,' said Tom shortly. 'I expect so.'

'Miss van Neef tells me that you're going to join the Order as well.'

'That's the idea.'

'You're lucky to have Brother Joachim as your – what do you call it? Tutor?'

'Tutor, yes. Do you know Brother Joachim then?'

'Only indirectly, Tom. Cecilia – George's mother – says that your Abbot speaks very highly of him . . .'

Tom could not resist any opportunity to praise his friend.

'I'm not surprised. He's the best. He can teach you without you even realising it. He just talks – you know, like normal conversation. I'm not all that bright and even I understand him . . . mostly. And you should see his carving!'

'Well, I'd like to. Perhaps I should take some lessons in theology from him, too. I've become a bit of a heathen recently! I don't suppose you've done much on that side of things yet . . . ?'

'Oh, I've done a bit.'

'Really? My main trouble has always been in believing that God would let His Son die on the Cross. The Redemption and all that. Seems almost too harsh somehow . . . don't you think?'

'Well, Joachim says . . .' But Tom remembered that he was not to mention what Joachim had said. (The wonderful Spirit, wide-eyed on its Cross, defying nails and thorns.) The stranger had leant forward fractionally in his chair.

'What does Joachim say?' Mr. de Vere's casual tone of voice contradicted his eager movement. There was something phoney about him.

'I can't remember.' He tried to cover the untruth by adding vaguely, 'I think doctrine may be slightly different in the Balkans.' Again the tell-tale movement in the chair.

'Where Joachim comes from, you mean . . .'

'Yes.' Tom no longer wanted to talk about Joachim. Something about the man's clothes did not go with the face or voice. They were too 'tweedy', too aggressively English; and the shoes, beautifully made from soft leather with thin soles, were hardly suitable for the country. He wanted to get back to George. 'It's funny that you should mention the Redemption. George said something about it in his letter. I think he was worried about it.' He gave a nervous laugh. 'He thinks we may all be damned!'

Mr. de Vere settled back in his chair. He looked a little bored now. 'Poor old George,' he sighed. 'May I have a look at the letter, Tom?'

'I'm afraid not. Brother Joachim has it – but you haven't told me how George is . . . I mean, is he better?' The man shifted about in his chair and suddenly sagged visibly. 'What's the matter?' asked Tom with genuine concern.

'Tom . . . I'm afraid George was more seriously ill than he thought.' His voice was unexpectedly gentle. 'I wish there was a way of making this easier for you . . . but I have to say that nothing could be done. George is dead.' The man took off his glasses and began to wipe them with great care.

Tom was not sure that he understood. He smiled politely and felt himself go very cold. A door must have been left open somewhere. The plump man looked rather comical: his eyes were sort of peering and myopic, like a mole's, wiping his glasses like that.

'Oh. Dead. I see,' he said sensibly. He felt his ears testing the word, letting it spiral through and into his head. A million little particles started trilling along the furrows of his brain. Sending messages no doubt. The sound was deafening for a while. You had to wait for it to die down, to drown in the creeping cold, before you could fit words to the movements the stranger's mouth was making.

'. . . suddenly. They still don't know what caused it, I'm afraid. But at least he's at peace . . .' It wasn't worth listening to such conventional silliness. It missed the point. You wanted to shut the man up, shut him out.

Tom closed his eyes. He hated this Mr. de Vere and all his deceitful questions. They were tiring. He just wanted to succumb to the cold feeling. He let it seep down, down until it struck him in the pit of the stomach and made him gasp. The world stopped spinning, the room slewed sideways without moving – the furniture seemed to spill out its insides, all its hard edges disappearing in a blur. Even the man was moving, blurring, melting into light. Not a strong light, but sad. It was flowing around his chair in shades of copper and green. Lovely colours like spring and autumn mixed; like hope and despair. He wasn't really hateful; just hurt and lonely.

He could hear the door opening and the rattle of cups. He was surprised to find his eyes closed – he must have dropped off for a second. His mother and the man, Mr. de Vere, were talking in low voices, earnest and respectful, as though *he* were the one who . . . not George. He opened his eyes. The chubby man was standing, shifting from one foot to another. He didn't want his coffee, he was going.

'Goodbye, Mr. de Vere. Thank you for coming.' Good. At least he had remembered his manners. Doors opening and closing. George's face, luminous and smiling. Dead. Mother's arms around you. No need for a lot of fuss, Mum. Mum? He's dead, *dead*. The ugly word squatting there like a great black stone. You couldn't do anything about it, you couldn't move it. Ever. It made you bloody furious.

In his heart he knew that he had been putting off this moment. He could not delay it any longer. Although in the realms of thought and theory Father Vittorio was an adventurous, even daring man, in matters of physical risk he was woefully timid. The sense of his own inadequacy

164

was heightened by the new oversized Wellington boots. They smothered his short legs. Just when he needed to appear impressive, he looked ridiculous.

Clumping along the gallery – his room was last on the right – he stopped outside Hannah's door. He could hear the busy stutter of her typewriter. He knocked twice and the typewriter stopped. Since her expeditions had been curtailed by the foot-and-mouth restrictions, Hannah had taken to writing up her notes quietly in her room. The door opened.

'Sorry to interrupt you, Miss van Neef, but I need your help. I want to visit the Abbey and, in particular, the workshop where one of the monks lives. Brother Joachim.'

'Tom's hero?' she smiled. 'Yes, he might be more communicative than the Abbot!'

'But I don't know where the place is. Can you tell me?' He gave no reason for wanting to go there. Hannah was the sort of person who would see straight through any elaborate justifications. His direct approach worked; she seemed to accept the request as the simple impulse of the tourist.

'I can do better than that,' she said. 'I can show you.' She beckoned him to follow her down the stairs and into the drawing-room.

Hannah led him across the wide room and, pushing past her embroidery stand, pointed out of the window overlooking the valley.

'You see the Abbey? Well, if you look to the left, you can just see a roof and chimney sticking up from the other side of the hill. You have it? Good. I believe that is the workshop where our monk hides. I see you have beautiful new rubber boots. That's fine – you will need them!'

Vittorio thanked her and turned to the door. His eye fell on her embroidery. His breath caught in his throat with a soft rasping sound. He bent over the pattern. The serpent in the centre, so much larger than in the frontispiece, seemed to wink at him.

165

'A most unusual design,' he commented vacuously.

'Yes, I thought so too. I'm quite pleased with it.' Hannah seemed oblivious to the bombshell she had dropped on him. But was she really? What on earth had made him believe that she was innocent of any connection with the Cathars? She could be in up to her neck, for God's sake. But, if so, why would she openly display the device? The questions flooded through his head. He heard himself speak too loudly, to cover up the clamour of his beating heart:

'Yes. *Most* unusual. What does it represent?'

'Don't ask me. Some arcane philosophy, perhaps . . . I don't know. I just copied this.'

'From one of your old manuscripts, I suppose . . .'

'No, no. It was my friend Tom who brought it to me. Wasn't it thoughtful of him? Look.' She opened the drawer of an adjacent writing desk and pulled out a leather-bound volume. Vittorio clenched his fist in an effort not to snatch it from her.

'How interesting,' he murmured. 'May I see?'

'Of course. Take it if you like – I've finished with it. As long as you give it back so that Tom can return it to his library.' She opened the book and pointed to the red words NOT TO BE REMOVED.

Vittorio handled the book as though it were fine porcelain. The title page read *Thesaurus Catharorum*.

'You're fond of old books?' Hannah asked sharply.

'Yes . . . yes, they're a hobby of mine.' He was already edging towards the door. Disappointingly, his sudden interest in her craft had just as suddenly evaporated. 'Well, I must be off. Thank you.' His boots could be heard lolloping up the stairs. A door banged. He really was an unpredictable little man – he had forgotten all about his trip to the Abbey.

Elizabeth found it difficult to gauge the depth of her son's grief. He continued to sit in his chair, perfectly still except for the occasional shiver. Her attempts to comfort him were neither accepted nor rejected: he simply did not pay them much attention. He seemed to be turning things over in his mind, struggling to assimilate his first real contact with death.

For a while, knowing that Tom would feel better if he let go of his emotions, she tried to coax him into talking. But he answered her in monosyllables, or not at all, until she was forced to give up. She sat quietly with him instead, her heart going out to him, wishing that his troubled unseeing eyes would release their reservoir of tears.

At last, to her immense relief, Tom turned to her and spoke. She was surprised rather than worried by his matter-of-fact statements, like a policeman reporting a shocking accident. But although she understood the words, she could not make sense of what he was saying. Ideas, people, events – real or imagined – were all scrambled together. Nothing seemed to follow on. The foot-and-mouth disease was mixed up with the Abbey; George was confused with Joachim; the Pope appeared in a description of Bloxbury Ring, and so on. Above all, Tom was obsessed with Brother Ambrose. All the tangled threads seemed to lead back to the Abbot; and, even making allowances for the shock he had sustained, Tom was levelling some really wild accusations at him. Elizabeth realised that it was time to call Eugene.

The doctor came straight over, took one look at the strained, exhausted boy and prescribed sleep. At the sight of the pills Dr. Kelly produced from his black bag, Tom became exasperated, insistent and, finally, alarmingly strident.

'You don't understand what I'm saying. You didn't read George's letter. Ambrose is behind it all – can't you see he's everywhere? Even Joachim can't do anything about him . . . I don't think he *knows*. He's too . . . too *good*. He can't see. No one can *see*. Look what Ambrose has done to the cows – didn't you hear them? He can do anything! Stick knives into himself . . . anything. For

God's sake, look what he's done to George. Oh George knew all right. Joachim could've protected him but he wasn't *there* . . . at the Ring. Ambrose wouldn't let him . . . George saw it all and – don't you see? The Pope's coming. Ambrose could just stretch out his hand and . . . we must do something – *anything* . . .'

Elizabeth was bewildered. It was nearly as painful to hear Ambrose being slandered as it was to see Tom in such a pitiful state. Any attempt to calm him down only made him more hysterical. Fortunately, Eugene took the matter in hand. He ground up two of his pills, sprinkled them in some hot tea and ordered Tom to drink it, promising that they would discuss everything later. It was clear that Tom did not believe him; but, at the same time, he seemed to want to. The violence of his speech seemed to have frightened him into exhausted silence. He was ready to welcome the oblivion which the tea would bring and he quickly drank it down. Within twenty minutes he was fast asleep in his bed.

19

The sun had already dropped to the level of the window-sill – the winter days seemed so much shorter than in Italy – and the room was filled with shadows. Vittorio did not want to switch on the light; it might attract attention. He dragged a table in front of the window and sat down with the book in front of him. There was enough light to read by. Nevertheless, the priest hesitated.

As a writer himself, he knew what powerful weapons words were. Better minds than his had been raped by books; greater souls damned. He was afraid of what he might find. There were some things it was better not to know. On an impulse, he sprang up and fetched his large homely Bible – he favoured the old Douay Version – from his suitcase. It could do no harm to perform a small ritual, to counter words with words. He opened the Bible at random and read aloud the promise which Jesus had made to the fisherman; '. . . And I also say unto thee, that thou art Peter, and upon this rock I will build my church; and the gates of hell shall not prevail against it. I will give unto thee the keys of the kingdom of heaven . . .'

The quotation was a happy accident, a timely reminder that the Church could not be destroyed. It had been built on Peter, the Rock, and it was still being built on Pope John the Twenty-Fifth, St. Peter's successor. Vittorio experienced a surge of relief: even if he failed utterly, no heretic – not even hell itself – could prevail against the Church. He had Christ's word for it.

With a lighter heart, the priest turned to the first page

of the book. He saw at once that he was faced with a longer job than he had anticipated. As well as coping with the Latin, he had to decode Brother Anthony's obscure, quasi-poetic style which was obviously designed to discourage the casual or unworthy reader. Patiently, he settled down to translate.

'First Circle: Let the Aspiring One beware! . . . Tortuous as the serpent is the way out of the *Tumulus*, grave are its dangers . . .'

At first Vittorio was inclined to dismiss the whole book as the product of a wild – possibly deranged – imagination. But the contents were described in such deadly earnest that they commanded the highest respect. The six chapters, which corresponded to six 'circles', outlined a series of rituals for closely simulating the conditions of death. The first 'circle', for instance, described how the Cathar initiate (the 'Aspiring One') was laid in a 'Mound' while a symbolic burial ceremony was held around him. When at the end he walked out of the mound, the act symbolised the soul's leaving the body at the moment of death.

The next 'circle' was more serious: with the aid of meditation and prayer, the initiate was taught how to enter a state of trance. With each successive 'circle', the trance became deeper and the body was brought closer to a death-like state. At the same time, the initiate's colleagues performed certain rites. These rites constituted the Treasure. In other words, the Treasure was a set of formulae – words and actions – which were so valuable and important that they were known to very few people, or perhaps only one person. Even Brother Anthony did not know what they were; but he knew what they did.

The rites of the Treasure acted directly on the entranced initiate so that his soul was able to rise from his body *without physical death*. As each 'circle' was reached, the bonds between soul and body became looser and the soul could be divorced from the body for a longer duration. As long as the invisible link between them held, the soul was prevented from flying off into its immortal element – that is, it could not join the Divine Spirit, but remained tied to Earth. Nevertheless, the soul's relative freedom allowed it a fleeting contact with the Spirit so that every time it was reunited with the body, it brought back more of the Spirit's power.

Vittorio's ears, finely tuned to the continuous sounds of the old house, picked out an alien noise. A creak outside his door. A footstep. But it was not Hannah's confident tread, nor Mrs. K.'s shuffle. It was heavier and more tentative, belonging to a man who was not sure of his way. Vittorio cursed himself for having neglected to lock the door. There was a single knock. He shot out an arm and, grabbing the Bible, laid it over the book so that it was hidden. It was not a moment too soon. The door had opened and a large hairy man with a red face was filling the doorway.

'*Do* come in,' said Vittorio.

The big man seemed unconscious of the priest's sarcasm. He was smiling broadly.

'Mr. de Vere, is it? Hello! My name's Kelly – Doctor Kelly. I heard you'd arrived and thought I'd drop by and have a look at you – if you don't mind. I've been appointed to check up on everyone around here as long as this dreadful foot-and-mouth business is going on. Not much of a welcome, I'm afraid, but perhaps my companion can do better . . .' He stood aside to let another man through. He was a monk, short and powerfully built, with the hair close-cropped on his large bony head, and very deep-set eyes. 'May I introduce Brother Ambrose? He's the headmaster of Bloxbury School and, of course, the Abbot. The two of us are not much of a committee, I know! But we have to try and take every precaution to stop the disease spreading.'

'Yes, I understand,' murmured the priest. 'It's a tragedy for the farmers. I suppose it has disrupted life at the school as well, er, Brother Ambrose?'

So this was Ambrose. His whole mission could depend on his performance over the next five minutes. The Abbot was smiling.

'Fortunately, our term ended before the outbreak and all the boys are at home. But I must say, it's pleasant to find that Bloxbury can still attract visitors. They are often thin on the ground at this time of year . . .'

Vittorio saw that his visit was being questioned. The best thing was to be conventional, not say too much. He gave a light laugh.

'Yes. That was the idea – to get away from it all. The pressures of business and so on. I thought it a good chance to keep my hand in – '

'At fishing. Quite.' The Abbot completed the sentence abruptly and moved towards him. He stood very close, still smiling. 'But, forgive me . . . you're not English, are you? It's a double pleasure to welcome visitors from abroad.'

Vittorio was ready for him. 'Half-English, actually. My father was French. It's extremely useful. I divide my time equally between London and Paris, which is the only way to make ends meet in the wine trade . . .' He innocently returned Ambrose's smile. The Abbot appeared to accept the story; he nodded and, glancing at the doctor, moved away towards the window. A tiny trickle of sweat ran down Vittorio's side. He was about to follow the monk and stand casually between him and the book, when he was interrupted by Dr. Kelly's firm hand in the small of his back. He was steered to the edge of the bed and had no choice but to sit down.

'This won't take a moment, Mr. de Vere. It's just routine.' The doctor removed his glasses and, pulling down the lower lids began peering into the priest's eyes. He smelt of strong drink. Ambrose became a distant blur.

'Surely this isn't necessary,' Vittorio protested. 'I can hardly have caught foot-and-mouth!'

'Not at all. But I have to make sure that you leave with the same diseases that you came with! Now, have you got anything at the moment? Are you taking any medicine or pills?'

'No, no,' said Vittorio, anxiously screwing up his eyes to catch a glimpse of Ambrose. He seemed to be looking down at the table. He had seen the Bible already; he must not look any further.

'In fact, Brother Ambrose, I'm especially glad to see you since it saves me a trip to the Abbey. I was wondering if I might come to Mass tomorrow? I could join you for Vespers – if that would be convenient?' Suggesting the early evening service was an inspiration; it coincided with the time of the Pope's arrival.

The Abbot left the table. 'I'm afraid that's impossible, Mr. de Vere. We don't say Mass at that hour – and besides, our chapel is temporarily closed for redecoration. But if you're still here next week, when it's ready, you'll be most welcome to join us in worship. It's refreshing to see a businessman such as yourself making the time to attend Mass regularly. And to read the Bible, I see . . .'

He had replied coolly enough, and it was understandable that he hadn't mentioned the Pope – he and the Cardinal had agreed to keep the visit secret. Nevertheless, Vittorio mistrusted him. He had a way of strolling around the room as if he owned it.

Dr. Kelly was about to apply his stethoscope to the priest's chest when Ambrose stopped him.

'Leave that,' he said sharply. Then he added more genially, 'I'm sure Mr. de Vere is not a source of infection. We mustn't interrupt his Bible studies any longer.'

The doctor grumbled, packed his bag and stood by the door, waiting for the Abbot.

'Thank you for your concern, Doctor Kelly,' said Vittorio, and he turned to the monk. Ambrose walked quickly towards him and, stretched out his arm as if to shake hands, appeared to change his mind. He raised his hand with the first two fingers pointing upwards.

'Bless you, my son.'

173

Vittorio was thrown mentally off balance. More used to blessing than being blessed, he coloured slightly and lowered his head.

'Thank you,' he muttered.

To his surprise, he felt the Abbot reach out and lay a hand on the crown of his head. A sudden tingling warmth, like a tiny electric charge, made him jerk his head slightly to one side. Embarrassed, he said, 'Till tomorrow then,' and seized the hand, still partially held out, to shake it. The hand was dry to the touch, and as hard and cold as a stone.

The little priest locked the door behind the two men and breathed out. He had dealt with the Abbot pretty well, he thought. He could report to the Cardinal that he had survived their first meeting unscathed. Now it was time to get back to the book.

Here ends the circle which is the last of the six Dark Nights of the Flesh. Now may He who alone is most Perfect in spirit proceed to the seventh circle where, in truth, He must dare the one Dark Night of the Soul. If the rites enshrined within the Sacred Treasure be performed with perfection (and if God is gracious), then shall He come again, crowned in glory, from the Mound of Living Death and take his rightful seat upon the Throne of Immortality. Here begins the Circle of the Serpent . . .

But here the seventh chapter – the so-called Serpent's Circle – did not begin. The pages had been torn out. Vittorio snapped the book shut in frustration and leaned back wearily in his chair. Whether he had caught a chill or strained his eyes reading, or both, his head was throbbing painfully, and burning. Already his throat was dry and sore, his neck swollen and stiff to move; and now a seam of pain was being sewn across his shoulders, so that he shifted about irritably in an effort to find a comfortable position.

According to Brother Anthony, the sixth 'circle' carried the soul momentarily into the presence of God. This was extraordinarily dangerous simply because the vision was so glorious that the soul could hardly bear to be reunited with its body. Only the most resolute and perfect soul could choose to turn its back on the Presence and, as it were, voluntarily return to Earth. But once it had done so, it brought back supernatural gifts: the initiate was henceforth endowed with an awesome power over the natural world.

The seventh 'circle' had to remain a mystery. The book seemed to suggest that it was separate from the other six 'circles', a kind of leap into a wholly different state. The other 'circles', for instance, each required a 'Dark Night of the Flesh'; the seventh appeared to exact an even more arduous, more spiritual task – the one 'Dark Night of the Soul'. Vittorio could not imagine what this was.

Something else puzzled him as well. On the diagram, the words 'Here lies the Treasure' were inscribed in the centre of the seventh circle. This implied that the 'Treasure' was twofold. On the one hand it was the *means* of reaching the seventh 'circle' – a series of secret rites; on the other hand, it was also the *end result* – a gift of revelation, perhaps, which placed the successful initiate on 'the Throne of Immortality'. Once again, whatever that was, was anybody's guess.

All in all, the book had not been as helpful as Vittorio hoped. There was still nothing to connect the Little Brothers with the Cathars. Nor was there anything which could be pinned down as hard fact – with one possible exception: the *tumulus*, which he translated as 'mound'. It played a crucial part in each one of the 'circles' and was variously referred to as the 'burial mound', the 'holy mound' and so on. Only at the approach of the seventh 'circle' was it called the 'Mound of Living Death'. Vittorio was convinced that whatever its description, it was the same place. But was it a fictional place, a mere poetic image? Or did it actually exist?

Vittorio could not tell; but if by any chance the Little Brothers possessed such a mound, there would be a positive link between them and the Cathars. Where on earth could such a God-forsaken place be found?

The priest looked at his watch. It was nearly ten o'clock already. Time to make the phone call.

The hotel's telephone arrangements were primitive. A single old-fashioned payphone installed under the boar's head in the hall was shared by the guests. The drawing-room door was open, but Vittorio did not want to shut it for fear of offending Hannah. Besides, since the hall was dark and he did not know where to find the switch, he was glad of the light which enabled him to see the dial.

There was a 'ting' as he picked up the receiver, and then he paused to clasp his burning head. How could he be so stupid? He had remembered everything, including Cardinal Benetti's London phone number; but he had forgotten that he needed small change. Neither of the two coins in his pocket fitted the call box. He was about to ask Hannah for change when he had a better idea: he would make a collect call (was that what the English said? Or was it just American? He couldn't remember.) The notice stuck above the call box told him he had to dial 100 to reach the operator.

'Number, please.' An adenoidal female voice, bored. The priest spoke close to the mouthpiece, not wanting to be overheard. His throat was painful, making his voice sound husky.

'I want to call London, er, collect, please.'

'A reverse-charge call,' the operator said pityingly. 'Number please.'

'Two, two, two. Eight, six, seven, four.'

'What's the name, please?'

'Mr. de Vere.'

'Mr. Veneer, hold the line please.'

Within seconds he heard the Cardinal's familiar decisive voice. It sounded so near and so thoroughly

176

down-to-earth that he felt almost happy. The Cardinal was agreeing to pay for the call, and then he was through. At the same moment the priest was plunged into darkness; the drawing-room door had been closed.

'Father? Is that you? Are you all right?'

'Yes, it's me. I've caught a cold, I think.'

'What?' The Cardinal was not in a sympathetic mood. Vittorio had hoped for something more friendly.

'It doesn't matter.'

'So you made it then? Are you satisfied?' Vittorio wondered what he had done to make his superior angry.

'I don't know.'

'Speak up, Father. What d'you mean? You've had twenty-four hours already. More . . . You'd better get back to London as soon as possible.'

'I think not. There may be something. I have to be sure.'

'For God's sake man. What's going on? Where are you? You sound terrible.'

'It's the line.'

'What?'

'It doesn't matter. Listen . . . I'm at the hotel. Don't do anything until I contact you tomorrow.'

'It'd better be sooner than that, Father. I'm running a very tight schedule. Have you found anything wrong? Yes or no.'

'I'll do my best.'

'I'm trying to be patient, Father.'

'Goodbye.'

He put down the receiver and sighed. He could not suppress a feeling that he had somehow been betrayed. It was a lonely feeling. Not an auspicious start to what was going to be a long night.

20

As soon as she heard the 'ting' of the telephone, Hannah left her embroidery and went to the door, wondering who could be making a call at that time of night. She peered across the hall and saw her plump fellow guest huddled over the call box. His voice was low and anxious. Not surprising – he was trying to make a reverse-charge call. Hannah was amused to hear that the number he wanted was the same as the registration number of her car at home in Amsterdam. Except for the three twos, of course. As it was not in her nature to eavesdrop, she shut the door and went back to her work. There was just time for a few more stitches before going to bed.

She was startled by the sound of someone clearing his thoat. Mr. de Vere had come in quietly and was standing in the middle of the room, trying to look nonchalant. He was plainly dying to speak to her. She felt like teasing him.

'Good evening. Did you want something, Mr. de Vere? Our dear Mrs. K. was here earlier, but she's gone to stay with her sister who, apparently, had has "one of her turns"!' She pulled a long face. 'I shudder to think what this implies . . . I've been left in charge, as usual. It's very trusting of her. I could steal the silver, if she has any, or her stuffed boar's head.'

'Yes. I suppose so.'

The little man seemed to have lost his sense of humour. He was obviously preoccupied. Maybe the phone call had brought bad news and, if so, he might be wanting to talk about it.

'Did you get through all right?' she prompted.

'What? Oh, the phone call. Yes, thank you.' He moved behind her chair and twitched back the curtain. 'They're still up,' he said irrelevantly. Across the black valley, lights were flickering in the Abbey.

'That's their chapel,' she explained. 'They're probably saying their prayers before snuggling down in their cells with hot cups of cocoa.'

She still could not raise a smile from Mr. de Vere, who turned and said unexpectedly, 'Have you come across what I might call a . . . *mound* near the Abbey?'

'What? There are hundreds! Every kind of tumulus in this part of England – long barrows, round barrows . . . molehills. Take your pick.' She regretted her flippancy instantly. The poor man did not look at all well. There were beads of sweat on his forehead and he was having trouble speaking.

'I . . . I meant some sort of . . . special mound. Or something,' he stuttered.

'Yes. As a matter of fact, there is. Behind the chapel, there's Bloxbury Ring. Do you know what that is? It's an ancient circular earthwork. I don't know the exact period yet. But there's a long barrow inside the Ring, so I'm told. That would be very rare and possibly very special indeed. How did you know?'

'I . . . didn't. It was just something I heard. Thank you.'

He wanted to leave now, in a hurry. He even stumbled against a card table on the way out. What a comical man he was.

High winds had dispersed the day's cloud and the single eye of a huge moon gazed placidly down on the priest as he stepped out of the dark hotel. No longer trusting his memory, he paused to check his jacket: the torch was in the side pocket, the Cardinal's official letter was in his wallet. He had also remembered to push a letter of his own under Miss van Neef's door. If for any reason he was held up, he could trust her to send a telegram for him.

The sharp wind carried the distant bellow of a cow; a banal sound made poignant by the imminence of death. The priest shivered in spite of his growing fever. He could hardly believe that he was actually going through with this insane, one-man crusade at dead of night. It didn't suit him, he wasn't built for it, he was ill, the whole thing was unreal. But it had to be done, not for the Church – that was a long way from his mind – but for the sake of the Holy Father. Pope John was not only a good man; he was also something just as important – a lovable man. He must not be exposed to the scandal of a troop of heretics.

Father Vittorio began to trudge unsteadily towards the Abbey to do his duty.

Six pinpoints of light on the hilltop signalled that some of the monks had not yet gone to bed. He hurried past the gates, keeping to the shadow of the wall, until he found what he was looking for: a section of cracked and partially crumbled masonry. The climb would have been easy for someone young and nimble; the priest was neither. He hauled himself grimly to the top, hung there uncertainly and then dropped like a sack of potatoes on the far side. He sat, winded, on the damp ground and waited until his arms, weakened by fever, had regained some strength.

The terrain between the wall and Bloxbury Ring was a mixture of woodland and overgrown but more open ground. Instead of heading directly towards the Ring, Vittorio began to skirt around the edge of the grounds, keeping as far away from the Abbey as possible. The woods were comparatively easy going; but, even so, he treated them like minefields, picking every step with care and freezing at the slightest sound. The open ground was more of a problem. Several times he had to wait until a scudding cloud had blotted out the searchlight of the moon, before wading as fast as he could through the tangle of brambles and bracken. Occasionally, he took his bearings from the Abbey lights which, one by one, were extinguished until he was left disoriented and alone in the dark.

After more than an hour, he reached the shelter of a small copse where he sat down, exhausted, with his back against a beech tree. He needed to rest before the final assault. He fumbled mechanically in his trouser pocket for his rosary; reciting the certain words and hearing the vital click of the beads often had a soothing effect. But the rosary was gone. He smiled grimly; he had forgotten something after all. He vaguely remembered having heard the beads drop to the floor when he hung up his other trousers in the wardrobe. It was no great loss. He needed something stronger than the rosary's gentle sedative in any case. Beating off the hopelessness which, as usual, threatened his attempts to pray, he solemnly asked Mary, the Mother of God, for guidance and strength; he also asked, with his characteristic irony, for luck. The bright words drifted away from him on the wind and were snuffed out in the darkness.

Then, as if in miraculous reply, Father Vittorio heard the distant chime of disembodied voices, singing in harmony. He started, straining forward to listen. He thought at first that the sound was inside him, a cruel distortion of the fever which was singing along the wires in his head. But he heard it again and it was real. His only illusion, induced by a trick of the wind, had been the harmony. The chant which assailed his ears was a far cry from the choiring of angels; it was high and wild, like souls wailing in torment. It kept breaking up into the shrieks of gulls, only to re-form into the deadly precision of a psalm.

The priest scrambled to his feet and followed the sound, which led him like a will-o'-the-wisp to the edge of the wood. Crouched behind a tree, he found himself looking, across a wide expanse of grass, at Bloxbury

Ring. Lights flickered dimly in the giant yews which lined its walls, while all around the chant was rising higher, climbing into a weird ecstatic region of its own. Straining upwards, it gathered force and struck a single note of excruciating beauty and terror – then died away. The wind dropped, and a long electric silence held the priest breathless by his tree. The lights in the Ring were fading, giving way to the ghostly gloss of moonlight on the open field.

A whisper of leaves in a nearby drift suggested that he was not the only creature to be disturbed by the sudden quiet. The whisper was answered by more whispers, and more, until the noise swelled into a frantic rustling. In every direction the copse was seething with life. Underneath his feet, there was a shiver of premonition in the roots of the tree. Tiny shapes were swarming openly out of the ground and scampering away through the undergrowth; birds were beating off through the branches; the field was twitching with the shadows of rabbits, streaking out of their burrows and away from the Ring.

Deep in the earth, too low for human hearing, an immense bass note sent a series of shocks through the soles of Vittorio's feet. A larger creature, oblivious of his presence, crashed past him with eyes still blinded by winter sleep. The amazing whiteness of its fur was turned to shining silver by the moon – and then it was off, flashing through the trees on short, powerful legs. Vittorio was abandoned, the only animal too senseless or stubborn to flee. He stoically held his ground and watched.

Out there, at the base of the Ring, a black wave began to travel across the field. No, *the field itself was moving*. Casually shaken out by the hand of God, the wide carpet of grass was rippling and undulating towards him. The priest closed his eyes and ordered himself to pray: 'Hail, Mary, full of Grace . . .' A muffled roar, like a great beast waking at the Earth's core, heralded the arrival of the first wave ('. . . blessed is the fruit of thy womb, Jesus'). The ground swayed, turned to liquid, surged up angrily, sending him down on his knees ('Holy Mary, Mother of God . . .'); hearing the trees groan, sensing the heaving and wrenching of rock, expecting the Earth at any second to slide apart and swallow him as though he had never been. *Pray for us sinners, now, and at the hour of our death.*

The earth tremor had been a small one, lasting two or three minutes at the most, but long enough to shake Father Vittorio's view of the world. He did not count on many certainties but, when the solid earth betrayed a lifetime's trust, he was appalled. He felt sick and beaten, all sense of duty driven out of him. What compelled him to stagger to his feet was a much older impulse: his curiosity. He had to find out what was hidden at the source of the tremor.

There was no way round the open field. The priest could only walk across it, straight to the Ring. By the wide ditch which surrounded the walls of the Ring, there was no light and no sound to suggest that anything had happened. He inched up the steep slope, carefully negotiating the exposed roots of the yews, and peered over the edge.

The circular crater was silent and lifeless. The embers of a large fire glowed red against the pale light. In the centre lay the smooth hump of a long mound. The priest had expected it; but he was surprised by the massive column of stone which protruded from its domed roof. It seemed unusually luminous as if, instead of reflecting the moon, it had absorbed and stored the light and was shining from within. A movement in the mound's opening made him tear his eyes away from the stone.

A shape had emerged from the low doorway. A dark-robed figure whose head and face were hidden in a deep cowl. Its back was slightly bowed under the weight of something it was carrying. Another, identical figure appeared alongside, and another, until six had appeared. They were holding between them a long, bulky object on a stretcher. Vittorio adjusted his glasses. There could be no mistake. Underneath a dark cloth, the outline of a body was clearly discernible. In spite of his revulsion, he was filled with a rush of insane glee: all his suspicions were vindicated – he had been right all along! In a sense, it no longer mattered whether they were Cathars or not; the fact remained that, in the black heart of an ancient burial mound, these cowled figures – The Little Brothers of the Apostles – had committed murder. He was convinced of it with all the force of a revelation.

More shapes, like prehistoric ants, were climbing out of the mound to join the obscene procession. One of them held a box, or small chest, bound in gleaming steel; another – the last – cradled in his arms an enormous chalice with two handles and an ornate lid. The others paused, waiting for him to fall in behind, and then set off as sedately as pall-bearers towards the far side of the Ring.

Vittorio waited until he was sure they would not return before pulling himself over the brink and slipping quietly down the inner slope. He had to collect, if possible, the final evidence. He stepped into the clearing. It was like standing on the surface of the moon. The high ramparts topped by their dense yews imparted an eerie stillness to the Ring; even the atmosphere seemed thinner, more difficult to breathe, but he put it down to the hot numbing pain which spread across his chest. He waited for a slight spell of dizziness to pass and crept to the entrance of the mound. Then, satisfied that he was alone in the clearing, he crossed the threshold into darkness.

21

Gradually surfacing from his drugged, shallow sleep, Tom felt himself being tugged unwillingly into consciousness. He opened his eyes to find the blankets pulled well over his head.

He pulled back the covers and sat up. His room was outwardly the same as when he had gone to sleep; but although everything was in its proper place, familiar objects were behaving strangely. Evidently he was still dreaming. His mother's photograph was clicking up and down on the bedside table, the wardrobe door was swinging open, the windowpanes rattling, the oak beams creaking.

He climbed out of bed and stood stupefied in the centre of the room. The sudden animation of lifeless objects was threatening. Even the walls were vibrating – he could sense it rather than see it in the darkness. In the distance there was a crash, people calling out to each other, a dog yelping hysterically.

The trembling stopped. The room returned to a friendly state of calm. Tom crossed to the window overlooking the village street and looked out. Lights were springing up in the night, doors and windows opened and slammed shut, people exclaimed in excitement tinged with fear; somewhere a baby was crying; the yelping dog began to bark monotonously. A small group of men could be seen contemplating a pile of slates which had fallen from a roof and smashed on the ground. Opening the window, Tom could hear their low nervous laughter wafted on the night breeze.

Slowly the hubbub died down. The men dispersed to their homes, windows and doors were closed and, one by one, the lights went out. The frightened child was soothed into silence. Before long, the village had settled comfortably back to sleep as though nothing had happened. Nothing stirred except a solitary dog sniffing its way between the cottages.

The past impinged more closely on his room, peeping over his shoulder like the ghosts of its medieval occupants. He felt a certain kinship with them, and with their firm belief that cosmic events mirrored the affairs of men. Whenever plagues erupted and the earth quaked and fiery comets seared across the sky, they would tremble and cross themselves to ward off the death of friends and the birth of monsters.

Just then the dog stopped, tensed, pricked its ears. It turned and looked at something behind it, every muscle quivering. Then it uttered a low growl and ran helter-skelter up the street and out of sight.

A person came into view. A monk, judging by his long, shadowy robe. At first, Tom thought he might be ill because of the way he was moving. Long shivers seemed to ripple down his body, while his head wobbled from side to side like a puppet's, as if too loosely attached to his shoulders. At the same time, he was walking strangely – gliding over the stone street without a sound. Tom was fascinated.

As he moved nearer, the monk paused and turned, tilting his head to look up at the brilliant moon. Tom nearly cried out. It was Joachim! Why had he not recognised him at once? He wanted to call out to his friend, but Joachim's face forbade it: it was wearing an alien expression – distant and rapt, as though he were seeing the moon for the first time. Tom kept very quiet, ashamed at having witnessed such an intensely private moment.

There was something else that bothered him about Joachim; but before he could pin it down, the door opened.

'Tom? Ah! So you're awake.' His mother was smiling in the doorway. 'Did you ever hear of such a thing!' She was quite breathless with excitement. 'A real earthquake, here, in England! I've never known anything like it – I thought the roof would cave in. Whatever next!'

Seeing that he was still groggy from the effects of the sleeping pills, she helped Tom back to bed and tucked him in. He gave her a dazed smile and she blew him a kiss as she turned to leave. 'Whatever next,' she repeated, shutting the door behind her.

Tom realised that he must have drifted back to sleep, for the next thing he knew was that the moon was higher in the sky, striping his bed with bars of light. He remembered immediately what had bothered him about Joachim. Or had he dreamt it? It was all such a muddle . . . But it seemed to him that the monk had cast no shadow on the street. He sat up and said aloud, 'I'm *sure* he didn't have a shadow.'

Downstairs in the hall the telephone began to ring. Perhaps that was Joachim, calling to find out if everything was all right. It would be typical of his kindness, just as it had been so like him to patrol the streets after the unheard-of tremor, making sure no harm had been done. Besides, who else would phone in the early hours of the morning?

Immediately beyond the opening, the floor sloped away in a kind of rough-hewn ramp. Vittorio took a few tentative steps forward and listened. He had to be sure that all the monks had left. There was complete silence except for the blood pounding in his head. He began to feel his way down, not yet daring to switch on his torch. The dim light from the doorway quickly disappeared, giving way to a profound darkness. The muffled echo of his footsteps sounded very loud. The air became thicker and warmer, smelling stale and rather sickly. His feet struck level ground. Holding back the first stirrings of claustrophobic panic, he fumbled for his torch and switched it on.

The weak beam made less of an impression on the darkness than he would have liked. He swept the light in an arc from left to right and found that he was standing in a stone chamber. It was surprisingly large and almost circular in shape. The walls were partly hewn out of solid rock and partly composed of stone slabs, so beautifully cut that they fitted together exactly, without mortar. They curved upwards and over to form a domed ceiling about three metres high. At the far end, the chamber was slightly elongated, giving Vittorio the sensation of being enclosed in a monstrous egg.

In the middle of the chamber there was a large obstacle. Vittorio concentrated the thin beam of light on it and saw that it was a stone pillar which appeared to grow out of the floor and straight up through the ceiling at its central and highest point. He realised that the standing stone which thrust through the roof of the mound was really the apex of the pillar. On either side of the monolith, the chamber was bare. It seemed to have no other function than to surround the pillar which, in turn, supported it.

The little priest went up to the column of stone and examined it. Its colour was unusual – a light blue-grey, completely different from the surrounding walls. Although its shape was irregular, the surface was so smooth that it might have been polished. Vittorio could not resist putting out a hand to stroke it. He instantly received a mild shock: the stone was evidently charged with something like static electricity, in which case it had to be a very peculiar stone indeed.

On the other side of the column a large horizontal stone stretched out from its base. Its surface was uneven and slightly concave, as though it had been worn down or hollowed out. At the point where it joined the column, however, the surface was still level with the sides, suggesting a rough stone pillow.

Father Vittorio bent over the slab excitedly. It was decorated with carvings. He guessed that they were immensely old – at any rate, they were extremely crude. He could only decipher a few of the images: some figures, for instance, with branched headdresses like antlers; an impressionistic tree with snakes for roots; a skull with ears of corn growing out of it. They all seemed to be symbols belonging to a primitive, complicated ritual. Just then, the light flickered and went out.

He tapped the torch irritably on the side of the slab, which he now reckoned was a kind of pre-Christian altar, and the light came on again. It shone on a rust-coloured stain just below the 'pillow' at the top end. Vittorio tested the stain curiously with his index finger. It was some sort of sticky liquid. He looked at his finger closely in the feeble light. It was smeared with blood. He recoiled in disgust, backing against the wall to put more distance between himself and the offensive liquid. He was suddenly highly conscious of where he was, and of the weakness in his legs and the dryness in his mouth.

He stifled a shout – his feet had got tangled in something. He pointed the torch down and saw that it was only some rope. He gasped with relief. The rope was attached to a metal ring driven into the wall. He traced its length with the beam of light and saw that the rope stretched up diagonally to the ceiling. There was a pulley and, above that, a glint of steel. He moved nervously back towards the slab. Hanging directly above it was a vicious hook. It was obviously designed to be lowered and raised like the hooks that carried carcasses in a slaughter-house.

Vittorio had seen enough. The blood and the hook turned his stomach. He stumbled back to the opening into the chamber and had barely begun to stagger up the ramp when his torch went out again. He swore out loud and struck it against the stones. It refused to work. The darkness pressed around him; he could not breathe. Dropping the torch, he rushed blindly forward, arms outstretched, ricochetting from one wall to the other until at last he saw the doorway.

He knelt in the clearing, trembling and gasping in the pure air. His throat and chest were painfully constricted; his whole body raged with fever. He doubted whether he had ever felt so exhausted and weak. But at least the ordeal – the long nightmare – was over. There would be telephone calls, the reassuring voice of the Cardinal, the police . . . an end to the madness. All would be well.

He stood up slowly, relishing the night air and the cool moonlight. His eyes rested on the tall stone dominating the roof of the mound. The Mound of Living Death – he would probably never know what that meant. He was not sorry. He began a dutiful prayer of thanks, but was stopped in mid-sentence. His mouth fell open. Either he was going mad or *there was someone standing behind the stone*.

A short black figure stepped into view and casually pointed at him. His scream came out of his swollen throat as a low animal rasp. He whirled round and forced his legs to carry him towards the wall of the Ring. High up on the parapet a shadow detached itself from the trees and began to move towards him. He changed direction and another dark shape began to descend the slope. All around him hooded figures were converging with the slow and merciless tread of predators. The little priest was at the end of his strength. There was no escape. His last thought before he passed out was that, for him, the nightmare was only beginning after all.

22

Tom dressed quickly and crept downstairs. All the lights were out, but he could hear his mother in the drawing-room. She was still crying. She'd refused to tell him what Dr. Kelly had said on the phone – the reason for her outburst of grief – but that only made it worse. He had to find out; he was going to find out.

There were no lights shining at the front of the house, but a chink of light at the surgery window announced that Dr. Kelly had not gone to bed yet. The curtains were partly drawn and the doctor's legs were just visible, stretched on the floor, with a whiskey bottle lodged between them. He banged on the window and was greeted by a gruff voice telling him to go away.

'It's me! *Tom*. Let me in,' he shouted and banged again.

The legs stirred, knocking over the bottle. Eventually the doctor lumbered into view and, pulling back the curtains, pressed his face against the glass.

'Is that you, Tom?' His voice was slurred and wary.

'Yes. Let me *in*.' He was losing patience with the old drunk. The moment the window was opened, Tom vaulted into the surgery. Dr. Kelly peered anxiously out of the window before shutting it and drawing the curtains again, more tightly.

'You're on your own, then?' he said, swaying slightly. His eyes were unfocused and bloodshot. He shook his head slowly.

'I'm sorry, Tom . . . so sorry.' The huge head went on shaking from side to side with its own momentum. 'I

shouldn't have told your ma, but I had to – didn't I? – I
had to . . . *confess*.' The doctor's voice trailed off dully.
Tom's anger faltered against the maudlin wall of regret.

Dr. Kelly leant against a filing cabinet, closed his eyes
and took a long pull at the whiskey. When he took the
bottle away, his eyes were fierce. With sudden violence,
he shouted, '*Damn their eyes*! They'll rot in hell!'

Tom shrank back, momentarily afraid of the big man
who, fortunately, was sliding down his former position
on the floor.

'What d'you mean, Doctor Kelly?' he asked. 'Who'll
rot in hell?'

'*What?* Come here a minute. Come *here* till I tell you a
thing or two about me.' He beckoned wildly and then
pressed his fingers to his lips. 'Sssh. Mum's the word,
Tom. You'll not say anything. I know. I *know* you.' He
pulled the boy down beside him. The stench of whiskey
was overpowering.

'Listen now,' he whispered conspiratorially. 'Years ago
there was a boy . . . about your age. Up There. I can see
him now, lying there. He had red hair, I remember . . .
red like yours. I can't say I liked him, Tom, I can't say
that – it was always "Yes, doctor" and "No, doctor" as
good as bloody gold. And he was for ever fiddling with
his rosary and looking up at me and saying "I'm sorry to
mention it, doctor, but it still hurts . . ." "Go on taking the
medicine," says I. Oh God, he got me down. The next
day – *listen*. The next day – oh Lord, Lord – he died. I let
him die. Too much of this' – he waved the bottle – 'and I
didn't see it. His bloody appendix ruptured – died in
agony. Up There. I let him die.'

The doctor lapsed into a morose silence, staring at his
large limp hands. Tom was utterly bewildered.

'Why are you telling me all this? About the boy with
the red hair? I'm sorry about it . . . really. But it's over
with now. It's finished.'

'It's not finished,' Dr. Kelly snarled with renewed
energy. 'It'll never be *finished*. Don't you see? They knew

I'd let the boy die. The Brothers. Ambrose fixed it . . . they promised not to tell. I was so grateful – I'd have been struck . . . struck off, you see. There would have been nothing left, *nothing*. I said I'd do anything for them . . . for *him* and now *this* . . . How could I ever guess this could happen? Sweet Mother of God. He was a decent fellow. The best of the lot.'

'Who?' Tom almost shouted in frustration. Dr. Kelly seemed surprised; he focused his eyes with difficulty.

'Who? Who d'you think? Brother Joachim, that's who. The question is . . . *why*. Why did they do him in?' His head slumped down. Tom seized it between both hands and forced the doctor to look at him.

'Are you saying that Joachim's hurt? That the Brothers have done something to him?'

'Not hurt. Dead.' He nodded towards a door which led to a small annexe at the back of the surgery. Tom pushed the doctor away in disgust, sprang up and ran to the door of the annexe.

'Tom!' Dr. Kelly shouted. 'Stop! No one should see him. He's in no condition – ' but it was too late: Tom was through the door and standing in the small bare room. On one side was a kind of steel trough or bath, some large glass jars of colourless fluid and a set of sharp, shiny dissecting instruments lying on a table; on the other, a human shape lay on a metal trolley, covered by a dark cloth. Tom grasped the cloth and pulled it back.

Two eyes stared straight at him out of Joachim's white, white face. He saw at once what had happened: there'd been a monumental mistake, they'd thought that Joachim was dead and covered him in a cloth. But he wasn't dead, he was just hurt, hurt so badly that he couldn't speak; only his eyes were left, pleading for help. Tom gazed deeply into the eyes, to make Joachim see that he understood. The eyes gazed back glassily, devoid of humour, intelligence or even sadness; devoid of life. There was no mistake. Joachim was dead.

He pulled the cloth farther back, marvelling at the

preternatural whiteness of the flesh. A gaping slit exposed the monk's throat from ear to ear. Farther down still, a ragged cavity in the abdomen revealed the secret softness of vital organs, which glistened moistly for a moment. Tom turned away, avoiding the stare of the ghastly blank eyes.

The doctor was leaning against the doorpost and when he spoke, his slurred voice was high and filled with wonder. 'They cut his throat, Tom. They took away his liver. See where it's been torn out. And look – there's not a drop of blood left in his body. Not a drop . . . They tried to steal his soul.'

Tom pushed past the doctor, who followed him out of the surgery and along the narrow corridor. He was still talking, but it didn't bother Tom. He wasn't listening particularly.

'Take this, Tom. It fell off when they brought him in. He'd have wanted you to have it. They were looking for it, Tom, looking everywhere – but I kept it safe, I kept quiet.' He pressed something small and hard into the boy's unresisting hand. 'You won't say anything, eh? Please . . . please.'

Tom had reached the front door. He opened it mechanically and without a word passed into the night like a sleepwalker.

Eugene Kelly reeled back to his bottle of whiskey and looked at it as though he were carefully reading the label. Then he hurled it with all his strength against the wall. He swayed on to his heels, head bowed, arms dangling. The door to the annexe was still open. He blundered violently towards it and slammed it shut. Finally he went to his surgical cupboard, took out another bottle of whiskey and sank to the floor. He hugged the bottle close to his body, rocking to and fro for a long time. Then he opened it.

It was an exceptionally clear and beautiful night. The wind had diminished to a riffling breeze and a light frost glistened on the doctor's lawn.

194

Tom lifted his eyes to the infinitude of sky where galaxies lay like diamond necklaces against dark blue velvet, and big planets hung low on the horizon, sparkling like crystal pendants.

He saw straight through it. He knew now what a sham it all was, so much tinsel to conceal the real desert of interstellar dust where nothing ever happened, unless you counted the endless, random, futile collision of dead grey particles. It was sad to think that there was no point to anything after all.

In the distance, there was the sound of glass smashing. It did not signify anything, it was just something else breaking, shattering into fragments.

The world, having no alternative, continued to turn; gravity went on demonstrating its laws; time passed.

Gradually he became aware of a hard object in the palm of his hand. Yes, Kelly had given him something. He opened his fist and looked at it without interest.

The tiny eye of the snake glinted. The ring felt so strange and warm in his cold hand that it might just have left Joachim's finger. It was his inheritance, passed on to him by his Teacher. The ring which could only be removed at death.

Although he had seen it with his own eyes, Joachim's death was not something he could believe in. Until now. The little snake was living proof of it.

He was amazed at how enormous his tears were, and how hot. And the pain in his left side . . . He vaguely wondered if it were true – that it was possible to die of a broken heart.

23

In his dream, Father Vittorio was sitting at a table in an intimate and sunny piazza; he was drinking chilled white wine. There was a fountain playing and the sound of laughter. Over the rooftops he could see the huge dome of St. Peter's which, he noticed approvingly, had been refashioned out of gold. The reflection of sunlight from the dome was dazzling. Suddenly a gong sounded; it was so loud that it made his wine tremble in its glass. The sky darkened and the dome lost its brilliance. A crack appeared in its smooth rounded surface and out of the crack flew a tiny bird. It headed straight to where Vittorio was sitting and as it approached it grew larger and larger until, with a tremendous beating of wings, it alighted on his table, towering over him. It was completely black and had a cruel hooked beak. Vittorio could not move, could scarcely breathe. As the bird lowered its head towards him, he knew something terrible was going to happen. He woke up gasping and drenched in sweat.

He could see nothing at first – the darkness was impenetrable – but he could feel that he was flat on his back with the upper part of his body imprisoned in a steel vice so tight that he could move no more than his fingertips. His legs were not bound, he guessed, but they were aching so much that he had to summon all his strength to shift them.

As his eyes grew accustomed to the darkness, he could see the faintest suspicion of light shining above his head. He was in a small bare room with a heavy, steel-bound door. There was a table and possibly a chair, against the wall; and he was lying on a hard narrow bed. He guessed that he must be in the Abbey in a cell – what an appropriate word – belonging to one of the monks. The light was starlight shining through a tiny window. He could also see that he was not tied or bound in any external way, but held by the invisible chains of his fever which had all but paralysed him.

He could no longer pretend that the creeping illness was some natural infection which could be shrugged off in time. He recognised the symptoms – they tallied with the descriptions of Brother Anthony's disease and with Giorgio's. He could trace the origins to that apparently insignificant moment when Brother Ambrose had blessed him. If he had not been so preoccupied and so pleased with his own coolness and guile, he might have seen that it was not a blessing, but a curse. It began to look as though the legendary powers of the Cathars were not just imagined by credulous peasants. But in all the accounts he had read there had not been a single mention of any harmful action by the Cathars. At what point had they begun to pervert their power, begun to kill instead of cure, begun to commit casual murder in pagan burial mounds?

Vittorio felt curiously detached and unafraid, although he knew that this was probably part of the strange euphoria induced by the illness. It was the picture of Pope John arriving that day which made him sweat and strain against his physical enslavement. The old man was smiling benignly at Ambrose, raising a hand in benediction, looking round at dark-robed figures closing in, his mild face clouding over with puzzlement, then disbelief, then fright.

As he drifted back into his delirium, a last brightly-lit picture flashed before his eyes: Hannah van Neef sitting, composed and competent, at her embroidery. His unspoken words to her were like a prayer. 'Oh Hannah! Dear sensible trustworthy Hannah! You'll remember

197

the telegram, you'll send it straight away. I know you will, you *must*.' And as he sunk into unconsciousness, it seemed that she turned to him and rolled her eyes comically as if to say, 'Don't be silly! Of course I will.'

There was no need to say anything. Elizabeth took one look at her son's face and, putting her arms around him, held him tightly. He was shaking uncontrollably. She took him into the drawing-room, wrapped him in a rug and sat him in an armchair by the newly-lit fire. Next, she went into the kitchen and heated some milk, which she gave him to drink having added a large shot of whiskey. Between sips she wiped the tear streaks from his face with a damp flannel, as though he were a child again.

The strong potion made Tom gasp; but he gradually stopped shaking and his face relaxed, returning to something like its normal colour. His mother sat on the arm of the chair, gently stroking his hair. He was grateful. While dark anguished waters swirled around him, carrying away everything he held dear, his mother withstood the torrent like a rock. She was warm and comforting and, above all, immovable. He was overcome by drowsiness but he fought it off; he had to make his mother *understand*.

'It's true, Mum. He's dead. Jo . . . Joachim's dead. He's all smashed up. Look. This is his ring. He wore it always, it couldn't be taken off.' He stroked the ring compulsively. 'What's happening, Mum? God Almighty – ' He choked back the beginnings of a fresh spate of sobs.

'It's all right, Tom. It'll pass. Gently now, gently . . .'

'No, Mum, it's not all right. Really. You don't see how it fits together. First, George – you didn't see the letter. He was made ill, driven mad, killed. *He* killed George and now he's killed Joachim.'

'Who, Tom?' Elizabeth asked wearily. She realised, with a sinking heart, that he was going to start all over again, babbling about the Little Brothers.

'Ambrose, of course. The Brothers. They're all in it – George thought they were out to get the Pope. Now he's dead. Joachim must've known or he'd still be alive. Don't you see? They're all *mad* – they could kill us all. Only Joachim was left . . . he hated violence, wouldn't hurt a flea. So they slit his throat, opened him up . . . Oh *God*.' He buried his head in his hands.

Elizabeth tried – tried to concentrate on what he was saying, tried to take it seriously. She could not deny that there seemed to be a sort of jinx attached to the Pope's visit. George had died of an illness far away in Italy; the foot-and-mouth had broken out; now Joachim had met with a ghastly accident. At least Eugene had said it was an accident. But none of these things were connected. They were tragic coincidences which could not justify Tom's wild talk, his blasphemy.

'Ssh, darling. Try not to talk like this. You'll feel differently soon. I promise.' She managed to sound calmer than she felt. After all, Tom was her son; and he wasn't hysterical like the day before. He knew what he was saying.

Tom uncovered his face and breathed deeply. He was struggling to keep his voice at an even pitch.

'You don't understand. Doctor Kelly – Eugene – told me about the Brothers. He's been under their thumb for years. Ask him.' He took hold of her hand and looked into her troubled eyes. 'You must believe me. It's all out of control now – it's all got too big. There's only us left. We have to tell somebody . . . the police – *anybody*. We have to stop them before the Holy Father comes.' He began to shiver again. 'They'll be after me, Mum. I know they will. I'll have no chance against them . . . against Ambrose. He knows everything, sees through everything. I'm so scared. I . . . I . . .' He did not trust himself to go on. His mother patted him gently, anxiously. After a while, he spoke again in a low determined voice. 'I'm going to phone the police *now*. We'll tell them everything, Mum. Won't we? They'll know what to do. If I can just get them

over to Doctor Kelly's before they take J . . . Jo . . . take
his body away, then they'll *see*.' He started to get up
excitedly but Elizabeth restrained him. She looked at
him uncertainly for a moment and then made up her
mind.

'It's O.K., Tommy. Just you relax – I'll phone. It'll be
all right . . . Just stay there and keep warm,' she said
firmly.

As she left the room, closing the door behind her, Tom
sank back in his chair, overwhelmed by relief. Now that
his mother was convinced, it must all come right. The
Little Brothers of the Apostles would be stopped, called
to account, made to pay for what they had done to
Brother Joachim. As he gazed into the fire, the image of
those empty eyes, that black gash at the neck, floated in
the flames. He closed his eyes; he would never forget that
image. No one could replace the most extraordinary man
he had ever known, and the best friend; but at least he
and his mother could bring his death, and his life, to
light. After that, they could go away – it didn't much
matter where – and begin again. He could get a job, in a
factory or something; it didn't matter.

The fire fizzed and murmured reassuringly. Tom felt
the irresistible drowsiness steal over him, and this time
he succumbed. He could hear his mother's voice in the
hall as he drifted off. The police would arrive soon
enough and he would be ready to tell them everything.

The ringing of the doorbell made him jump. He had no
idea how long he had been dozing, but it must have been
a while judging by the fire which had burnt down to a
steady glow. A pillow had been placed behind his head
and the rug tucked around him. The door was ajar.

Tom swallowed nervously, rehearsing in his mind
what he would say. Not too much at first, perhaps. The
main thing was to persuade them to visit – 'raid' was
better – Dr. Kelly's. He got up and walked to the door.
His mother was clearly framed in the narrow opening.

She was undoing the chain on the front door. She was opening it, greeting someone in a low voice, politely. A shadow fell over her. She took a step back.

Then she did something so unexpected, something so intrinsically alien, that Tom could only suppose that the woman standing there was not his mother at all, but a working model of her, a kind of robot or humanoid creature. She might just as well have sprouted horns, or smiled to reveal the long yellow teeth of a vampire.

Quite simply, she was bowing. Once, twice, three times. Tom could not place where he had seen that movement before; but some instinctive part of him remembered very precisely, and was terrified. In a few silent bounds, his legs carried him through the door and up the stairs. He sprang into his bedroom, locked the door and crouched behing it like an animal, panting and listening. He fancied he could hear long robes swishing up the stairs. He was caught in a trap of his own making unless . . . He sped to the window and fumbled with the catch for an eternity. It flew open at last and he was out, clinging to the branches of his cherry tree. He clawed his way down like a cat, scanning the darkness for unfamiliar shadows. It looked safe. He dropped to the ground and was running over the deserted fields towards the ridge of woods.

By the time he had reached the comparative safety of the pine trees, the land all around was being drained of darkness, leaving a residue of dull grey light which prefigured the dawn of the shortest day of the year. Tom threw himself down on a cushion of pine needles. No matter how he tried to distract himself, he could not prevent a black void from enveloping him; a void so vast and penetrating that he could not tell whether it was inside him or he was inside it. In the end he lay on his side, knees pulled up to his chest with his arms around them, and felt himself wholly abandoned, floating through a dark immensity.

He did not even blink when the reluctant sun opened its indifferent eye on the horizon, shooting its level beams the length of the valley and heralding the day when the infallible mouthpiece of God, Pope John the Twenty-Fifth, would arrive to bless his good and faithful servants, the Little Brothers of the Apostles.

24

'I can't think where he's got to. He was here a moment ago. Asleep on that chair.' She pointed to the armchair by the fire. The hard unsmiling faces of the monks made her nervous. Why didn't they say something? She addressed Brother Ambrose directly, appealing to him. 'I did the right thing, didn't I? Calling you? Tom was very upset. I thought that you would explain everything to him . . . put his mind at rest.'

The Abbot cast his eyes around the room. Without looking at her, he said, 'Well? We're wasting time. Where is he?'

'I . . . I don't know. I told you. In his room, perhaps; I'll go and see.' She made for the door.

Ambrose stopped her in her tracks. 'No! You stay here.' He pointed to the chair.

Elizabeth sat down. His voice had made her go all to pieces. He nodded at his companions.

'Find him. Bring him to me.' Without a word the impassive monks left the room. She could hear their boots on the staircase. There was a long silence until she couldn't stand it any longer.

'I *did* do the right thing, didn't I? Brother Ambrose? I mean, Tom hasn't done anything . . . anything wrong. Has he? It's just that he was so terribly worried. He was going to call the police. I . . . I didn't want him to cause any trouble, you see.' The Abbot ignored her.

'You mentioned a ring,' he said.

She felt like crying, but eager to please him she blurted

out, 'Yes. Yes, he has a ring. Brother Joachim's, he said. He showed it to me – he didn't steal it or anything. Eugene gave it to him, I think.' She might have been talking to a statue. She began to panic. 'You won't hurt him, will you?'

'It may not be necessary, provided that he gives up the ring,' Ambrose replied grimly. 'You had better get it into your head that the snake-ring is immeasurably old and valuable. It's an amulet of power, sacred to the Order. It grows into the wearer like a living thing, a vital bond that holds his body and soul in tension until he can't live without it!' He lowered his voice emphatically. 'But even as the ring holds his life in the balance, it confers gifts you can't even dream of . . .'

The Abbot was interrupted by the sound, from upstairs, of wood splintering under the crash of heavy boots.

Elizabeth began to cry. 'Stop them. Please. They're breaking up my house.'

Ambrose was not listening. He waited until one of the monks shouted down, 'He's not here!' Then he frowned and walked across to Elizabeth's chair. Standing over her, he said urgently, 'I must have that ring. It belongs to me. You've always been a good believer, a devoted servant of the Perfect . . . Now will you tell me where Tom is.'

'He must've run away,' she said in a tiny voice.

The Abbot sighed and, casually stepping forward, hit her without anger in the face.

'Obviously,' he said. 'The question is: *where* has he run away to?'

'I don't know.' Elizabeth put up her arms feebly, as if they could protect her from futher blows. Her cheek throbbed painfully and her whole head was ringing. She knew she must have done something extraordinarily wicked for Ambrose, of all people, to have hit her; but she couldn't work out exactly what. Terrified as she was, she was more frightened for her son.

'Please don't hurt him. He didn't mean –' She broke off

as the two monks returned. Ambrose glanced at them enquiringly. They shook their heads in unison.

'Elizabeth,' he went on in his former icy tone, 'Tom will come to no harm if he returns the ring. From now on, we'll be looking for him. But make no mistake – ' he raised a finger – 'if he forces my hand I won't hesitate to have one of the Brothers break every bone in his body. Do you understand?' Elizabeth could not speak or move her head, but the expression on her face appeared to satisfy him. 'Good.' He signalled to his companions and all three of them left the house.

Elizabeth made her way painfully upstairs. The sight of Tom's shattered bedroom door increased the sensation of nausea which told her a migraine was coming on. The room was a mess, turned over half-heartedly in the fruitless search for the snake-ring. She picked up Tom's pyjamas from the floor and absently folded them. The window at the back of the room flapped idly in the breeze; she went across to shut it.

The world was caving in on her. She touched the side of her face to test the extent of the swelling. It ached intolerably. She saw again the expressions of coldness and anger she would never have been forced to see if Tom hadn't run away with the precious ring. She didn't know if she could forgive him for that; and yet . . . his defiance of Ambrose was unquestionably brave. She realised that she had always been a little afraid of Brother Ambrose.

Looking out at the grey light which oppressed the window-panes and made the garden, the cherry tree, the fields seem unreal, she decided to leave the window ajar, just in case. The pain in her head was blinding. Without even the strength to fetch her pills, she sank exhausted to the floor by the bed and, resting her head against the mattress, wished that Tom would by a miracle be safely returned to her.

The morning was bright with watery sunlight filtering through the trees and sparkling on the fields and roofs of the cottages. A sharp breeze tossed fluffy clouds in a pale-blue translucent sky and, sifting through the pines, carried the tang of resin to where Tom lay huddled in his trance of grief.

The aroma seemed to penetrate his stiff, frozen body and, like tiny plants pushing up through a rocky desert, signs of life began to appear. His nose wrinkled, his legs began to stretch, his stomach registered a gnawing emptiness distinct from the greater void which engulfed him. He was surprised that he had survived, and ashamed – ashamed that he was still alive when others were dead, ashamed that his body could still make demands on him as though there was still a future.

From his vantage point he commanded a panoramic view of the valley with its patchwork fields, pretty village cottages and streets, and the pile of Abbey buildings on the opposite hill. It was no longer the happy valley of yesterday's childhood, but a mirror-landscape of sinister reversal where the meek turned into vicious murderers, where the pure in heart were killed; where family doctors were broken on the wheel of their past and changed into criminal accomplices. Where mothers betrayed their sons. It was a nightmare world where at any moment a tap on the shoulder might confront you with a grinning Double, looking at you with cold and knowing eyes out of your own face.

A movement seen in the corner of his eye, a fleeting black shape, electrified him. In a split second he had jumped behind his tree, his body braced and ready for fight or flight. It was only a young fir tree shivering in the wind. But it served as a bleak reminder that, like hunger, fear was still alive and flourishing long after the demise of more delicate emotions. No doubt the lower part of him – stomach, abdomen, legs – took a little longer to freeze than the heart.

More out of curiosity than anything else, Tom began to probe the aching void which occupied him, to see if any further feeling had survived the devastation. He was rewarded with an unexpected warmth which gushed into the vacuum of his heart and brought sudden strength to his limbs. It was hate. He knew it was a sin to hate Ambrose as much as he did, but he didn't care. Sin belonged to another time, when God still ruled over a benevolent universe.

The hatred gave birth to an heroic idea. He would break out of Bloxbury, make for the nearest town, raise the alarm; he would mobilise the forces of law and order, intercept the Holy Father, prevent him from stepping into the snake-pit; he would forgive his mother and together they would watch Ambrose being handcuffed and carted off to prison. Later, he would talk to the journalists and television crews – not about himself, not even about Ambrose – but about Brother Joachim. Something at least could be salvaged from the wreck.

Intoxicated with his daring scheme, he reached into his pocket, pulled out the snake-ring and put it on his middle finger. The tiny sphinx-like eye was full of reproach. Tom regretted his rashness immediately: wearing the ring was a kind of sacrilege, a violation of Joachim's memory. He removed it from his finger. The ring was as hard as reality, bringing him face to face with the hopelessness of his fantasy.

He remembered how far it was to town and how much open ground there was on the way; he remembered the roadblocks and the surly men patrolling the village limits. He knew it would take too long to get through and, even supposing he did, he knew no one would believe the wild story of a dishevelled sixteen-year-old. And even if he did manage to persuade them, who would support him? George was gone, his letter was gone, Joachim was gone. Kelly would lie through his teeth to protect the Brothers and save himself. Even his mother – Tom could not think about his mother, did not trust himself to recall her abject bowing and scraping before that man. Realising he was shaking with hatred once more, he forced himself to fix his attention on the ring. The enigmatic serpent was mesmerising; its carved perfection sublime. In spite of himself Tom was transported, compelled to reflect how strange it was that the ring had withstood centuries of change, watching with supreme indifference as, one by one, its brilliant owners had crumbled to dust.

Apart from midsummer, the winter solstice was Hannah's favourite day. She had always mistrusted the modern dating system. To her mind it was arbitrary and impoverished compared to the rich meaning of the old pagan calendar, which clung faithfully to seasonal rhythms and was embodied in her beloved stone circles. Today the sun was in its last decline, showing its face for a bare eight hours at the most. Tomorrow would bring not just a new day, but a New Year when the reborn sun would begin to loop higher in the sky and lengthen the days downhill towards summer. The beauty of the morning suggested to Hannah that the sun was hastening joyfully towards death, eager for its resurrection the following day.

Striding briskly down the track, she was ready to be a friend to everyone on such a morning. Even to the exasperating Mr. de Vere who had not come back to the hotel. But she drew the line at the two men who were walking towards her round a bend in the track, their thick black boots ringing on the sparse stones. One was young and sharp-featured; the other was older, and as large and shaggy as a bear. Both were dressed in gloomy dark-blue habits. She quickened her step, annoyed at herself for allowing the sight of the stiff unsmiling monks to bring a chill to the day.

The two men moved apart slightly, blocking the narrow roadway and forcing her to slow down. She twirled her walking-stick up to her shoulder and let it rest there.

The younger monk greeted her. 'Lovely morning, Miss van Neef,' he remarked. She was surprised that he knew her name; she was sure she had not seen him before. 'I wonder if by any chance you've seen young Reardon this morning?' The corner of his mouth twisted into a smile. Both the monks had stopped. They obviously did not mean to let her pass without further disrupting her harmonious mood.

'It's a little early for socialising,' she said pointedly. 'You might have better luck at his house.'

The large monk took a step forward. Her hand tightened involuntarily around the stick. The young monk made a slight gesture, and his companion stood still.

'That's the problem,' the monk went on. 'He's not at home and hasn't been all night. His mother is very distressed. We said we'd do what we could, didn't we, Brother Gregory?' The mass of black hair nodded slowly.

'We did,' said Brother Gregory.

'So if you see him perhaps you'd let us know?'

Hannah reckoned it was time to counter with a question of her own. 'And if you see Mr. de Vere, perhaps you'd tell him that I'm looking for him?'

'Mr. de Vere . . . ? Ah yes. Your fellow guest at Mrs. K.'s.'

'Yes. I thought he might have spent the night at your Abbey. He seemed very interested in it.'

'Did he? Well, we do have rooms for lay visitors but I don't think . . . Have you seen Mr. de Vere, Brother Gregory?'

'No.' The word was muffled by the bushy beard.

'Oh, well, never mind,' said Hannah. 'It's just that he left – ' On second thoughts, the little man's letter was none of their business.

'Left what?'

'Left last night and didn't return. Most mysterious. Now if you'll excuse me, gentlemen . . .' She lowered her stick and pointed it firmly at the space between them. They moved apart to let her through.

Further down the hill she noticed that all the curtains were still drawn in the doctor's house. She felt unaccountably shaken by her meeting with the monks.

She arrived at the post office just as it was opening. She asked the postmistress for a telegram form and pulled the letter out of her jacket pocket. Mr. de Vere was apologetic, courteous and brief. If by any remote chance he was held up (she couldn't imagine what business would detain him all night in Bloxbury!) he would be eternally grateful if she would send a telegram to his business partner, Charles Bennett. The address was in London; the message was succinct. It had to do with cancelling a shipment of wine.

Folded inside the letter was some money – far too much – which she gave to the postmistress along with the completed form. The woman gave the change without a word. Hannah thanked her and left the shop to continue her walk. On the hillside, three – no, four – dark figures were walking in a line across the fields towards the woods. It was a depressing sight. She hoped that the monks' sudden passion for early morning exercise would be shortlived, and that they would have disappeared by the time she reached the high ridge.

As she set off, she found herself wondering why on earth the silent old postmistress insisted on wearing that ridiculous feather hat indoors as well as out.

The contemplation of the ring cleared his head. The way the serpent endlessly devoured and regenerated itself seemed like a promise of permanence in the midst of change; more than that, it perpetual cycle of death and rebirth seemed to stand as an emblem of immortality. Slowly Tom emerged from the black tunnel of his hatred. The snake-ring was showing him the futility of personal emotion. He had to be detached and remorseless – as ruthless as Ambrose. Tom saw at once that, apart from its symbolic worth, the snake-ring could well be a powerful weapon. It was important to the monks, according to

Kelly. They had been looking for it everywhere; but even in death Joachim had managed to keep it from them. It was encouraging to find that Ambrose and his henchmen were fallible . . . Tom experienced a sudden dark elation. Maybe Ambrose had made another mistake – by not killing him sooner. For, deprived of everything he loved, left empty and alone, he had nothing to lose except a life he no longer valued. Naturally, in a physical sense, he was still afraid of death; but at a deeper level he was indifferent to it. The knowledge was strangely liberating. Breathing more freely, he decided that he was not going to make it easy for Ambrose to get rid of him.

Making an effective plan was a different matter. All his attempts to think were disrupted by vivid memories of Joachim, either lying dead on the trolley, with blank staring eyes; or alive and gliding loosely down the street. He could not reconcile the two pictures. But since the first one was a fact, he had to accept the second as imaginary, or else the result of some odd aberration of his second sight. Either way, there was no time to speculate. He gave up the effort of thinking and simply concentrated on the ring, letting himself be drawn into its timeless circle. The chaotic images were banished from his mind, all feeling hung suspended. He stood at the centre of the void, waiting.

He did not have to wait long. He was already on his feet and jogging warily through the woods before the idea had fully materialised. He did not trust de Vere (he had learnt his lesson on that score) but the man was at least an outsider. It was even possible that he knew something about the Little Brothers – his questions had been suspicious enough. But above all there was his light. The melancholy combination of copper and green ruled him out as a hero or saint, but they hinted that he was, at worst, essentially harmless. He was a long shot all right, but Tom had nothing to lose.

Beyond the plantation of firs and pines was the small forest of oaks which extended almost to the rear of the hotel. The giant trees were stripped of leaves and widely spaced so that he had to dash from one to the next, looking round each time for signs of the monks. It was slow going, but at last the red-brick walls of the hotel came clearly into view below.

25

There was a sizeable distance between the last oak and the hotel, whose overgrown gardens would in any case be difficult to run across. Tom checked his watch and calculated that Hannah would be out on her regular walk by now. The chances were that Mrs. K. would not be there either. It meant that the foreigner was probably on his own, unless the Little Brothers were also inside, lying in wait. The windows at the side of the hotel told him nothing, but serenely reflected the sunlight and the blue sky. He would just have to risk it.

Preferring speed to caution, he shot out from behind the tree and sped through the long grass, jumping over weed-strewn flowerbeds, dodging through shrivelled rosebushes, until he reached the rambling house. He paused for a moment, pressing himself against the brick walls and breathing hard. Then he began to edge round to the back door, which gave on to the kitchen, ducking below each ground-floor window as he came to it. The door was locked. There was no choice but to go in boldly by the front. At the corner of the building he sneaked a look round to make sure the coast was clear, and ran to the door. It yielded to his first push and he was inside, standing in the gloomy hall.

Tom strained every nerve to detect any sound from the kitchen or drawing-room, or from upstairs. The hotel was as quiet as a tomb. He tiptoed to the wide staircase and began to climb it, keeping to one side of the steps where, he hoped, the boards would be less likely to creak. At the top he was confronted by nine identical doors. There was no way of telling which one was Mr. de Vere's. He wondered if he was making too much fuss and that perhaps he ought simply to call out. It was still early and Mr. de Vere could easily be in bed. But the silence was dense and, as he thought, forbidding.

Putting his ear to the nearest door and hearing nothing, he tried the handle. It was locked. He tried the next and it opened. He could guess from the contents of the room that it belonged to Hannah. He was debating whether to leave her a message of some sort when the sound of a drawer being opened in the last room on the right made him stiffen for a second, and then relax. Mr. de Vere was getting up.

He went quickly along the gallery to the door which was open a crack and pushed it wider. The room was dark except for a single strip of light which shone through the narrow gap between the drawn curtains. It was enough to see that the place was a mess. The floor was littered with a jumble of clothes, bedclothes, books, paper – all the occupant's belongings. Tom was afraid that the little man had thrown a fit.

'Mr. de Vere . . . ?' he called tentatively. A man standing in shadow by the table turned in surprise. He had a book in his hands. He and Tom recognised each other simultaneously; they both froze.

Brother Paul was the first to recover. He gave Tom a sidelong, almost amused look and began to walk casually towards him.

'Hello, Tom. I'm glad to see you. You've been causing us some . . . concern, you know.'

Tom backed towards the doorway; he had the absurd impression that both he and the monk were behaving like gunfighters in a Western.

'No. Don't run away,' Paul went on conversationally. 'I'd like to show you this book. I think you'd find it especially interesting . . .' He held it out, smiling his crooked smile.

214

Tom remembered the gunfighter's advice: never look at the gun – always look at the eyes. 'Don't come any closer,' he said thickly, ignoring the book. 'Where's Mr. de Vere?'

Paul stopped, but went on talking in the easy-going, hypnotic way that made it difficult to think. 'Don't be afraid, Tom. *I'm* not going to hurt you. How could I? Come in and we'll have a chat . . .' Watch the eyes, thought Tom, even though Paul's stare was drilling into him almost painfully. '. . . you know perfectly well that you have something I want, don't you? Be sensible. We'll talk about it. Don't worry about Mr. de Vere. We're looking after him . . . he's quite safe . . .' The young monk had taken another two steps forward. *Watch the eyes.*

Without moving his head or changing his expression Paul flicked his eyes to the right. Tom hurled himself sideways just as the huge bulk of Brother Gregory lunged at him from behind the door. His mouth was open, a red gash in the mass of black beard.

The ring was already in Tom's hand. He held it high above his head and, as the Mad Monk grabbed him, he yelled, 'Get back! I'll smash it! *Get away.*' The monk's heavy paw hesitated and withdrew. 'I mean it. I'll break the ring against the wall!' He sounded more certain than he actually was that the ring's brittle stone would break. He prayed that the monks would not test him. Paul's face was white with rage; Gregory backed away.

It worked! They couldn't touch him while he had the ring! Tom was possessed by a thrill of power, a lightning flash before fear re-asserted itself. He shuffled towards the door still shouting mindlessly, 'If you move, I'll *smash* it . . . Stay where you are or the ring's gone!'

He slammed the door behind him and looked around in terror. How many more of them were in the hotel? He had no time to be cautious – his legs were already buckling under him. He sprinted for his life out of the hotel.

*

215

'The car has now been waiting for half an hour, Eminence.' The Pope's chaplain could not keep a trace of petulance out of his voice. In his opinion, the Cardinal was acting in an extremely high-handed manner. There was no denying that he was a master of organisation, so why was he keeping the Holy Father waiting?

'I know, Father Giulio. Be patient.' Sitting behind his desk and blowing smoke-rings, Carlo Benetti's calm exterior successfully concealed his inner agitation. He knew that he must appear to be behaving unreasonably, but no one could know that he was waiting for Father Vittorio to contact him. He was still angry with the little priest and had wanted to proceed as planned, letting Vittorio look after himself. But an innate caution had held him back. One word of reassurance was all he wanted; but although he had camped all night beside the telephone, it had refused to ring.

'With respect, Eminence, I don't think His Holiness will wait much longer. If you could perhaps give me a *reason* for the delay . . . ?'

The Cardinal stubbed out his cigarette. He wished he could stub out Father Giulio. The pompous young priest had been a thorn in his side right from the start. At the same time, his efficiency, intelligence and, above all, his devotion to the Holy Father were undeniable points in his favour.

'I'm afraid I can't, Father. And by the way, I think that His Holiness will wait as long as I ask him to. He knows that I – like you – have his best interests at heart. We would never inconvenience him without good cause, would we?'

The chaplain's face coloured, indicating that he had taken the point. He shuffled his feet uncomfortably but went on undeterred. 'I'm sorry, Eminence, but I really must – ' He was cut short by the door flying open. A breathless Father Dominic burst into the room.

'Eminence! The telegram! I came as fast as I could . . .' He was excited and his head was moving nervously from

216

side to side. 'It's addressed to "Charles Bennett", just as you said!' The presence of the Pope's chaplain had a sobering effect on him. He paused and, straightening his cassock, handed the envelope to the Cardinal.

The two chaplains, one Italian, one English, eyed each other curiously as Cardinal Benetti ripped open the envelope. Then they turned in unison to watch his face. His expression did not change. But suddenly he was springing out of his chair, issuing orders.

'Right. Father Dominic! Stay here and man the office. You, Father, follow me!' His long legs carried him out of the office in five strides.

There was someone in the hall. Hannah bolted out of the drawing-room, calling out 'Mr. de Vere! Mr. de Vere!' His absence had brought her to an unaccustomed state of anxiety. She hated mysteries which she could not solve by measurement, calculation and scholarship.

'Was you wanting somethin', Miss Vaneef?' Mrs. K.'s broad country accent preceded her out of the cubbyhole, which served as her office, across the hall.

'I thought you were Mr. de Vere. Have you seen him, Mrs. K.?'

'Can't say I 'ave, Miss.'

'He didn't come back last night, you know. Nor this morning.'

'That's as may be,' said Mrs. K., folding her arms disapprovingly under her lumpy bosom. 'It's no business o' mine.'

'Do you know when he's supposed to be leaving the hotel then?' Hannah asked despairingly.

'I do.' She settled complacently into her large and shapeless body.

'*When*?'

'There's no need to take that tone, Miss.' She adjusted her bosom with dignity. 'As a matter o' fact, he's already gone.'

'What? When . . . you must have seen him then!'

217

'Not at all. He left my money – quite a generous gen'leman – and slipped off quietly as you please. Never made no fuss about it.'

'Impossible!'

'As you like, Miss.'

Hannah strode to the staircase and began to take the steps two at a time.

Hannah saw immediately that Mr. de Vere's room was far too neat to be occupied. There were no objects strewn about on the table, no clock or photograph beside the bed, no suitcase, not a single shoe or slipper. Even before she pulled open the first drawer, she knew it would be empty.

He had obviously left while she was out walking – although how he had managed without a car she could not imagine. However, she was less concerned with *how* he had left than with *why* he had left without saying a word. She supposed that it was silly of her to expect thanks for doing him a small favour, but it did not seem like him to have disappeared without even mentioning the telegram. He had always been so correct and, besides, she had grown to like him. Their isolation at the hotel had bred – or so she thought – a mutual understanding, a kind of *camaraderie*.

Irritably, she pulled open the rest of the drawers to check that he had left nothing behind. They were all empty. She went to the wardrobe and threw open the long door. It was bare except for a handsome collection of coathangers. But as she was closing the door again, something on the floor at the back caught her eye. It looked like a bracelet or necklace. She reached it and picked it up. It was a miniature crucifix with a string of beads attached. A rosary. She would never have guessed that Mr. de Vere was a Roman Catholic. During their early discussions about ancient rites and religions he had never once mentioned sin, guilt, confession, judgment, hell or even the Virgin Mary.

218

She scrutinised the rosary. The little figure of Christ looked to be made of silver and was welded to a wooden cross. It was quite a professional article. She turned the cross over. A name was etched in fine script on the back. *Padre Vittorio di Rivera.* The rosary belonged to a priest – an *Italian* priest. It took her a moment or two to spot the interesting coincidence. Victor, *Vittorio;* de Vere, *di Rivera.* The resemblance between the names was striking. Could it be that . . . ? She had heard of spies posing as priests, but the reverse was simply ridiculous. Mr. de Vere was an Anglo-French wine importer. Although he could be an *Italian* importer . . .

Hannah was close to confusion, a state she was not accustomed to. A longer talk with Mrs. K. was in order. But when she went downstairs, she found that Mrs. K. was gone.

26

The light shining through the narrow slot of window threw a thin rectangle on the bare wall at the end of the bed. The remainder of the room was swathed in semi-darkness, but Father Vittorio sensed that he was not alone, that someone was standing in the shadows, watching him. He had no idea how long he had been unconscious – it could hardly be called sleeping – but the day had to be fairly well advanced to judge by the height of the light rectangle on the wall. He dimly remembered having woken at some point, only to realise with deep humiliation that he had wet his bed. Shortly after, strong hands had lifted him and washed him and changed his bed clothes; and, after that, he had been fed some soup as if he were a baby. He could feel too that his clothes had been changed. By a great effort he moved his head a fraction and saw that he was wearing a dark-blue monk's habit.

Wood scraped on stone. The unseen presence in the cell was stirring. A large, bony head bent over him; he recognized the face of the Abbot. His fever instantly seemed to take a greater hold on him.

'Good afternoon, Mr. de Vere. I expect you'd prefer to be called "Father Vittorio" from now on. You see, I know a little more about you since I took the liberty of examining your belongings. Don't worry – they're quite safe. I've had them moved from the hotel while you're staying here at the Abbey. We've tried to make you as comfortable as possible . . . under the circumstances. You do see that I had no choice? The arrival here of a pious Catholic could scarcely have been a coincidence, so I couldn't take a chance, could I? You can imagine my relief when I found out who you were! It meant that my action – and your . . . condition – were entirely justified.

'I must say that I'm impressed by your ingenuity. It is always pleasing to find that human beings can still spring the occasional surprise. I would never have guessed that you could have stumbled on the Order's true identity . . .' The Abbot held something in front of the priest's face. It was a book whose leather binding was instantly recognisable. He removed the book and continued his monologue:

'Yes, Brother Anthony's book is quite entertaining – although I don't suppose it was much use to you, Father. It's all true, of course . . . but only as far as it goes. Anthony was an interesting example of how vulnerable we have always been. Let me explain . . . It's a curious irony that for all these centuries the Order has been virtually immune to corruption from the *outside*, while remaining sensitive to *internal* crises. You see, we play the part of devout Catholic Brothers so convincingly that every now and then some of it rubs off on a member of the Order. He becomes infected by your faith which, we must admit, is very similar in many ways to the true one. It's not long before he is tempted to leave the Order and possibly reveal its secrets.

'Anthony was the most notorious of these traitors. But luckily he came at a time when the twin gods of Science and Reason were raising their ugly heads in Europe. So, despite a brief *furore*, no one took his book seriously. It was a simple matter to suppress it, but a mistake, I now see, to retain a copy ourselves – as a reminder of the possible dangers that can threaten us from within. I won't be so tactless as to ask how you came by the book, Father. I prefer mysteries.' He gave a grating laugh which sounded like an instrument grown rusty through lack of use.

Ambrose paused and began to pace up and down the narrow cell, hands behind his back. He appeared and disappeared as he walked in and out of Vittorio's limited range of vision. He seemed self-absorbed, his expression absent-minded, almost musing; but the blue squiggle of vein on the side of his head pulsed faintly, betraying some inner excitement.

Abruptly he turned to the priest once more. 'Father Vittorio. You are a dying man. I expect you've already guessed as much. But you still have the consolations of your faith. I'm afraid you may not have them for long. In recognition of your efforts, I've decided to answer your questions. Oh, I know what they are. You are not the first to seek the Cathars' Treasure; but you will be the first to know the whole story. I assume you already know what is commonly available – the massacres, the siege at Montségur, the removal of the Treasure and so on? Of course you do. I will begin at the base of that dreadful cliff which the four Perfect climbed down at dead of night . . .

'One of them carried the Treasure. His name was Guillebert. It was easy to carry because it was all in his head. He was the Guardian of the rites whose effects are so luridly described by Brother Anthony. Guillebert also carried something else – a ring formed from a snake eating its own tail. This ring had been intimately connected with the Treasure right from the beginning, and it was said to possess exceptional powers . . . Together with another Perfect, Guillebert travelled to a place remote from Montségur where he hoped he could not be traced. He was successful. After long years and much hardship, during which his companion died, Guillebert founded the Order of the Little Brothers of the Apostles – in Bloxbury. He was an extraordinary fount of learning and wisdom, perhaps the greatest Cathar of them all. He not only contrived the Order's disguise; he also introduced many innovations to preserve – and enhance – the Cathars' power. It was he who hit upon the idea of adapting ancient sites in the service of the Treasure;

222

he had studied the secret properties of such places and knew their value. The unique configuration of Bloxbury Ring, the Mound and Stone have enabled the Order to deploy the Earth's energies to its personal, spiritual advantage.

'However, we must not forget the two remaining Perfect. For safety's sake, and to increase the odds in favour of Cathar survival, they decided to break with the Guardian and take their chances elsewhere. They also adopted Guillebert's plan and likewise founded an Order of apparently orthodox monks in the Balkans. The second Order of the Little Brothers. But before they parted from the Guardian, he gave them a token of the spiritual bond which united them, the last four Perfect Ones . . . He gave them the snake-ring. And it has been worn by the Abbots of the Balkan Order right down to the present day. Indeed, the ring seems to have given formidable powers to the wearer – the Abbots in the Balkans have even outshone our own with their spiritual feats. Certanly, the Little Brothers in Bloxbury have always believed that, when the snake-ring is reunited with the Treasure, the Perfect will come again openly to rule the hearts and minds of men . . .'

The Abbot walked to and fro, to and fro. Half the time he seemed to be talking to himself. At other times his talk took on the intimate tone of the confessional, perhaps because in addressing Vittorio, he saw himself as already communing with the dead:

'You know, the flame of our missionary zeal has never been dimmed – we have always felt that in the long run there was a surer way of regaining our former glory . . . that God would not desert us. I never dreamt that I would be the one to accomplish the task . . . after all the years, the long years . . .

'You must remember, Father, that until recently it was unheard-of for a Pope even to contemplate stepping on to largely Protestant soil. So how could we hope to succeed? Then something *momentous* occurred: a Brother arrived from the Balkan Order. And he brought the snake-ring with him. Within a short time, a Pope was to come to this country for the first time. It was nothing less than a sign from God, a sign that the time of the Perfect was approaching . . . I did not fail to discern the hand of Providence – and I opened negotiations with that cesspool called the Vatican. The rest is history – or will be.'

He looked down at the priest's tortured face with the impersonal concern of a doctor. Then he went to the table and poured some water into a glass, which he pressed to Vittorio's lips. Even as his body shrank and tightened under the Abbot's touch, Vittorio was moved almost to ecstasy by the coolness of the water on his red-hot, rigid throat. He uttered a series of pathetic grunts. For a second, he and Ambrose were united by the closeness of sworn enemies, and then the monk's recognisably human face retreated behind its cruel mask.

'Good,' he said. 'We don't want to lose you yet. But don't think you can escape death, Father. Even I cannot reverse the fever I've given you. But you will not die in your pitiful state of self-delusion – I personally guarantee you a glimpse of the great truth which you soft little priests have never been able to face. And, incidentally, if you're harbouring any secret hope that the Holy Father – as you so quaintly call him – will be prevented from coming . . .' He went back to the table and fetched a piece of paper which he held close to the priest's eyes. 'Do you recognise this? It was not difficult to guess who "Charles Bennett" is. I'm afraid I had to send another, more encouraging telegram to our friend the Cardinal – on your behalf, of course.'

Behind his glasses, Father Vittorio's eyes rolled upwards, showing the whites. When they returned to their normal position, two large tears had gathered in the corners and begun to roll slowly over his cheeks.

Down below, in the secluded courtyard, a black car was parked in front of an insignificant entrance. It was a fairly large comfortable car, but by no means in the limousine class. Apart from the windows whose glass was tinted to hide the passengers from prying eyes, it might have passed for an ordinary family saloon. A big man, slightly balding and with very broad shoulders, was leaning against the door on the driver's side. He was wearing a three-piece brown suit and, every now and then, he glanced at his watch. Father Dominic surmised that the man was Commander Komit from Special Branch.

The policeman's name was the occasion of endless tiresome jokes amongst his colleagues who called him a 'high-flier', a 'regular ball of fire', and so on. The jokes were accurate: the only son of Polish immigrant parents (who had abbreviated their real name by three syllables and cut out at least two 'z's), Commander Komit's meteoric rise through the ranks had been as remarkable as it was deserved. He was smart, tough, honest and discreet. He was also a Roman Catholic, which fact, combined with his other qualities, had made him an automatic choice to look after the Pope for a day or so. Although it was one of his easier assignments, it was also the one he was most honoured to be asked to carry out.

Father Dominic watched as the small door opened and Cardinal Benetti appeared, a tall imposing figure in his long black soutane. He called to the Special Branch man who hurried around the car to meet him. They exchanged a few sentences, during which Komit opened his jacket to show the Cardinal something hidden underneath. The Cardinal shrugged and went back inside. Komit opened the back door of the car and walked up and down beside it, looking keenly in every direction including upwards, at the top-floor window of the Archbishop's residence where Father Dominic was posted. Then he returned to the door.

An old man in long white robes came out. Komit

bowed and attempted to usher him into the car. The old man would not be hurried, but stood at the open door chatting to the policeman and introducing him to the young priest who had followed him out. Then he offered Komit a frail hand which the policeman took with clumsy reverence, and, bending low, kissed. By this time, the young priest – Father Giulio – had become agitated and was fussing around the Holy Father. Dominic smiled to himself as he saw the old man refuse the chaplain's offer of help and climb unaided into the back of the car. The chaplain got in after him and Commander Komit, having spoken briefly once more to the Cardinal standing in the background, went round to the driver's seat and took his place behind the wheel. Dominic knew that, just outside the courtyard, two unmarked police cars were waiting to escort the Pope to the outskirts of London, where they would be replaced by two police motorcyclists. He was prevented from watching the Pope's departure by the ringing of the telephone. He answered it.

'Hello. Cardinal Benetti's office . . .' The ringing continued. He had picked up the wrong phone. It was the Cardinal's private direct line which was ringing. He answered it more cautiously.

'Hello . . .' A woman's voice was speaking. He listened. 'No, madam. I'm afraid I've never heard of Mr. de Vere. You must have the wrong number.' He was about to ring off, but the woman's urgency stopped him. She was talking about a priest now, a Father Vittorio. The name meant nothing to him. He was growing impatient when she mentioned a third name. Charles Bennett. He wished the Cardinal was in the office; it was he who knew about Mr. Bennett – or *was* Mr. Bennett. The Cardinal was full of contradictions.

Dominic decided to cover his confusion by adopting a firm line with the mysterious female caller. 'May I ask how you came by this number? It's not listed, you know.' The woman explained coherently enough but it made no sense to him – something about overhearing the de Vere character and remembering the registration number of her car. It seemed to be her turn to express impatience and it made the young priest nervous. His head began to twitch. The woman was pretty intimidating once she got going. He remained business-like only with an effort. 'I'll certainly pass on your message to my superior . . . yes, it's quite possible that he can help you . . . If you'll leave me your name and number? Van Neef. Yes, two words, I've got it. Did you say *Bloxbury*? No, no, it's just that . . . well, I can't say at the moment. Yes, I said I'd get him to call you back. No, he'll tell you his name himself . . . Yes, he'll be back shortly. Bloxbury two seven seven, yes. Goodbye, Miss . . . er . . .' The woman was still talking when he put the receiver down.

Vittori's curiosity had survived his bodily affliction intact. He had listened intently to the Abbot's strange tale which seemed to take place on an altogether separate timescale, where centuries were compressed to mere decades and years to months. He had talked about events of 1244 as if they were still fresh in his memory. But any idea that Ambrose was simply mad had to be dismissed – unless madness could be systematically formulated and transmitted through twenty generations of monks. Besides, he was so much in control, so confident of his divine righteousness, that Vittorio had nearly come to believe that he was himself the lunatic, not Ambrose.

The revelation that the telegram had been discovered was an almost intolerable blow. With all his hopes dashed, the little priest steeled himself for a last attempt to reason with the Cathar leader. If he could reach, for one second, the human he had glimpsed inside the heretic, perhaps, perhaps . . . The water's cool refreshment helped. He struggled for a long time, the veins standing out in his neck and head, inarticulate noises issuing from his mouth. Ambrose watched him with interest. At last the words came, forming an appeal all the more eloquent for its childlike simplicity.

'John . . . is a good . . . man. Inno . . . cent. *He* . . . did not . . . kill . . . Cath . . . ars. Not . . . responsible. Give up your . . . grievance. Forgive. No *point* killing . . . John. Nothing gained. Please . . . *please* leave . . . him – ' His words were lost in painful gasps. The effort had exhausted him.

'I understand you perfectly, Father,' said Ambrose. 'But are you really as naive as you pretend?' He resumed his pacing up and down. When his face next came into view, it wore the frown of someone who is striving to explain a simple fact to an idiot.

'It puzzles me, Father – it *upsets* me – that a man of your intellect should think of us as no more than a base species of terrorist. Surely you must admit – from personal experience – that we could be highly effective assassins? We could have disposed of any number of Popes if we had wanted to. You still fail to see that our divine mission is nowhere near so crude – it's not political at all, except in the broadest sense. It is a wholly spiritual affair, ordained by God.'

His face appeared again, unclouded, the frown replaced by a distant, almost noble look of exaltation. His voice grew low and resonant.

'Father, you don't seem to appreciate the honour I'm conferring on you. You're not going to die in darkness, like a rat – you're going to witness the Treasure, the secret of immortality! It will be a moment unrivalled since our Lord Himself graced the Earth . . . a moment when Time will be embraced by Eternity and, at a stroke, the repulsive propaganda of two thousand years will be swept away! You'll *see*. At last the power of the Popes – those Anti-Christs! – will be broken and returned – O Lord of Light be praised – returned to the True Faith of the Perfect Ones, the creed of the Cathars . . .' The face hovered over the priest; it was radiant with a dark secret joy.

Vittorio was shaken to his bones by the sheer power of the Cathar; a howl of protest rose up through his body, but it emerged as feebly as the whisper of a dying man's last words:

'*No . . . for the love of . . . stop . . .*' His lips went on moving soundlessly.

27

It was still comparatively early in the day, but already the waning moon was as high in the pale sky as the declining sun. The winter solstice was drawing to a close. The last of the tall pines threw long shadows across Winston Powell's fields, beyond which the village road gleamed dully like gunmetal in the dying light.

Tom stood motionless at the edge of the pines. He had spent hours in the woods, either lodged in the branches of trees or crawling through thickets, always alert, always silent. The monks had come close to him twice, but they were no match for him in his chosen terrain. Their noisy boots had given them away or else their dark garb had stood out like scars against the mellow woodland colours. He had had little trouble in keeping his distance, coolly picking his next point of cover and reaching it each time with the utmost economy of movement. He no longer noticed the hunger in his stomach or the tension in his limbs; if anything, they had been pressed into the service of his greater instinct for survival and had helped to refine his senses to such a pitch that he could distinguish between the rustle of a fieldmouse and a sparrow at fifty paces. He was existing now on pure adrenalin.

As the monks had advanced, he had circled away on to higher and higher ground; and when they retreated, he had tracked them back down the hillside. He was sure that they had left the woods about an hour before, leaving him almost at the spot from which he had started that morning – it seemed like light years ago – trembling on the brink of the trees. They could still be out there, hiding behind hedgerows, waiting to take advantage of the open ground.

He swept his gaze methodically across the fields until he had covered every inch. There was not a single movement to arrest him, not even a breath of wind to ruffle the grass. The cattle were all gone – slaughtered and hauled into a pit. He could clearly see the enormous black gash in the green field, with white lime and disinfectant spread for yards around it. The impenetrable hedges were the problem; they had to remain an unknown quantity. He turned his attention to the real objective: the road. Nothing would pass along it until the Holy Father arrived – the men at the barriers would see to that – and the time of his arrival was imminent.

Tom was not certain how or when the decision had crept up on him. He only knew it was there, and it was all that was left him. Joachim's death had devastated his fragile beliefs and deprived them of both substance and comfort. He had tried out of loyalty to find strength in the immortal Spirit of Christ, but without his friend's persuasive certainty its power was diminished and its glory faded. He had to act from the standpoint of the void, and he could see only one starting point: the fact that a man's life was in jeopardy. He alone was responsible.

As surely as if a giant hand had been laid across his shoulders, he felt the pressure of a deeper responsibility than simply saving a man's life. The man was a Pope; and as long as there were souls to be saved, the Pope's fate was intimately bound up with the fate of Christ. But decisions of that nature would have to wait: like a battleship captain, Tom was doomed to venture far out into unknown waters and there, hovering over fathomless deeps, open sealed orders.

He shrewdly calculated the distance from the trees to the road, and then the distance at which he would first see the approaching car. He dared not show himself until the last minute. How fast would the car be travelling? He mentally pictured it coming into view and began counting. He saw it moving slowly down the road, gathering speed as it left the barrier behind. When it drew level with him, he clicked his imaginary stopwatch. Twenty-three. Disastrous. He knew he could never make it across the field and on to the road in twenty-three beats. He would have to get closer – and there was only one possible point of cover.

It was not time to be squeamish. He took a deep breath, and, balancing himself for a moment on the balls of his feet, broke cover like a fox and dashed, head down, across the open expanse of grass. He expected the hedge on his left to bristle with dark emerging shapes, to ring with shouts of recognition, but he heard only the sound of his own gasps and the light thud of his feet. Within seconds he was at the edge of the pit. He jumped in and landed on something soft.

'Miss who?' Cardinal Benetti stifled a yawn. His leisurely lunch at the restaurant had been expensive, certainly, but excellent – it was not true what they said about English food. It had been his first piece of self-indulgence for weeks, and, since his day had begun at dawn, he was ready for a quick siesta before resuming the round of phone calls necessary to finalise the arrangements for the second phase of Pope John's tour.

'Miss van Neef, I think she said,' replied Father Dominic. The Cardinal yawned again; she was probably one of those female columnists for the popular press who delighted in speculating on what the Holy Father ate for breakfast and what time he went to bed.

'Do we know this Miss van Neef?'

'She's not on any of the lists, Eminence, but she did call on your private line.' Cardinal Benetti leant forward, wide-awake.

'Go on.'

'Unfortunately, I couldn't really understand what she

was saying except that she was trying to contact someone who knew a man called Mr. de Vere. She thought that, perhaps, this was Charles Bennett's number . . .'

The Cardinal felt a pricking sensation on his skin. He said something under his breath. It sounded like 'Oh God!'

'She left a number,' Father Dominic went on eagerly. 'Bloxbury two seven seven.'

'Bloxbury.'

'Yes, Eminence.'

'What time did she phone?' The question was shot out with sudden force.

Dominic was taken aback. 'About . . . about an hour ago . . . I think.'

'Think harder.'

'It may have been more . . . Yes, I remember. You were seeing His Holiness to the car.'

The Cardinal looked at his watch. Then he reached for the phone on his desk.

'I did look for you at the time, Eminence . . . but . . .'

Carlo Benetti was not listening; he was dialling.

At first Tom thought that he would not be able to bear it. There were so many of them, so huge and heavy and dead. He was quite unprepared for the sheer mass of the carcasses, piled up anyhow, hooves sticking out awkwardly, legs oddly contorted and painful-looking.

But gradually he grew accustomed to them. Wedged down between the back of one cow and the belly of another, he even derived a little warmth from their soft hides. For it was cold in the pit; the weak sun had made no impression on it. Just as well perhaps because the cattle had not yet begun to putrefy, although one or two had started to swell ominously. Tom shivered at the thought of their internal rotting, the bursting of their bloated skins, the escape of hideous gases.

The worst thing now was the stench. Tom could feel the ammonia burning into his nostrils and up into his brain. He had to breath through his mouth to prevent himself from retching. He eased himself on to his knees, balancing precariously on the carcass underneath him. It shifted slightly. Tom had to suppress a cry – he was seized with the irrational feeling that somehow the beast was still alive. He forced himself to dismiss the thought and, carefully rising to his knees, peered over the edge of the pit. His heart lifted; he could clearly see the whole road and it was nearer than he had calculated. The Little Brothers couldn't stop him now! He slid back to his niche among the cattle.

The sun continued on its flat trajectory across the sky, tingeing the horizon with orange. Tom grew nervous. He had not bargained for this waiting. Nor for this abysmal charnel-house. As the darkness gathered around him, Tom became increasingly aware of the eyes. They glimmered white on every side, rolled back in fear, reflecting the agony of the death throes. He tried to ignore them by running through in his mind what he would do when he heard the Pope's car. He would have to be quick; he must not let it pass – dared not let it pass. If only he knew how fast it would be going . . . The eyes stared at him blankly.

A vivid memory leapt into his head: the image of those other dead eyes, and the awful whiteness of the body sprawled on the trolley. He quickly shifted his gaze, noticing for the first time the mouths of the cattle, the disfiguring blisters on their poor dumb muzzles. They looked sad and vulnerable. Here was another item in the catalogue of crimes to be held against Ambrose through all eternity.

Pacing up and down in front of the impressive portals of the Archbishop's residence, Carlo Benetti was in a rage of impatience waiting for the car he had begged from the Italian Embassy. Father Dominic's bleating offers to fetch his coat for protection against the cold wind fell on deaf ears. The Cardinal's lean body seemed oblivious of the weather; all his strength was bent on willing the car to arrive. He was gambling on the assumption that, in the time it would take to cut all the red tape and persuade the authorities to act, he could with luck overtake the Holy Father himself. Besides, what reason could he give for mounting an attempt to intercept the Pope? He only had the evidence of an unknown woman that the telegram he had received was not the one she had sent. What the hell was Vittorio playing at? And where, where was the damned car? The one thing he could not bear in a crisis was inaction.

The official car rolled sedately round the corner. Before it had even stopped, the Cardinal flung open the door and shouted to his chaplain:

'Right! Get in, Father Dominic, I might need you!'

'But, *Eminence* –' He had not realised he was going too. Wherever they *were* going.

'Get in, man.' He turned to the surprised driver. 'Can you drive fast?'

The young man grinned and tipped his peaked cap to a jaunty angle. 'Just give me the chance, sir!' This Cardinal fellow was obviously not the average, thirty-miles-an-hour bigwig.

'You've got it. Head west. We want the M3 motorway – and make sure you drive like the devil!'

'Yessir!' The driver had secretly dreamt of this moment. With a squeal of tyres, he pulled straight out into the bustle of traffic and steered directly into the rays of the sinking sun.

From the highest tier of the new wooden gallery, to the left of the chapel doors, Father Vittorio looked down on another world. Whereas he was hidden in deep shadow, the far end of the chapel from choir stalls to altar was lit by a brilliant array of candles. Their flames danced and flickered in an invisible draught, bestowing an air of unreality on the dream-like figures who moved within the magic circle of light.

He had been propped against the wall like a sack of

vegetables, and the cowl of his habit had been pulled over his head to hide his face. He could no more move than if he had been tied in a straitjacket. His neck and head especially felt as though they had been clamped in a white-hot vice; he did not even begin to know how to speak. His eyes alone moved, darting rapidly from left to right, drinking in every detail of the scene below.

He counted eleven monks. Each appeared to have an appointed task to perform and every movement was executed according to a prescribed pattern. They fetched and carried the accoutrements of the altar, lit and re-lit candles, swung the censers which sweetened the air with pungent smoke. As one of them stopped to kneel before the altar, so another would rise to take his place in the ritual. There were never less than seven kneeling monks, who were responsible for the precise, but uncanny, chant. It wove an incessant thread of murmured sound which bound the movements of the monks together, forming them into a whole and perfect rite.

At the heart of the ceremony, in his elevated position behind the altar, stood the square, imposing figure of the twelfth monk, the twelfth Apostle. Brother Ambrose. He remained rooted to his spot throughout, while all around him the Little Brothers revolved like stately dancers at a sovereign's ball. Yet nothing escaped him. Every act, every gesture was subject to his scrutiny; everything was ordered by him. It was obvious to Father Vittorio, the only witness to the sacred drama, that the will of the Abbot was being done.

Pope John the Twenty-Fifth, Vicar of Christ and successor to St. Peter was dozing peacefully, his head on one side and his mouth slightly open. Father Giulio gently pulled the rug further over the white robes. It would not do to let the Holy Father catch a chill. He smiled affectionately at the old man; how the Holy Father hated his fussing! But someone had to look after him – the doctors had been very specific about that. There was no cure for the Pope's condition which was easily described: after a long and strenuous life, his heart was simply wearing out. He needed care, rest and good clean air. Father Giulio looked out of the window at the peaceful countryside. It seemed to be the ideal place.

Just beyond the large sign which carried the single word BLOXBURY, the two motorcyclists were talking to a group of men at a makeshift roadblock. One of them was holding a shotgun. Commander Komit was standing in front of the car and, when two of the men came forward with large cans of disinfectant and spraying apparatus, he waved them back and indicated that they should give their equipment to the policemen. The men stood in a huddle, staring at the car, as the motorcyclists sprayed the wheels. Komit climbed back inside and leant over the seat.

'Everything O.K., Father?' The Pope's chaplain put his finger to his lips and nodded.

The planks and oil drums of the barrier were moved aside and the policemen re-mounted their motorcycles. One of them raised his hand in a signal to the Special Branch man and simultaneously the group of men stepped back respectfully. The shiny black boots of the policemen kicked the powerful machines into life. The old man in white stirred slightly at the roar of the bikes as they accelerated away down the road. The black car moved off more slowly. One of the roadblock men bent down to try and peer through the darkened glass of the window. He straightened up again and smiled at the man standing next to him. Father Giulio took no notice; he was lost in admiration for the sun which was hanging low over a distant hill like a huge ball of fire, streaking the sky with crimson.

28

Tom thought at first that the humming was in his head. But, as it grew louder, he scrambled to the rim of the pit and looked out. Something was moving on the road. He screwed up his eyes, forcing them to penetrate the fading light, and was just able to make out two dots approaching at speed. They disappeared behind a hedge and, when they re-emerged, he could clearly see that they were motorcycles. Some way behind them was a black car. Tom cursed his stupidity. Of course the Pope would not be travelling alone; there would be an escort. Police probably. He glanced wildly around him for signs of life – for figures in dark robes – but the area was deserted. He braced himself to dash out into the road, to stand fast in the middle and stop everything any way he could. He wished he were bigger, wished he had something to wave.

The sound of the vehicles grew louder. The motor-cycles were dead ahead. Perhaps he should risk it now – no one could stop him in full view of the Holy Father. His legs tensed themselves for the spring; but still he waited. There was so much to lose. What if the policemen caught him, bundled him away, gave him no chance to explain? It was too terrible to contemplate. They were less than three hundred yards away now. The car had dropped back a little as the motorcyclists enjoyed the open road. He could just do it if he timed it right.

Coldly Tom judged the distance between the oncoming motorcyces and the car. He pulled himself half out of the pit, poised in readiness. The massive bikes roared past in tandem, shattering the silence of the fields. Tom held his breath and counted. One-two-three-NOW. He flung himself towards the road and the big car which purred smoothly along it.

The ritual was reaching its climax. The monks continued to rise and kneel with perfect precision, carried forward on the carefully modulated wave of incantation. Even Vittorio, trapped and burning in invisible flames, was taken out of himself. He had to admit that the spectacle was impeccable. Too impeccable, perhaps. There was something inhuman about the elaborate dumbshow of the ceremony. Like the courtly mating dance of certain exotic insects.

All at once Ambrose raised his arms. The vibrant chant abruptly ceased. It was so quiet that the wind could be heard moaning gently at the corners of the chapel. The candles guttered and flared, throwing a trembling net of shadows over the silent monks. To the left of the altar stood two Brothers. Each carried a large vessel. Vittorio recognised them at once: the first was the same cloth-covered salver and the second, the same enormous loving-cup that he had seen being borne in procession from the mound at the heart of Bloxbury Ring.

The deep voice of the Abbot rang through the chapel: 'IT IS TIME.'

The monks answered in unison.

'We pray that we are worthy witnesses.'

'ARE ALL HERE OF ONE MIND?'

'We are all of one mind.'

'ARE ALL HERE PURE IN SPIRIT?'

'We pray that we are pure in spirit.'

'BRING FORWARD THE SACRIFICE.'

The two monks stepped up to the altar and placed the huge chalice and covered salver in the centre. Then they took their places in the semicircle of kneeling monks. The Abbot's head was thrown back, his cowl around his shoulders, his eyes closed in prayer or ecstasy.

When he opened them again, they appeared as bright

239

pinpoints of light which seemed to shoot the length of the chapel, piercing the gloom and battening on Vittorio. The little priest felt his body obey the will of the Abbot, coiling more tightly round itself until he thought his heart would burst.

Again the voice rang out: 'LET US HEARKEN TO THE WORDS OF THE SPIRIT, THE CHRIST, WHO LIGHTS OUR PATH TO PERFECTION.'

'Let us hearken to the words.'

One of the monks – the oldest, by the look of him – stood up and walked forward. He mounted the dais and took his place beside Ambrose at the altar. He was carrying a large book which he put down next to the heavy pewter cross and opened. To Vittorio's surprise, he began to read aloud Jesus's famous pronouncement from the Gospel of St. John. The tremendous words were both infinitely familiar and infinitely strange within the context of the Cathar rite:

'. . . Truly, truly, I say to you, unless you eat the flesh of the Son of man and drink his blood, you have no life in you; he who eats my flesh and drinks my blood has eternal life, and I will raise him up at the last day . . .'

While the passage was being read, Ambrose took a small silver ladle and dipped it into the huge chalice. He drew it out and poured the dark viscous contents into another smaller cup before adding communion wine. Next, he folded back the cloth on the salver to reveal a freshly-baked loaf of unleavened bread. '. . . For my flesh is food indeed, and my blood is drink indeed. He who eats my flesh and drinks my blood abides in me, and I in him . . .'

The elderly monk closed the book and returned to his place in the rank of Little Brothers.

The Abbot paused and then cried out: 'WE BIND OUR POWER TO THE BODY AND THE BLOOD.'

'We bind our power.'

One by one the monks approached the altar and, kneeling reverently before it, passed their hands over the small chalice and the loaf of bread.

'O LORD OF LIGHT, MAY THESE HOLY SACRA-
MENTS CAST OUT THE ENEMY AND REDEEM THE
TIME FOR ALL ETERNITY.'

'Redeem the time for all eternity.'

The booming echo died away.

Ambrose spoke in his normal voice, but with absolute
finality:

'We are ready.'

Flanked by two of the Little Brothers, he marched
down the centre aisle of the chapel and, without even a
glance at the priest, went out through the wooden doors.
He was closely followed by two more monks who,
between then, carried out the enormous lidded chalice
whose purpose, apparently, had been fulfilled.

The sudden screech of tyres woke Pope John the Twenty-
Fifth with a start. The car swerved violently and he was
jolted sideways against Father Giulio. At the same
moment he glimpsed a boy in the road, waving his arms
wildly and shouting. The Pope raise an automatic hand
in blessing. He was quite used to displays of pious
enthusiasm, even extreme ones.

As the vehicle careered past the boy, narrowly missing
him, he leapt forward again and dealt the roof a mighty
smack with the flat of his hand. 'STOP!' The anguished
cry tore at the heart of the old man. He leant forward to
speak to the driver, who had quickly regained control of
the car. His chaplain gently restrained him.

'The young idiot!' he muttered, and then soothingly to
the old man in his care, 'Don't worry, Holiness, the boy is
all right.'

'Yes, yes. But shouldn't we – '

'We cannot stop for everyone, Holiness.'

The Pope craned his neck round to peer out of the rear
window, a look of concern on his face. The boy was
running down the middle of the road, still waving for all
he was worth.

The Commander was speaking. 'I'm sorry, Holiness.

He came from nowhere. Just leapt in front of me. I nearly killed him.'

'I saw what happened,' interjected Father Giulio. 'You did well to miss him. The young *idiot*.' He was furious that the Holy Father had been unnecessarily alarmed. 'Are you all right, Holiness?'

'Yes, yes.' The boy was receding into the distance, his arms still moving feebly up and down. The Pope was struck by how forlorn he looked. For an instant he regretted the high office which had put him out of reach of so many people. Especially the young, whom he loved. In the old days he could have stopped – the boy meant no harm, he was sure of that. The words of the Saviour came to him, like a reproach: 'Suffer the little children . . .' The old man felt the weight of his years and a great weariness fell over him; yet he had duties to perform still. The Little Brothers of the Apostles, his brothers in Christ – they would see no trace of weariness when he stepped from the car to greet them.

Tom hauled himself through the branches of the old cherry tree and eased open the bedroom window. His sharpened sense of hearing could detect only the tick of the antique clock in the hall downstairs, reminding him of how the minutes were slipping away. Apart from the moment of sheer desolation on the road his failure, far from deterring him, had instillled in him a relentless determination – an obsession even – to pursue the Holy Father at all costs and alert him to the machinations of the monks. He pulled himself over to the window ledge and dropped quietly into the twilit room.

He darted across to the cupboard where he kept his clothes and opened it. There was a mirror attached to the inside of the door and, as he began to rummage in the cupboard, he caught the reflection of a movement in the corner of his eye. He spun round, grabbing the ring from his pocket and holding it in readiness. He spoke quite calmly.

242

'Stay where you are or I'll destroy the ring.'

He edged around the bed, keeping close to the wall. A person was sitting on the floor, head resting on drawn-up knees. It was his mother.

'Stay where you are. Don't try to stop me.'

Elizabeth lifted her head and slowly shook it from side to side. She winced as though the simple gesture had caused her enormous pain. Tom recognised the symptoms of her migraine, but he was shocked by her gaunt, beaten appearance which suggested a much deeper pain. Mother and son appraised each other briefly, like strangers. Tom saw that he had nothing to fear from her now. He returned to the cupboard and pulled out his cassock and surplice. Then he opened a drawer and took out the security pass which Brother Paul had given him to gain admittance to the Abbey.

Elizabeth looked at him wonderingly as he brushed his hair and scrubbed at his face with a spit-moistened handkerchief. He seemed so different – decisive and grim and so much older. More like a man than a boy. He obviously knew exactly what he was doing, but she could make no sense of his actions and clung to the belief that she must protect him, especially from himself.

'Tom,' she said softly; it hurt her to speak. 'Tom, give up. Brother Ambrose promised not to hurt you. Just give him the ring and we'll go away from here quietly.'

Tom was pulling the cassock over his head. He appeared not to hear her, but asked bitterly, 'I take it that there aren't any Brothers hanging about here?'

Elizabeth hung her head with shame.

'Well?' The single word was rapped out, demanding an answer. She had never remotely heard him speak like that before.

'No . . . *no*, Tom. They've gone. Back to the Abbey . . .'

'Good. I don't suppose you'd like to tell me why you did it?' he said coldly.

'Oh, Tom. I *had* to tell Brother Ambrose. I thought it would be for the best. Don't you see? He's been everything to us . . . to me. He brought me into the true faith, made a Believer of me. I suppose you'll never understand now. I don't think I understand anything any more. Oh, if only this hadn't happened . . . if only you'd become a Little Brother . . . Can't you just give Ambrose what he wants? It may not be too late . . . *Please*, Tommy. For pity's sake, he promised – '

' *"He promised"*.' The scorn in her son's voice made Elizabeth flinch. 'Mum! Can't you see what Ambrose does? He lies and kills – that's what he does. He's probably raving mad for all we know!' He softened slightly at his mother's distress and went on with weary patience, 'I don't even care any more. All I know is that the Holy Father's here. I've seen his car. I can't just do nothing . . . not after what *they've* done, what they're *going* to do. I doubt if I can help, but I've got to try. So no more of this talk . . . please. Just leave me alone.'

'But where are you going? What are you going to do?'

He paused. 'What they least expect. I'll turn up for the Blessing Ceremony – the closer I get to the Pope, the better. What I'll do then . . . God knows.'

He walked towards the door, then turned and said in a matter-of-fact tone, 'I'm telling you this in case something happens to me . . . so that you'll *know*.' He shrugged and, looking into Elizabeth's face, held her eyes for a second. 'Don't betray me again, Mum.' He went swiftly out of the room and down the stairs.

'What about the boy?' Brother Gregory had bent his head and was hissing in the Abbot's left ear. 'He can't have got far. We must find him.'

Ambrose did not answer him immediately. He was busy savouring the moment.

Standing in front of the Abbey's main doors, he commanded a clear view down the drive to the gates a quarter of a mile away. They were being opened by two policemen whose motorbikes were parked in the road. An unostentatious black car was driving through.

Ambrose delicately moistened his lips with the tip of his tongue. He spoke calmly, in a low voice, without taking his eyes off the approaching car.

'After today, Brother Gregory, the whole world will not be big enough to hide young Reardon. So don't worry – he's a nuisance, nothing more. However, we may not have to look that far – '

'But the *ring* – '

'Don't interrupt, Brother Gregory.' The Abbot's eyes were following the car passionately, as if he could draw it up the hill by the strength of his gaze. 'As I was saying . . . I have no doubt that he will bring the ring to us when he is ready.'

'What do you mean, Brother Ambrose?'

'What I say. Reardon has nowhere left to go. But I know the boy. He still has his sense of duty, the pathetic child – and he will still want to receive the blessing of the . . . Holy Father.' He smiled. 'Oh yes, he'll come in good time. Don't concern yourself, Brother. I'll vouch for the return of the snake-ring. Make sure that Brother Paul knows that I want the Blessing Ceremony conducted as normal. If I'm wrong, no matter. We have all the time in the world . . .'

The gates had been closed again and the two policemen were standing guard, as Ambrose had instructed. The Pope's car was drawing up in front of the Abbey. Ambrose glided smoothly forward and opened the rear door.

'Welcome to Bloxbury Abbey, Holiness,' he said. 'I . . . we have all prayed for this moment.'

'In a bit of a hurry are we, sir?' The policeman was speaking to the driver at the open window. In the back of the car, Cardinal Benetti's knuckles went white as he clutched the upholstery. The driver said nothing. 'I don't suppose you'd care to guess how fast you were going when we overtook you, sir?' The heavy irony was too much for the Cardinal. He sprang out of the car and drew the surprised policeman aside.

Father Dominic began to perspire heavily as he saw his superior gesticulating earnestly in his direction. The police officer was nodding. The flashing red light on the police car illuminated their faces in a series of stills. They appeared to be sharing a joke. Countless cars hurtled past on the busy motorway. The driver drummed his fingers on the steering wheel.

Suddenly the policeman ran to his car and spoke to his partner who, in turn, spoke into the handset of his radio. Carlo Benetti paced up and down, taking deep breaths. The policeman returned. He spoke briefly, gave a self-conscious salute and all at once the Cardinal was back. 'Follow those police officers,' he ordered the driver, 'And hurry!'

'Yessir!' The driver pulled out into the stream of traffic, following in the wake of the police car's wailing siren. He was thoroughly enjoying himself. This Vatican man was a hell of a guy – one minute they were stopped for speeding, the next, they were being escorted!

'What did you tell the police, Eminence?' Dominic asked nervously.

'I told them,' he replied serenely, 'a pack of lies.'

'*Lies*, Eminence?' The chaplain's head began to wobble.

'I merely informed the officer that you are the Holy Father's doctor and that we are pursuing him with some important medication – heart pills, I think. You know how forgetful His Holiness can be. Fortunately, Mr. O'Malley is not only a good policeman; he's a good Catholic. He immediately requested permission to escort us part of the way . . . You will confirm my story if the need arises.'

Doctor? Pills? Dominic was bewildered. He studied his superior to see if this was a joke. Cardinal Benetti was sitting on the edge of his seat, teeth clenched and staring straight ahead. There was no trace of humour. Dominic gave up.

'As you say, Eminence.' His head moved sadly from side to side.

29

Tom took the long carving knife out of the kitchen drawer. With the snake-ring he had at least one strong card to play; all he needed now was something to inflict real damage if necessary. The knife fitted snugly into the long baggy sleeve of his white surplice. He practised whipping it out and slashing at Ambrose's face. He imagined his cold fury guiding the point of the knife through flesh, through muscle, striking bone. He imagined twisting it slowly round.

It was no good. He could not convince himself – the knife felt clumsy and hostile in his hands. It called to mind a fragment of George's delirious letter: '. . . he's pushing the knife *into his stomach*. I can't take my eyes away, they hurt, his eyes burn me. He doesn't mind the knife it sticks out it doesn't hurt he smiles . . .' The words made Tom shudder. '. . . It's not a dream, it's real *real*.' He could believe it all right.

He threw the knife back in the drawer and beat his arms against his sides. There had to be something he could threaten Ambrose with, the man wasn't invulnerable, he *was* a man. Wasn't he? While he was thinking, he took a lump of cheese out of the fridge, tore a wedge of bread off the loaf on the sideboard and stuffed them ravenously into his mouth. Then, still chewing, he slipped out of the back door and hurried to the garden shed.

He soon found what he was looking for: the paraffin lamp for use in emergencies or power-cuts. He emptied a bottle of weedkiller and poured the paraffin into it, securely stuffing the neck with a piece of old rag. He had seen it done on television – they were always making Molotov cocktails. He had no idea whether or not he had made it correctly, but it was better than nothing. He hid the bottle in his sleeve and set off for the Abbey, running easily, pacing himself so as to be ready for his blessing, or his ordeal.

Wandering in a daze through the empty house, Elizabeth found that she was incapable of focusing her thoughts through the mist of pain. Every time she fought off the migraine long enough to concentrate, frightening images thronged her head. They resolved themselves into just two: the majestic, glowering face of Ambrose and the pale stricken features of her son. So intense was the vision of the two conflicting faces that she experienced them as physical presences, like twin prongs probing her body, goading her to make some crucial choice between strength and weakness. She was appalled at the implications of such a choice. And yet she had to find some deliverance from the intolerable sensation of being cut loose and cast adrift over dark swirling waters.

Slowly Elizabeth felt herself inexorably drawn to the one who had watched over her, the source of her solace and spiritual nourishment. Only he could rescue her. She picked up the telephone receiver and dialled the number of the Abbey. It rang. Tom's face swam on the tears before her eyes; he was laughing, as in the old days when they were happy. A voice answered, calm, expectant. Without a word she replaced the receiver.

Her mind shifted; the pain moved from the centre to somewhere on the periphery of her being, and began to dissolve; the world took on a shape again. The dilemma had been deeper than she knew. A choice between power and love. Elizageth guessed that she had, come what may, chosen well.

'Yes, but alert him to what?' Hannah asked the question out loud as she stumped down the muddy track for the second time that day. The man had not said. He had rung off. Either he was what he claimed to be or he was a lunatic. She had to admit that he had not sounded mad – disturbed, yes, but not mad. All the same she was beginning to regret the moment of pure caprice when she had rung the number which she had overheard Mr. de Vere (Father Vittorio di Rivera?) asking for. The evasiveness of the man who had answered was infuriating enough; but it was nothing compared to what she had felt when, after a long wait, 'Charles Bennett' had phoned her back. The call had begun politely, with an exchange of mutual caution; but as soon as she had mentioned the contents of the telegram she had sent, all hell had been let loose. In a few tumultuous seconds she had been asked to believe that Mr. Bennett had not received the telegram – or not *her* telegram at any rate; that Mr. Bennett was really a Cardinal; that Mr. de Vere was, yes, a priest; that the Pope was coming to Bloxbury.

Nor was this all. Charles Bennett, or Cardinal Benetti – or 'Charlie Bravo' (his code-name, apparently, as head of the operation) – instructed her (instructed *her*) to alert a man travelling with the Pope, a special policeman with the unlikely name of Comet (spelt Komit). She was to trust no one else, repeat *no one*, especially the monks. Avoid them, he had said, like the plague. Nettled by the man's presumption – his arrogance – she was about to point out that, if Roman Catholic churchmen wanted to cut each other's throats, it was no business of hers (in fact, it was not a bad idea); but she did not get the chance. He was repeating that she should rush to Komit, tell him that 'Charlie Bravo' had sent her and alert him. Then he rang off. Alert him to what? She had sat stunned for five minutes at the end of a disconnected telephone line.

After its brief performance, the exhausted sun was sinking through a trap-door in the horizon, changing the main street into a no-man's-land between light and dark. Hannah's stick clicked on stone as she mounted the pavement which ran parallel to the Abbey walls. In her sensible and forthright way, she had wanted to reject the so-called Cardinal's story out of hand. It was against all reason. Her attempts to piece together a less fantastic, more acceptable version were thwarted by yawning gaps – gaps which tended to fill up with enigmatic men in dark-blue robes. All the arrows had pointed to the Little Brothers ever since she first saw them that morning, wandering in the woods or heading up the track towards her hotel. But she could not grasp the significance of them. She was left with a brooding sense of unease in which she was conscious of her own uncertainty. The Cardinal had been definite – not in his story, but in his earnest, impressive tone of voice. And it would not be difficult to check on the arrival of a Pope . . . and wherever the Pope was, there – according to 'Charlie Bravo' – would be Commander Komit.

The light was fading so fast and Hannah was so lost in thought that she did not immediately notice that two people were walking across the street from her, and in the same direction. They were not out for a stroll. Their feet were full of purpose, striking the ground in unison. A third pair of footsteps joined them. Glancing over the shoulder, Hannah saw that a heavy man was following her through the dusk.

Father Giulio walked along the colonnade and joined the man who, despite the chilliness of the oncoming night, was standing stock still in front of the chapel doors. He peered at the inscription carved into the stone lintel.

'Be ye perfect . . .' he remarked.

'What's that?' said Stanislav Komit. (His friends called him Stan.)

'Nothing.'

A sliver of flaming sun remained on the western horizon. Enough light to see that a group of people had already foregathered at the gates down below. Commander Komit looked at his watch.

'No need for you to stay out, Father. It'll be really cold

in a minute.' As if to demonstrate his point, he removed the overcoat from his arm and put it on. Father Giulio did not reply; he seemed preoccupied.

Stan Komit had already checked the Holy Father's quarters, of course. They were a trifle spartan, but absolutely safe from intruders, casual or otherwise; that was the main thing. The chapel might also have been designed with security in mind. It was built like a fortress. Taking nothing for granted, he had circled it twice. Nothing could get inside except through the doors; and he would be standing in front of those. Predictably, everything was in order and on schedule.

'How long you reckon they'll be in there?' He asked the question to be sociable. He already knew the timing of the Mass and the following Service of Thanksgiving, give or take a minute or two. A lot depended on whether he double-checked the villagers' passes. He had already decided that he would.

'Not long. An hour or so altogether, I should think,' said the Pope's chaplain. Half to himself he added fretfully, 'His Holiness must be tired after the journey. Thank God he doesn't have to say Mass . . .'

'I thought that was the whole point, Father,' said Komit, surprised.

'No, no. The whole point is that he's here out of humility. He thinks the monastic and teaching Orders have been neglected for too long. He means to celebrate Mass with the Little Brothers as an equal, for his own private spiritual benefit . . . Only after he has received the Holy Sacraments will he become Pope again – at their request – to bless the village representative and afterwards, in the presence of all the local people, to consecrate the chapel and give thanks for the continuance of the Order . . .' He lowered his voice. 'Here they come now.'

The cloister door had opened and through it came a single monk. His hood was pulled over his reverently lowered head and he was ceremonially carrying a key.

He was followed by another, rather shorter monk. Behind him came two rows of five similarly cowled Brothers, their hand piously concealed in their sleeves. The Holy Father was walking between the two rows of men as though he were being shielded by their bodies. Another single monk brought up the rear.

The procession moved sedately along the colonnade. The two spectators stepped aside to allow the leading monk to unlock the doors. The monk with the key was the last to cross the threshold. As he did so, he raised his head slightly so that his mouth was visible. He was smiling at the policeman and the priest with a crooked smile. Komit nodded in return. He heard the key grate in the lock as the smiling monk inaugurated the private service. Komit took up his position again and pulled out his copy of the Cardinal's document. The number of monks attending the Mass was there in black and white, submitted by the Abbot of the Order. Thirteen. All present and correct. Komit was a man who liked symmetry; he found it displeasing that there were not twelve Little Brothers of the Apostles, like in the Bible. He switched on his two-way radio and muttered into it. His officers could let in the villagers now.

As the sun dropped behind the hills, a tide of darkness swept across the land. The powerful car flashed through the narrow lanes, following the twin beams of its headlights. A rabbit, trapped in the sudden light, zig-zagged crazily ahead of the car before swerving into a ditch. The miles burned away under the wheels.

The three men inside had barely exchanged a word since the police had waved them off the motorway and into the labyrinth of side roads that led to Bloxbury. Dominic was simply too frightened as the driver flung the car around corners and over hillocks, wholly absorbed in keeping to the road. An oncoming car, horn blaring, passed within a hair's breadth on the twisting lane. Its headlamps briefly revealed the Cardinal sitting forward, hands braced on the seat in front, eyes fixed glassily on the road ahead. From time to time, he rapped out a command: 'Right here!' 'Now left!' 'Good man!'

The driver obeyed without question or comment, as if he were in silent communion with the mind of Carlo Benetti. Once, he missed a turning and, shuddering to a halt, had to reverse; the car revved to a high-pitched scream. The Cardinal said nothing. Only his left hand, beating involuntarily on the back of the seat, betrayed his frustration and anxiety. He did not even accept his chaplain's offer of a cigarette.

More people were coming towards her out of the night. She could see shadowy figures slipping out of the cottages and joining the swelling stream. No one spoke or laughed; there was only the sound of feet, heading towards the crowd which had already gathered at the gates of the Abbey. Two men in shiny black boots were letting people through one at a time after inspecting a white card, like an invitation. Hannah knew then, beyond a shadow of a doubt, that the Pope was up there. Never had she felt so strongly that she did not belong.

It was too late to back out, and besides she was already caught up in the mass of bodies, edging forward. Her reluctance to move was greeted with curious stares from big farmers in stiff collars or thin women in hats. She managed to break free and pluck at the elbow of a policeman.

'I have to see Commander Komit,' she whispered. The man stopped checking the white cards to look at her. The crowd grew restless and a low murmuring sprang up. He indicated to his partner that he should go on checking, while he drew Hannah aside.

'Let's see your pass please, madam,' he said.

'I don't have a pass. I have a personal message for Commander Komit.'

The policeman detected her Dutch accent; his boots creaked suspiciously. 'Are you from the village?'

'Yes. No – I'm staying at the hotel.' She noticed that one or two villagers were throwing sidelong, hostile glances at her before entering the Abbey grounds and starting to climb the slow curve of the drive.

'Just tell me where Komit is, will you?' she demanded with a hint of desperation.

'What is all this about, madam?'

'I *told* you.'

'Well now. You tell me the message and I'll see the Commander gets it. Can't say fairer than that, can I?' Hannah brought her stick down with a crack.

'You don't seem to understand, officer. The message is personal. Does the name Charlie Bravo mean anything to you? He telephoned me.'

'Telephoned, eh?' the policeman said, as if that were the crucial point. He stared over her shoulder for several seconds. Then, making up his mind, pulled out a radio.

'What's your name, madam?'

'Van Neef. Hannah van Neef. But he won't know my name.'

The police officer had turned away and was holding the radio close to his mouth. Hannah could only hear snatches of what he was saying.

'. . . Yessir . . . Right . . . Vaneef . . . No, V for Victor . . . No, she hasn't got one but . . . Bravo . . . personal, sir . . . Yessir . . . hold her as long as you want, sir . . . Right . . . half-an-hour? . . . Right, sir . . .' But Hannah had heard enough. She was not going to be bogged down by hide-bound policemen and held, like a prisoner, before she could deliver her message. The Pope came before their protocol. By the time the policeman had finished with his radio and returned to detain her, she had crept off into the night.

He called to his partner, who was seeing the last of the villagers through the gate. 'You see where the lady went?'

'Her? Nah. Who d'you reckon she was?'

'Dunno. Crackpot maybe. Dunno.'

'What was she on about?'

'Wanted to 'ave a word in the Comet's ear.'

'Must be barmy.'

'I dunno. Said she knew Charlie Bravo. Said he'd been on the blower to her.'

'Strewth. Better get her. I'll hang on here.'

'Yeah.' He went.

The second policeman was startled by a boy who had materialised out of the dark and was standing in front of him.

'Bit late aren't you, son?' The boy looked at him suspiciously. He was wearing white church clothes; a choirboy or something. Looked as though he could use a good night's sleep.

'Got your pass?' The boy nodded and held out his white card. 'Good lad. Big day for you, eh?'

The boy did not reply. The look on his face could give a bloke the creeps.

The policeman watched him disappear like a ghost up the drive and then produced his radio. He'd better tell the Comet that the funny woman had changed her mind, but that his partner was after her anyway.

30

From his eyrie in the outer darkness, Father Vittorio witnessed – as Ambrose had promised – the heretics' Mass. The candlelit chapel burned with a feverish brightness like the mouth of hell. As demure as model Christians, the Little Brothers had reformed their semi-circle and had once more set up a chant. It carried no suspicion of its former savage strains; instead, it was a Gregorian chant of flawless orthodoxy whose cool Latin words and exacting harmonies raised up calm pillars of sound around the altar.

A velvet cushion had been placed in front of the three steps which mounted to the dais. Kneeling on the cushion was Pope John the Twenty-Fifth. His white robes stood out amid the dark rank of monks with the starkness of a negative photograph. Only the Abbot had removed his cowl. He was facing the altar and preparing the Sacraments, assisted by a Brother who seemed to do no more than hover around him. Vittorio counted the monks. Unwilling to believe his eyes, he counted again. Including the Abbot, there were thirteen where before there had been twelve. Where had the thirteenth Apostle come from? Any why had he come? The little priest failed to understand and trembled to his bones.

Ambrose carefully raised the Host, heavy with more than mere bread, high into the air. The chanting grew piercing and sweet with adoration. He lifted the ordinary-looking chalice.

The Holy Father unclasped his hands, ready to receive

the Body and the Blood. The chanting stopped. The chapel was charged with a stillness as though, for the space of a heartbeat, the whole of Creation was holding its breath.

Ambrose came forward with the salver on which he had broken the loaf of unleavened bread. He picked up a fragment and placed it on the Pope's tongue. He offered the chalice. The old man took it and put it to his lips. He seemed to hesitate for a moment. The faintest sigh swept along the line of monks. Then he tilted the silver cup and drank. Brother Ambrose stepped to one side and stood quietly with his head lowered.

The enchanted stillness was broken by the clatter of the chalice as it dropped on to the stone steps. Red liquid spread like an oily stain on the floor. The old man tried to get to his feet, stumbled, and pitched forward on to all fours. The Little Brothers watched him, unmoved inside their deep hoods.

Kneeling next to the altar, the Abbot's assistant rose as though lifted by an invisible string attached to the crown of his head. A sudden current of air whispered through the chapel. The candle flames began to dance crazily; the shadows of the Cathars on the ceiling and walls danced with them. The monk began to glide in a curious boneless motion towards the Pope. At the head of the steps he paused to face the carved crucifix at the far end of the building. In spite of everything, Vittorio was riveted.

The apparition of the thirteenth Apostle was surrounded by a shimmering heat-haze which gradually grew stronger until it glowed white-hot and blossomed into silver light. His cowl was imperceptibly peeled back to reveal a face so dazzling that the priest's eyes hurt to look upon it; a face whose ageless features shone in silent rapture before the Cathar cross.

The Abbot jumped lightly off the platform and, seizing the Holy Father under the arms, lifted him easily into an upright position. The silver head of the monk made a final dislocated movement, like a bow, as he drifted over

257

the steps towards the Pope. The old man, clasped tightly from behind, flinched from the radiance of the face. His eyes narrowed and then opened wide with shock.

The monk gently embraced him like a long-lost friend. As he did so, he grew huge and luminous and then, in a blinding burst of light, he disintegrated, dissolved – and was gone. The white robes of the Pope billowed as if in a gust of wind. The candles sputtered and flared. The Abbot lowered the old man softly to the floor. There was not a single trace of the monk and his silver light.

A slight noise from the adjoining room penetrated Eugene Kelly's stupor. He heaved himself to his feet and staggered across to the door of the small annexe. Opening it, he rubbed his eyes and did his best to examine the contents of the room. Everything was in order. He was about to return to the surgery when he appeared to have second thoughts. Weaving like a man on the deck of a pitching ship, he went over to the trolley and paused with his hand on the cloth. He pulled it back.

Eugene looked at the face of the corpse. His head shook in disbelief. The stern marble face had relaxed and softened into an almost serene expression. The black slit across the neck was like a sinister smile. The dead man's eyes had closed.

Hannah was dismayed – the wall looked much taller than in daylight. She might even have been deterred, were it not for the sound of shiny boots crunching down the street towards her. With the gesture of someone making a final commitment, she flung her walking-stick over the top. She heard it land on the other side. Looking apprehensively in the direction of the footsteps, she quickly inserted the round toe of her sensible brown shoe into a crevice, and her fingers into a crack, and began to scale the wall.

It was as difficult to climb as she had imagined. But the stones had crumbled and come apart in places; and

Hannah was strong. The top of the wall was rounded and smooth and, as she struggled to swivel round and lower herself down the other side, she lost her grip and dropped too quickly.

She fell heavily on to her right ankle and twisted it badly. It was all she could do not to groan aloud with pain; but the heavy footsteps had stopped immediately in front of her on the far side of the wall. She bit her tongue and held her breath, hoping she had left behind no clue for the policeman to detect her climb. The boots moved off again. Hannah exhaled and, groping in the dark for her stick, found it and struggled to her feet. She could just make out the Abbey, looming in the distance through the trees. Leaning heavily on her stick, she began to limp through the tangled undergrowth towards her rendezvous – she could still scarcely credit it – with the Pope's bodyguard.

A kind of low unholy crooning had broken out among the Little Brothers. Ambrose silenced them and leant over the splayed body of Pope John the Twenty-Fifth. After a long moment, he straightened up and raised both his arms in the air.

'Let us praise the Lord of Light. The Anti-Christ is vanquished.'

The monks replied, *'We praise Him. May the Perfect Ones live for ever.'*

With military precision they formed a circle around the lifeless bundle of white robes and stretching out their arms in supplication, began to pace anti-clockwise around the Pope's body.

The Abbot urged them on, declaiming, 'O LORD OF LIGHT, LEND US THE POWER TO RAISE UP THE SOUL OF THY CHOSEN ONE, THAT THY TRUE WILL MAY BE DONE ON EARTH.'

'Thy Kingdom come.'

The inert form of Pope John stirred like a man waking from a deep sleep. The Little Brothers broke into their old chant, as controlled as before, but lower, more urgent, pleading. In accord with an unheard command, they paced faster round the body, their boots stamping out a background rhythm to the wordless, intricate pattern of sound. The body seemed to respond. It quivered and tried to thrust itself upwards, before flopping down again like a beached sea creature. For a long time it lay still. Unable to contain himself, Ambrose broke through the circle and began to whisper feverishly into its ear. With a violent spasm the body arched upwards again and, managing to rest on its elbows, opened its eyes.

The ancient oppressive stones of the Abbey cloisters were stacked on the hill like a natural outcrop of rock, blocking the starlight. A steady buzz emanated from the sombre horde of villagers which filled the colonnade. They were milling about impatiently, rubbing shoulders, seeming to produce the insect-like sound from the friction between them. They were shuffling into an order of precedence known only to themselves, each vying with his or her neighbour to be at the head of the queue for the Thanksgiving Ceremony.

Scared that they might try to turn him over to the Little Brothers, Tom approached the villagers warily, glad to feel the snake-ring nestling hard and warm in one closed fist while the other clasped the bottle of paraffin inside his sleeve. He began to push through the crowd. There were a few friendly glances and several looks of envy, but no one disputed his right to pass unmolested to the head of the queue. Clearly, his unique role in the proceedings carried weight.

His caution turned to contempt for the people who had let themselves be duped by the Order, mistaking the monks for men of God instead of the bringers of destruction and agents of chaos which in reality they were. The contempt gave way in turn to sadness, a grieving for the past when all the faces he knew so well had belonged to neighbours and not to Ambrose's army of zombies. One or two of the villagers reached out to touch him, as if for luck; their smiles of recognition froze on their lips under his scathing stare, and they looked away.

At last he was standing in front of the doors over which the words 'Be ye Perfect . . .' hung like a threat. Beneath them a broad-shouldered man was posted with a proprietorial air. Tom did not recognise him. It struck him that the man, who wore his strength as discreetly as his well-cut overcoat, was attached to the Pope. His heart pounded briefly; perhaps he could make the man understand . . . He pulled himself together, remembering bitterly that he had fallen into that trap before. Even if the man was not under Ambrose's influence, how could he (how could anyone?) possibly understand? Tom clung to the belief that the Pope's superior insight – and his alone – would enable him to see the truth clearly when the time came.

Just then there was a scraping noise from the other side of the doors and the rattle of a key in the lock. He glanced wildly at the burly man who nodded at him, smiled and stepped aside. Tom walked past him. Using his left arm to hold the bottle tightly against his stomach, he withdrew his right hand from the sleeve and hammered three times on the doors. The buzz of the crowd subsided.

In the glare of the headlights, Cardinal Benetti counted five men behind the barrier. Three of them were clustered at the left-hand end, talking to Father Dominic; the other two were standing a little apart in the middle of the road, keeping an uneasy eye on the car. One of them was holding a shotgun.

The driver pushed back his cap, 'I don't think he's having much luck. D'you want me to have a go?'

'No,' said the Cardinal. He lit a cigarette. It had not crossed his mind that his chaplain would persuade the men to let the car through, but it gave him a breathing space to decide his next step. Whatever it was, it would have to be quick.

Even at fifty yards the young priest's head could clearly be seen wobbling. He was turning away from the man and half-walking, half-running back to the car. He got into the back, a little out of breath.

'It's no use Eminence. We'll have to go back. Or find another way round. It's the foot-and-mouth disease, you see. They're not allowed to let us through. I can sympathise with them – '

'Father, you may as well know now,' interrupted the Cardinal. 'The Holy Father's life may be in danger. I haven't time to explain. I *certainly* have no time – nor inclination – to find another way through. Kindly go out there and get them to remove those oil drums. If necessary, knock them down yourself.'

Father Dominic blinked rapidly. He looked at the driver and then back at his superior.

'There are five of them, Eminence,' he said shakily.

'I know, Father. I wouldn't ask you to do this if I didn't have to.'

'Couldn't you . . . perhaps . . . ?'

'No. My rank would not impress them. And an Italian would antagonise them. I depend on you, Father. You have the full authority of the Church behind you. *Demand* that they remove the barrier or tear it down yourself. And, for God's sake, *hurry*.'

'Look. I don't mind having a crack at it,' said the driver who felt sorry for the nervous young chaplain.

'No. I have every confidence in Father Dominic. Go now, Father – and remember that *we* are not important . . . the Holy Father *is*.'

Dominic sunk his head. 'I'll do my best,' he said and, climbing out of the car, he walked with as much bravado as he could muster towards the waiting men.

The driver shook his head unhappily. 'With respect, sir, I don't think the Church is going to cut a lot of ice with those lads . . .'

'Of course not. Listen to me. I estimate that, with luck, we shall have about six seconds to reach the barrier. There's a sight gap between the right-hand end and the bank – you'll have to drive up it, of course – but we must get through that gap. Do you think you can do it?'

'What abour Father Dominic?'

The Cardinal said nothing. The driver sniffed.

'Is it true what you said about the Pope?'

'It's true.'

The driver pulled his cap down firmly. 'I think I can do it,' he said.

'Good. Start the engine. Go when I say.'

They both watched the roadblock. Dominic was waving his arms and arguing. He suddenly lashed out with his foot and dislodged one of the drums. The men exchanged glances. He shouted something and, grasping one of the long planks, threw one end of it to the ground.

'Nice one,' remarked the driver admiringly. He put the car quietly into gear. As the three men raced round the barrier to grab him, the priest ducked nimbly under the planks and, head down, cannoned into the two men remaining on the far side.

'Go,' said the Cardinal.

The young man revved the engine, slipped the clutch like a rally driver and hurtled towards the right side of the roadblock. The bright headlights picked out the figure of Dominic flailing wildly in the arms of three large farm-hands while two more looked poised to hurl themselves on to the front of the car. At the last moment the driver swerved skilfully up on to the bank and, with only two wheels on the road, hit the narrow gap at fifty miles an hour.

The front bumper clipped the first oil drum which spun harmlessly away; the one behind it had been weighted down. With a rending of steel, the front wing crumpled and its headlight exploded in a shower of glass. The force of the impact lifted the car free of the

263

grassy bank so that it hung in the balance on its side for a second, wheels spinning, before smacking down again. There were shouts, the loud report of the shotgun, a hail of metal pellets on the boot, the hiss of a punctured tyre – and the car was away, zigzagging towards the Abbey. The driver let out a triumphant hoot. Carlo Benetti picked himself up off the floor.

'*A good Christian seeks entrance to the House of God.*'

From sheer nervousness, Tom called out more loudly than he intended, but the effect was all the more impressive. He did not know which he feared most – to be refused entry or to be let in. There was a long pause during which even the villagers fell silent. Then the key turned in the lock with a hollow click as dire as a condemned cell being opened at dawn.

Brother Paul stood in the doorway, key in hand. He did not seem at all surprised to see Tom. But it was difficult to gauge any emotion behind the monk's hood. Only too aware of his last encounter with Paul, Tom stepped hesitantly across the threshold and waited. The door crashed shut behind him and was re-locked. There was no way to go now but forward, into the midst of the Little Brothers. With head lowered as though expecting a swift execution, he felt his neck tingle in anticipation of the monk's sudden blow. It did not come. Instead, Paul slid past him and began to walk down the central aisle, leading him into the presence of the Holy Father.

Tom tentatively raised his eyes, ready to shut them tight against the possibility of some unspeakable out-rage – dreading that he might see the bloody corpse of the Pope, or worse. The candlelight dazzled him, but the first thing he could make out was the Little Brothers kneeling in rows on either side of the steps. At the head of the steps, splendidly attired in white flowing robes, stood Pope John the Twenty-Fifth. He looked more youthful than his photographs, and somehow less bowed. He appeared to tower over the monks kneeling around him and to exude an authority – a holiness even – that made it suddenly unthinkable that he could be under any threat. His hand was casually held out in greeting or encouragement. Relieved beyond measure, Tom took new heart and confidently began to follow Brother Paul towards the altar and his Blessing.

31

Out of the depths have I cried to thee, O Lord; Lord, hear my voice. Father Vittorio repeated the prayer over and over again. He scarcely knew what he was praying; he could not remember what came after the opening words. He had passed beyond ordinary thought and feeling as though he had been melted down and returned to raw incoherent material. His silent cry out of the depths was only a reflex, the last spiritual twitching of his extinct religion.

He did not know what he had witnessed. In any case, he had long since passed the point where he trusted his own eyes and ears. But he knew this much: beside the subtle abomination perpetrated by the Little Brothers of the Apostles, the crudest human sacrifice would have been a blessed relief. The Cathar rite had enshrined a violation that a Catholic would have to beg forgiveness just for having seen. He had lived too long and seen too much; it would have been better to have died.

Unfortunately – and although he was not always entirely sure of it – Vittorio found that he was still alive. He knew it now chiefly because a boy dressed in a white surplice was coming into view down below. He recognised the boy from somewhere. Hadn't they once spoken to each other? Why was he now being led to the altar, as meekly as a lamb . . . ? Was there no end to the rape of innocent souls?

A last prayer formed itself inside him. It had no words; it had no hope. It could hardly be distinguished from the simple grinding of his heart. Yet it was there, a weak appeal to the Unknown by one who stood on the razor edge of sanity, and of life.

Tom was acutely conscious of Brother Ambrose's presence a little behind, and to one side, of the Holy Father. He was afraid to look at the Abbot directly and kept his eyes fixed straight ahead. He could not shake off the irrational notion that as long as he kept the Pope in view and avoided the Abbot, then somehow the monks would not be able to move. Everything depended on his remaining calm and steadfast.

Brother Paul bowed to the Pope and peeled off to the right to take his place in the row of Little Brothers. Tom was aware that the Holy Father was watching him, his wise face illuminated by a gentle smile. It would not be long now – a simple blessing, a few words, and then the chapel would be flooded with people bringing the safety of numbers. He knelt on the lowest of the three steps. His face was very close to the cool whiteness of papal robes. He prepared for his holiest of moments, a blessing from God's representative on Earth.

A pale hand was held out towards him, an old man's hand with brown freckles on the back. But it did not waver – it was firm with the power of the Holy Spirit. Tom bent his head in anticipation of the light consecrating touch which, he fancied, would be like a bond between them; almost an act of complicity against the monks. Just above the level of his eyes, the hand stopped, turned palm upwards, the fingers curling inwards at the tips. He heard his name spoken.

'Tom.'

It was an old man's voice, and yet its faint accent was so familiar that he was tempted to believe that he had imagined it.

'Tom. Give me the ring.'

The effect of the voice was devastating. He would have recognised its unique intonation anywhere in the world.

The breath whistled through his teeth in a sudden gasp and his head snapped back so that he was staring full into the face of the Holy Father. At the same time, the request for the snake-ring had been so unexpected that he began to draw his hand obediently out of his sleeve. He felt a tremendous pressure in his head as though his mind were being flattened against the back of his skull. Without any conscious decision on his part, the Pope's smiling face began to change according to the mysterious laws of his second sight. The flames of the candles merged and leapt into one great arc of holy fire; the Pope's robes glowed as white and immaculate as the Lamb of God, while the face . . . the *face*. It was changing, yes, but strangely. There was no burst of colour, no sudden revelation of light. It was being drained of life, freezing, turning as cold, as stiff, as ugly as the face of a corpse. But behind the fixed and empty smile, *someone else was smiling*. Someone else was looking through the Pope's glassy eyes, someone known and loved and mourned. Joachim. Joachim had taken possession of the Pope – *Joachim was the Pope*.

Momentarily deranged by the spectre of his dead friend grinning out of the Holy Father's deathmask. Tom scarcely knew what he was doing. He snatched back the hand that was holding out the snake-ring, and dived past the white robes to the altar.

A voice he dimly identified as Ambrose's seemed to reverberate across a vast distance. 'Seize him! Seize the boy.'

He did not dare to look at the Abbot. He did not have to look. He could sense the weight of the monk's malevolence bearing down on him like a thundercloud. He was past the altar and clawing at the tapestry which hung behind it. It was a hopeless exercise. He was trapped. He turned to face his enemy – and was confronted with the Abbot's light.

It was as powerful and radiant as Joachim's had once been, with a single chilling difference: it was not coloured silver – it was not any colour at all. It was an overwhelming absence, sensed but not seen; a quintessence of darkness and nothingness; a furnace burning without light. It swirled towards him like nerve gas, threatening to engulf and suffocate him. Tom screamed.

The scream seemed to banish the terrifying vision and return the Abbot to human size and shape. Tom grasped the stem of the huge ten-branched candelabra and heaved it over into the Abbot's path. As it clanged to the floor, he pulled out his bottle of paraffin and smashed it into the burning candles. The Abbot vanished in a sheet of flame so fierce that Tom felt his eyelashes shrivel in the blast. The Abbot was transformed into a human torch, his arms raised across his face, dripping flames. Then he was down and rolling over the edge of the low platform. His faithful Brothers gathered round him, frantically beating out the flames. His hoarse screech was all but drowned in the flare and crackle of the fire which had spread to the corners of the tapestry and was curling around the wooden choir stalls.

'*Leave me. Get the ring.*'

Eleven Little Brothers spread out into a tight cordon and began to move cautiously towards Tom. He grabbed the heavy pewter cross from the altar and wielded it like a club. Behind him, the smouldering tapestry exploded like the skin of a Zeppelin, showering him with fragments of burning fabric. But not even for a second did he take his eyes off the monks as they closed in from all sides.

A commotion in the crowd of villagers made Stan Komit reach instinctively inside his jacket and rest his hand on the bulge under his arm. Someone was struggling through the mass of bodies. The loud muttering was punctuated by exclamations of protest. It looked like more than a queue-jumper.

Komit eased the revolver out of its holster and backed up against the chapel doors, motioning Father Giulio to stand well away. A woman with scraped-back hair and a red face broke free of the crowd and limped towards him, leaning heavily on a walking-stick and breathing hard.

'Are you Komit?' she demanded. The Commander nodded. He had not been spoken to like that since his cadet days, and he did not like it. 'I've got a message for you from Charlie Bravo,' and she muttered irritably. 'Ridiculous name!'

Ridiculous or not, the name had a magical effect on the Special Branch man. He took her none too gently by the arm and, ignoring the protests of the villagers, pulled her into the shadow of the chapel. Hannah disentangled her arm with dignity.

'Where's the Pope?' she asked bluntly.

He jerked his thumb towards the door. 'Who are you?' he barked. 'Never mind. What's the message? Speak. Quick!'

'Apparently I am to "alert" you . . .'

'Go on.'

She shrugged. 'That's it. I assume there is some difficulty about the Pope. Don't *you* know?'

Stan Komit hesitated. 'I'll soon find out,' he said. Then he turned and raised his fists to beat on the door. Before he had landed the first blow, a scream sounded distantly through the thick wood. A boy's scream.

'Jesus,' he said.

At the precise moment that the Abbot was set alight, Vittorio's fever loosened its grip as if it had been abruptly severed from its power source. He was seized by the curious sensation of floating away from his body. He felt his mind clear and every part of him breathing freely. He was hovering beside himself, looking with pity at the body he once inhabited – a ravaged bag of skin, blood and bone he was glad to be rid of. If he had still believed in miracles, he would have said that his blessed release was truly miraculous. Even so, it was as nothing compared to the Voice.

270

At first he was annoyed at it for disturbing his new-found freedom and reminding him of the body he had just cast off like an old skin. He wanted to drift away, to rise lighter than air through the roof, up to where the restful darkness was waiting to embrace him. But the Voice would not let him. He was compelled by its beauty to linger, to listen.

To begin with, he mistook it for his mother's voice, warm as sunlight, gentle as a summer breeze; then it grew yearning and filled with love, like the voice of the sweetheart he had never known. Or was it perhaps a man's voice after all? The voice of a friend who knew him better than he knew himself, who forgave him everything, who would never leave him lonely again. The priest could not decide. He only knew that he could have listened to the Voice for ever. Unfortunately it would not allow him; it was asking him to do a hard thing. He knew that he would not refuse; and perhaps it would not take long. Then, there would be time enough. All the time in the world. Obediently he returned to his body.

As he sank down into the harsh excruciating fever, its brittle heat seemed to snap so that the sweat poured out of him, unclenching his locked muscles and lubricating his rigid limbs. Painfully he moved one foot and then the other. He weakly lifted a hand, an arm. He began to crawl inch by inch towards the brink of the high gallery.

The car veered up the drive on its cripped wheel. Carlo Benetti could see the chapel clearly. Its stained-glass windows were shimmering with a light too bright for candles. Before the car had even pulled up, he had opened the door and jumped out. As he ran towards the crowd of people, he noticed that they were milling around the colonnade, obviously agitated, like cattle about to stampede. But what struck him as more sinister was the ungodly din. They were collectively giving vent to a kind of mindless wailing, like primitive tribesmen grieving over the death of a king.

The Cardinal charged into the baying throng and began to thrust his way towards the chapel. Above the uproar, he heard a single sharp explosion – the fatal sound of a gun being fired.

The fire gathered momentum and, having devoured the choir stalls, was spreading to the rows of pews and shooting out long tendrils of flame towards the panelled walls. Tom was appalled at the havoc he had created. His only real weapon had done its work too well. His legs would not move, his hands holding the cross and ring dangled at his sides; all thought of self-defence was swallowed up in the numbing smoke that rose around the squad of advancing monks. There were too many of them, there was no way out, it was pointless to struggle any more. He vaguely hoped that the end would not be too painful.

Out of the smoke, there was a sudden swirl of white robes moving directly in front of him, and a loud voice crying out:

'You will not touch this boy. I forbid it.'

The encircling monks were halted, spellbound, before the stern figure. Behind them, Ambrose had hauled himself to his knees and was urging them on in his awful rasping screech.

'Seize the boy, you fools. We must have the snake-ring. Get him!'

The monks surged forward in a wave, only to be repulsed once again by the adamant outstretched arms of the majestic man in white. They grew hesitant and confused and, looking about them in amazement, appeared to wake up for the first time to the danger of the blazing chapel. One of them shouted in panic. It was contagious: the Little Brothers no longer heard the impassioned commands of their Abbot but, abandoning both him and the boy they sought to destroy, broke away and began to run the gauntlet of fire towards the doors.

The man in white turned to Tom and spoke to him in

his unknown yet familiar voice. 'Tom, please give me the ring now. No-one's going to hurt you, but there's no escape. You may as well hand it over. I need it, Tom . . . I depend on it to . . . to bind myself to this flesh – to keep my hold on Earth. Please, Tom. Without it I'm . . . I'm lost.'

For a second, Tom was strongly swayed by the imploring voice. If he had closed his eyes, he might have believed that it was Joachim appealing to him. But standing in front of the weird hybrid creature, he felt no compassion for his friend, only horror. He couldn't help such a monstrous undead thing, he wouldn't serve the Spirit who inspired it. Even as his failure to save the Pope stared him in the face, his soul craved forgiveness of the Christ who died for his sins. He dropped the snake-ring on the altar and raised the pewter cross above his head.

'*I know that my Redeemer lives,*' he whispered.

He brought down the cross with all his might. The ring fractured into three pieces. He hit it again and again until it was ground to powder.

The white-haired creature jerked forward, holding its head in its hands, and clutched the altar to prevent itself from falling. Tom dropped the cross and fled to the corner of the chapel which was furthest from the flames. He squatted against the wall and rubbed his stinging eyes. Through a screen of fire and billowing smoke he saw that, at the other end of the chapel, something extraordinary was happening.

32

Even under their habits and hoods, Tom had no difficulty in distinguishing one Little Brother from another. But he was sure that he had never seen the one in the gallery before – the one who had crawled to the very edge. He was small and stout and it some way maimed, humping himself along like a caterpillar. He lowered himself headlong over the edge and dropped full-length on to one arm of the great crucifix. It was all he could do to cling on, with all four limbs wrapped around the crosspiece. The whole crucifix began to swing perilously on the chain from which it hung.

Down below, the monks were clustering around the doors. One of them – Brother Paul – was brandishing the key and fighting his way through the swarm towards the lock. The cross swung to and fro like a giant pendulum – to and fro and then, with a terrible rending of metal and stone, the chain was wrenched from the wall and the cross plummeted down. The Little Brothers scattered; Paul alone was left, looking up in disbelief, the key in his hand an inch from the lock. The heavy base of the crucifix caught him on the shoulder, crushing it and hurling him sideways as easily as a doll. It crashed on to the stone floor.

The impact tore away the grip of the man on the arm and jolted him upwards. He seemed to hang in thin air for a moment, his dark robe spreading like a bat's wings, his eyes flashing red in the firelight – and then he folded and dropped in a graceful arc. His head bounced once on the flagstones. The tall shaft of the cross barred the doors, its twin arms lodged immovably behind the pillars of the galleries.

Cardinal Benetti burst into the space cleared in front of the chapel in time to see Commander Komit empty his revolver into the wood around the heavy lock embedded in the door. He understood immediately and, shoving people aside, waved to his young driver who brought the car up to the colonnade with the headlights pointed at the doors. Caught in the sudden glare, Komit did not even look round; he went on kicking fiercely at the splintering wood.

The Cardinal joined him. Komit did not seem surprised to see him, merely acknowledging his presence with a nod and another blow of his boot. They could dimly hear a frantic hubbub on the far side of the doors and hands scrabbling against the wood – which was beginning to give way under their combined assault. At that moment there was a terrific crash not three feet from where they stood. Komit and the Cardinal exchanged the briefest of glances, both fearing that – by the sound of it – the chapel was starting to collapse.

The right-hand door broke open and instantly struck something solid. No matter how they attacked it, it would not budge more than a crack.

'Something's blocking it. We need more weight!' Cardinal Benetti could not keep the desperation out of his voice. As if in reply, a female shout sounded behind him.

'Get out of the way!'

He swung round and saw a red-faced woman in tweeds limping towards him and cutting a swathe through the crowd with her walking-stick. A long heavy table carried by six burly villagers followed in her wake. A seventh man, slighter than the rest, strained under the weight of the table's front end.

'Good, Father Giulio, *good*.' The Cardinal leapt forward. His way was barred by the woman's stick.

'Who are you?' she snapped.

'Benetti.'

'Ah! Charlie Bravo. I'm Hannah van Neef.' She lowered her stick.

He nodded once and, seizing his share of the table, shouted like a sergeant-major, 'On the count of three . . . one – two – three – GO.'

The men ran clumsily forward and rammed the table into the door.

The heat was becoming intolerable. Tom tore at the buttons on his cassock and managed to loosen the collar, but it was not much help. He was alternately gasping and holding his breath as poisonous clouds of smoke drifted over him.

The falling of the crucifix had effected a profound change in the Little Brother's behaviour. Almost as though they saw it as a kind of judgment, they had retreated to the nearest pews and, with the fire bearing down on them from behind, they were kneeling in prayer. Each had withdrawn into his own isolation. They hardly seemed aware of the threat to their lives; but, apparently content to submit to their fate, they calmly prepared their souls – whether in pride or in penitence – for the final separation from their bodies.

Tom crouched lower on the floor, sucking greedily at the occasional pocket of uncontaminated air. His head was spinning, and he felt both intoxicated and curiously detached. He knew quite well that, mercifully, he would suffocate long before the flames vaporised him. He no longer had any control over his gift of second sight: he slipped out of ordinary perception and into his deeper vision – and back again – as easily as putting on and taking off a pair of glasses. For the first time he was able to see the elusive lights of the Little Brothers. Whether his gift had developed or their spiritual guards had dropped, he could not tell. Either way, the sight was unique even in his experience.

276

The lights possessed a ghastly power. Completely undimmed by any fleshly sin, they shone out in a glowing testament to the extreme self-denial of the monks' lives. At the same time, they were riddled with all the dismal colours of the damned. Menacing blacks, muddy jaundiced browns, ugly purples, jagged flashes of red, bile greens – a sickening iridescence which betrayed a secret hell of mortal sin, from presumption and pride to defiance of God and – the sickness unto death – despair. Tom watched as one by one the lights began to fade.

A scene from a nightmare was being enacted in front of the altar. A hunched and blackened creature was raving at the man in white. It was Ambrose. Much of his face had been flayed to a pulpy mass of burnt flesh, like smeared wax; he had no eyelashes or eyebrows and his hair had been largely scorched away. A few remaining tufts stressed the size and weight of his head so that he appeared deformed, like a dwarfish gargoyle. His habit hung around him in smoking rags. His eyes were dark hollows.

'You betrayed us, Joachim – destroyed us all. Why? Why? *Why* did you protect the boy? You had only to reach out a hand and crush him! Half the world was in your grasp – *we could have ruled half the world and more*. But you . . . you . . .' The man in white began to walk away. What was left of Ambrose shambled after him, plucking at his arm.

'*Why?*'

The bewildered scream received no answer. In a single imperious stroke, the arm shot out and swept the Abbot into the roaring heart of the fire.

Tom coughed and retched until his brain reeled; but he could not get rid of the black fumes which filled his lungs. Everything grew blurred and fuzzy as he struggled to fight off the faintness which threatened to overpower him. Out of swollen half-closed eyes he could just make out the shape of a man, firelight reflected off his white robes, lurching towards him through the fog. He was about to receive his punishment for denying the spectre of Joachim his precious snake-ring.

There was a distant tinkle of breaking glass. He was gripped by powerful hands and lifted high into the air. His feet struck stone and slipped up the wall until he was practically upside down, supported by a hand under his head and another on his shoulder. He kicked out and found nothing but an empty space. The hands deftly twisted him sideways and thrust him upwards with a mighty shove. A splinter of glass gashed his left thigh. He realised he was jammed in a narrow window. He began to writhe frantically between the stone mullions, his head buried in smoke, his legs thrashing the air outside. Gradually he eased himself through.

A cold breeze flowed over his head, clearing a brief tunnel in the thickening smoke. He looked down into the chapel. The face of his saviour was upturned towards him, an old smile on the new lips. Tom gazed into the sad, marvellous eyes of Joachim – and then, with a last frantic wrench, he was dropping through space.

He hit the ground hard enough to loosen his teeth, and rolled over. He was lying on grass, looking up at a glory of stars and filling his body with huge draughts of cold air.

The long table slammed into the doors for the seventh time. The crack was increased by several inches. Smoke belched out on a blast of heat. Whatever was barricading the entrance had at last budged. Komit and the Cardinal who together had been holding the table's front end, dropped it in unison. Komit quickly stripped himself down to his shirtsleeves.

Neither Hannah nor Father Giulio had been idle. The priest had organised those villagers who were in their right minds to collect containers and fill them with water – a variety of buckets, bowls and cans were lined up along the colonnade. Hannah had telephoned the fire brigade in the nearest town; she was reduced now to standing helplessly by, wringing her hands as Stan Komit attempted to squeeze through the narrow opening between the doors.

Carlo Benetti had judged the gap more accurately. He seized two buckets and drenched himself from head to toe with water. Next, he snatched Hannah's silk scarf from around her neck and, wetting it, tied it across his mouth and nose like a mask. He pulled the policeman away from the doors. Komit took one look at his lean, dripping frame and nodded. It was no time to argue.

The Cardinal seemed to aim himself at the crack and, taking a deep breath, launched himself at the lowest part where it was widest. His head disappeared into the chapel; he twisted his body and his shoulders followed. With astonishing agility for a man of his age and height, he squirmed like a slippery black eel until his entire body had vanished through the opening.

It was like crawling into a blast furnace. Pounded flat by the heat, the first thing the Cardinal saw – a bare two feet from his own face – was the face of Father Vittorio. His head was lying sideways on the stone floor, cushioned in blood. His glasses lay beside him; one of the lenses was broken. His expression, for the first time in his life, was completely unsurprised. Incredibly, he appeared to be smiling at some private joke.

Cardinal Benetti scrambled to his feet. He was greeted by an unnerving spectacle: there were monks all around, facing him. They paid no attention to him – nor to the tidal wave of flame at their backs. Those who had not succumbed to the smoke were kneeling quietly, lost in prayer or meditation; two of them had already caught fire and were silently burning like martyrs at the stake. Even as he watched, a third monk – larger than the rest – was set alight; his black, tangled mass of hair and beard fizzed like a Roman candle. The figure of Christ, wide-eyed and triumphant on his giant cross, presided over their deaths.

The central aisle had divided the blaze down the middle like waves in a Red Sea. Straight ahead, flanked by twin walls of fire, Pope John the Twenty-Fifth was face down on the floor, his arms outstretched as if he too were worshipping the Cathar crucifix. The Cardinal darted forward, grabbed the old man under the arms and dragged him roughly towards the door. His wet cassock was steaming and tongues of flame were licking at the edges; his skin bubbled in the searing heat; he could not find any air left to breathe.

Strong hands were waiting at the crack between the doors. They grasped the Pope and manhandled him through. Carlo fell to his knees and groped for the opening. He could see and hear nothing except the fire roaring around him. A terrible blackness began to steal over him. He felt a firm hand seize him by the scruff of the neck.

Sirens wailing. Tom half-raised his aching body. Far away, blue lights were flashing though the maze of lanes. He stood up and walked around the burning chapel. Across the wide sloping lawns he could see a crowd of people silently watching the fire; some of them were praying. Watching the crowd were the two motorcycle policemen.

Nearer to him, and set a little apart, was a smaller knot of people. It included Hannah, who was talking to the tough-looking man from outside the chapel; nearby, a tall dishevelled man in black was sitting exhausted on the grass; next to him, a priest was kneeling and, leaning back against him with his legs stretched out, was an old man dressed in dirty white robes. His chest was heaving. Although he was tired beyond belief, Tom felt his heart-beat quicken.

He walked uncertainly towards the group and stopped, almost shyly, a little way off. Hannah was the first to see him. She gave a small shriek and put her hands to her mouth. The others turned towards him. Red firelight and black shadows played across their faces. They were looking at him in an odd way. Hannah seemed to be limping as she hurried up to him.

'Tom! *Good God*. Look at you! Oh, *Tom*.' Unaccountably she began to cry.

He tried to smile at her, to tell her he was all right, but it hurt his face too much. Besides, he was more interested in the old man who was breathing regularly now and saying something to the man in black. The latter bent close to his mouth and listened intently. He straightened up and beckoned Tom over to him. His face was blistered with burns, but they could not mask his kindly concern.

'Hannah has told me about you, Tom. Are you all right? You've had a lucky escape. Please sit down. We've both been in the wars a bit, eh?' Tom nodded and sat down. 'I am Cardinal Benetti . . . Carlo Benetti. His Holiness tells me that we have much to thank you for. He says that you saved his life . . .'

Tom could not remember how to address a Cardinal. In the end, he said simply, 'I think he saved mine.' His voice sounded peculiar. A sort of croak. Cardinal Benetti looked puzzled and glanced from the boy to the old man.

The two survivors were watching each other in such a way that the Cardinal felt completely shut out. He went on talking, aware that neither of them was really listening.

'Anyway, we are grateful. Father Giulio and I think that he might have suffered a slight stroke, don't we, Father?' The priest who was supporting the old man nodded. 'But, thank God, it does not appear to be serious. Perhaps you can tell us what happened, Tom? How the fire started, for instance . . .' He gave Tom an acute look.

Tom shook his head. As he had hoped (as he had feared), the old man's face and form were beginning to change.

Carlo Benetti's voice was a faraway murmur. 'His Holiness is rather confused, you see. He remembers very little of what happened, Tom, except a dream. At least, he calls it a dream. He has told us that he "flew away to a beautiful place . . ."' (A light began to outline the head of the worn-out old man.) 'He claims that, somehow or other, it was you who . . . "called him back" – it's the shock, of course, and the effect of the fire.'

The old man soundlessly exploded into a cascade of light. Like sunlight ought to be, but never was. Pure molten gold shone around him, out of him, enveloping Tom in its glowing folds. He was bathed in blissful warmth and, closing his eyes, he glimpsed the peace that passed all understanding. He could rest now.

Pope John the Twenty-Fifth stretched out his hand and sketched the sign of the cross in the air.

'Bless you, my son.'

With a sound like thunder, the roof of the chapel collapsed, crashing into the inferno and throwing up a shower of huge sparks a hundred feet into the air. Scintillating like tiny stars, they spiralled into the night and were extinguished in darkness.